A REASON TO KILL

A JACK WIDOW THRILLER

SCOTT BLADE

Black Lion Media

ALSO BY SCOTT BLADE

1

JACK WIDOW HAD no reason to kill anybody.

Not now. Not recently. Not yet. Killing had been the last thing on his mind. He was traveling. Seeing. Experiencing. Touristing. Taking things in.

Making memories.

One memory, the one that wouldn't leave him, was two days ago. Back in a hotel room, Widow had been tangled in bleached sheets with high thread counts and soft limbs, and bare and naked with a beautiful woman in Las Vegas.

The impression lasted. He had a smile on his face for the entire two days that followed.

The feeling he held on to was the opposite of retribution. The reverse of reprisal. The contradiction of payback. The disagreement of disagreement.

It was sunshine in the dark.

He was the furthest thing from wanting to kill.

In the sweltering Texas heat, that was all about to change.

He first met Claire Hood outdoors in a bus depot in West Texas.

She was a nice old lady, as nice as old ladies come, like the catalog version of a sweet grandmother, and nothing else. She didn't have a mean bone in her body—not a mean word from her lips.

She was like a churchly grandmother who baked cookies for everyone on her block, and then returned after a couple of days to recover the plastic ware and ask if everyone had enjoyed the cookies.

She was the kind of woman who played bingo every Tuesday and Thursday night, routine. At least that's what she told her family. In reality, she was gambling. Playing pinochle, sometimes bridge, sometimes poker with her friends.

She belonged in a Kodak photo of a family picnic more than she did sitting on a hot, dry bus terminal bench close to the wasteland part of Texas on the long stretch of Interstate 10, somewhere between El Paso and San Antonio.

But that's where she was. She sat upright on the edge of her seat, back straight and chin up. Perfect posture. Her purse rested on her knees like a small dog. A perfectly pint-sized black hat rested on her head. Her gaunt hands were stacked, palm on top of palm, across her lap.

Her shoes were leathery and almost crinkle free, old but not worn to the point of retirement.

Her eyes were brown, and she had tan, paperlike skin. Lighter than her shoes, but not by much. She was a skinny thing: skin and bones, only more bones than skin. Her gray hair curled and coiled and merged with whiter strands of hair, all of which punched out from under the brim of her hat.

All the things Widow noticed about her had been his first and last impressions of her. Because twenty-one minutes after they met, after a long, revealing conversation, Claire Hood dropped dead.

THE CAUSES WERE NATURAL.

That was obvious, because she was ancient. No medical examiner in the world, no medical examiner Widow had ever worked with, would even go beyond a quick look over the body.

Ten medical examiners out of ten would agree. Right there on the spot. They'd all agree with one glance. Claire Hood was ancient. It had been her time. A strange place, no doubt, but your time was your time.

No question.

Claire Hood had died right in front of Widow. Right at that generic, sandy bus depot. Right at a place where she didn't want to die. Right at the time she couldn't afford to die. She had something left to do. She had unfinished business.

And the only person in the world who knew about it was Widow.

* * *

THE PRINCIPAL CALLED John Glock and waited for him to answer the phone. A static ringtone, an echoing whir, and then a hard voice that sounded like no one else on earth answered and said, "Yeah."

Glock's voice was unlike anyone else's on earth because eight years earlier, he had been stabbed in prison by a shiv made out of twenty-five pages of rolled paper, thick and ripped from a *National Geographic* magazine, fashioned and shaped into a great murder weapon. After its use, it could be unrolled and flushed down a toilet.

Three inmates in a Texas prison had tried to take him out. They had killed his friend, another former SEAL. But they had underestimated the man they were trying to put in the dirt. He had jerked the shiv out of his neck and whipped around and gored the closest attacker, twice, in his own throat. He'd jabbed the same shiv into the kidney of the second one as the attacker turned to run. And he'd killed the third attacker five weeks later, after he got out of the infirmary. Now Glock spoke with a rough and hard voice because some words were harder to pronounce than others.

Glock had a tattoo that paid tribute to his fallen friend. It was a frog's skeleton holding a trident, an unspoken symbol used by SEALs to honor their fallen friends. Glock had been a member of the SEALs for only four years, when he and his friend were discharged under less than savory circumstances. They had served their tenure and gone into business for themselves. That's when they had met the Principal, a wealthy man who shared their vision, which was a noninclusive vision for America.

Glock considered himself a patriot, and he considered the Principal to be a patriot. They had a plan to keep America safe. They shared a vision of taking back their country.

The Principal said, "It's me. I need your help."

"What's up?" asked Glock. He walked over to the small, thin-paned glass window in the trailer and pulled down the blinds with his fingers. He stared out over an enormous lot of construction vehicles and cement trucks and Caterpillars and unmanned bulldozers and giant excavators that stood monstrous and silent like dinosaur bones in a museum. And the site he was on wasn't the only one they owned, or even the largest.

"We've got a problem. Our business is in jeopardy."

"At what corner?"

The Principal said, "All of it. But primarily the Texas border."

"What happened?"

"James Hood."

Silence came over the phone. John Glock knew that name. And he hated the man it belonged to.

John Glock said, "Want me to call the Jericho Men?"

"No. We need professionals, not a bunch of militia idiots with guns," the Principal said. He paused a beat and said, "But put them on alert. Just in case."

"What do you propose?"

"You know what his being out means?"

"He's not dumb enough to have done anything."

The Principal said, "Think, John. Why else would he be out? The Feds know something. Or they're sniffing around. Or they're simply casting a net because they're bored. Whichever it is, we don't need them catching something with that net."

Glock said, "Don't be so paranoid. Maybe he's running. In which case, they won't find him. Either way, we'll handle it like we always do."

"We can't take that chance, and you know it."

Glock said, "Relax. We won't leave him out there. He'll be put down."

"And anyway, we made him a promise. Remember? If he didn't stay in for the full sentence, then we'd kill him and his family."

"I know," Glock said.

The Principal said, "We must keep our promise."

"We shoulda killed him way back then."

"I agree. You know where he'll go?"

"To see his wife and kid. And his mother, if she's still alive," Glock answered.

The Principal said nothing. Glock wasn't sure he was on board with threatening the lives of three innocent females just to prove a point to one guy that they'd kill anyway, but he wouldn't leave them alive. Not his style.

"I've called three others to help," the Principal said.

Glock said nothing. He didn't need help, but it wasn't his money. The Principal was the one with the cash. If he wanted to hire three other professionals to track and kill one man, then Glock wouldn't argue, and if James Hood was out long before his release date, that meant he was let out. And being let out by the Feds meant he'd made a deal.

"Meet with them and find the target. Kill him." The Principal hung up the phone.

Glock smiled. He was already in El Paso, Texas. If James Hood had just gotten out of prison, he'd have a head start, but that wouldn't matter. Glock would start with meeting the kill team members, and then he'd track James Hood down.

* * *

JEMMA COULD NOT REMEMBER the last time she had seen the driver of the car that she was in. But he looked like her daddy.

Jemma wondered where he was taking her. She still wore her good first-school-day clothes. She still had her lunch packed neatly inside a special lunch pail, special because her mommy gave it to her. It was a mint-condition collector's item from when her mommy was a little girl. It was made from cold steel, but colored with warm pinks and sunny yellows, and friendly whites.

Little ponies danced on the surfaces.

What did her mommy tell her it was called? *My Little Horsey?* Or *My Small Pony?* Or something like that. She wasn't exactly sure about the title. She learned new things every day, and it was hard to remember them all.

The lunch pail was named after toys her mommy used to play with when she was a little girl growing up in another country.

Maybe she had been Jemma's age. Maybe that's where Jemma got her love of horses from.

Jemma wasn't sure about what time it was. Not exactly. She didn't own a watch. Not yet. Because she was still learning how to tell time, but she knew it must've been around noon because she yawned again. Her legs dangled and waved back and forth over the edge of the front seat of the car.

The guy who looked like her daddy was tall, but all grown-ups were tall to her. There was nothing special about his height that she could see.

He had offered her Gummy Bears, which were her favorite. Not Gummy Worms. *Worms were gross*, she thought.

She wasn't supposed to talk to strangers. Or take rides from them. But her daddy was no stranger. He convinced her it was okay.

He said, "It was cool with mommy."

At first, she didn't trust him, but he had known her mommy. He knew her name. He looked like her daddy, maybe. So he didn't count as a stranger. Right?

It made sense to her. She had worked it all out.

He let her sit in the front seat. She loved that.

Her mommy never let her sit in the front seat of her car. Jemma had to always ride in the back seat. She hated the back seat. It was boring.

She was big enough to ride in the front. She thought so.

That's why she was glad to be in the front seat next to her own daddy.

She had felt she was old enough for over two years.

Jemma was about to have a birthday soon. She was going to turn seven, and she was very excited about the whole prospect.

She wondered if that's why her daddy was picking her up. Maybe he was surprising her for her birthday?

Jemma yawned again and stretched out her arms and hands as far as they would extend. She made a big deal out of it. All kinds of sounds and moans and groans, like she had heard her grandma do a million times.

Old people made all kinds of sounds, she thought.

Jemma twisted in her seat and stared at the guy who looked like her daddy.

She looked him up and down, and down and up, and back down, and back up, again.

He was her daddy. She was pretty sure. But he differed from what she remembered. Her daddy didn't have an arm tattoo. This guy had one—a big one. It was huge. She hadn't seen anything like it.

It was a dragon or snake or some kind of monster from Ancient Greece. She had learned about Greece in school. There was a book in the library she liked. It had plenty of pictures of monsters. There was one that looked like the one he had on his arm. It had three heads. Or ten heads. She couldn't remember.

The monster in her book had magical powers. If you cut off one head, another grew back in its place. Or two more grew back—something like that.

This arm tattoo was a little different. She only saw one head.

The guy who looked like her daddy looked down at her. A quick, brief glance, only he held on to it for more than a second. He seemed to stare into her face, hard. Then he smiled.

Under the stubble and the hard tan, she was pretty sure it was her daddy.

Almost sure.

Jemma wanted to talk with him and ask where they were going. She wanted to ask where he had been for the last two years. She wanted to show him she wasn't in a booster seat anymore. But he looked so serious that she decided not to bother him with what her teacher called "small talk."

Some grown-ups didn't like it, her teacher had said.

He had picked her up at her bus stop, where she'd been waiting in the early morning hours for the school bus.

It was her first day back at school. She was starting late this year because her mommy had been in the hospital. She was sick last year. And she was still sick this year, but her grandma decided it was time for Jemma to go back to school.

Jemma didn't want to go back. She didn't want the other kids to ask her why she'd been away for so long. Then she'd have to tell them about her mommy.

There would be questions. Kids liked questions. Especially the kids in her class. She'd have to explain to them why her mommy had lost all her hair.

They might pick on her for having a bald mother.

Her grandma had explained to her that her mother losing hair was a good thing because it meant she was getting better. The medicine did it to her.

Hair loss meant the medicine was working.

Jemma wondered if her daddy was taking her to meet her mommy somewhere, like a surprise. Maybe an early birthday surprise.

Even though part of her wanted to know, she didn't want to ask him. She didn't want to say a word.

She knew he was her daddy. He had to be. She was almost positive.

He looked like him. He acted like him, only quieter. It had to be him. Right?

She wanted to know, to be certain, but she felt tired. Her eyes felt heavy.

She yawned one last time in a long, over-the-top way. And she craned her head, and pushed up off of the seat with her knuckles, and tried to look at the terrain out the window, but all she could see was Texas wasteland.

She saw a sign that read a funny word. She wasn't sure how to say it, but she mouthed the letters anyway: "O-Z-O-N-A."

She looked at it as the sign passed. She mouthed it again, wondered how to pronounce it.

Sound it out, her teacher would've said.

She recognized the "Oz," like *Oz* from *Wizard of Oz*, one of her favorite books. It was better than the movie, she thought, because the book had action and blood and death in it. She liked that stuff.

The name of the town they just passed was *Ozona*.

It was a cool word.

Jemma yawned again.

The time must've been close to her regular nap time. Not at school, but at her grandma's house. Usually, her grandma would fix her a big lunch, and then she'd get so sleepy that she'd take a nap after.

This time, she had not touched her lunch. But she was still sleepy, like she was programmed to be.

She looked at the guy who looked like her daddy, one last time. He looked tired too. He looked like he hadn't slept in days. She was about to ask him if he wanted to take a nap with her.

Before she could, her eyes got too heavy to keep open, and she laid her head back against the seat.

She was out like a light in seconds.

3

BEFORE HE MET Claire Hood four days ago, Widow was in Las Vegas, a city he had always wanted to see and a city in which he had spent four days and three nights. It was a city he had never laid eyes on and still hadn't. Not really. He hadn't been to the world-famous Las Vegas Boulevard Strip, and he hadn't seen the fountain show at the Bellagio, and he hadn't ridden the roller coaster at New York–New York. He hadn't gone up the replica of the Eiffel Tower at Paris Casino.

Widow hadn't experienced the famous Fremont Street. He hadn't seen the canals at the Venetian or gazed at the lights that shot off the black pyramid known as the Luxor. Widow hadn't bungee-jumped off the Stratosphere, the tallest structure in Las Vegas. He hadn't seen a magic show or a musical or one of those topless burlesque shows—items on anyone's Las Vegas bucket list.

On his trip to Las Vegas, Widow walked on Route 161 after coming out of southern Colorado, where he had taken three different rides, all with male drivers. All of them had been decent guys. But the last one, a middle-aged guy driving a new black Ford Taurus like he had just bought it off the lot, took it on himself to pick Widow up instead of heading home to show his wife and neighbors his new ride.

The Ford Taurus driver drove the car, with Widow in the passenger seat, for the better part of seven hours, the bulk of Widow's trip to Las Vegas. And the guy hadn't asked Widow to drive, not once, which was something that Widow had expected him to do.

How often was it that a driver picked up a hitchhiker and then drove for seven hours and didn't ask that the rider pitch in his fair share of work for the ride? Or at least put up some money for the gas?

Widow had expected to take the wheel for at least half of the trip, which was no problem for him. He didn't mind driving. Sometimes he missed it. But the guy had never asked or even hinted at such a thing. And Widow didn't volunteer. He never volunteered for anything. That was a sailor's basic rule—*never volunteer for work*—and he had been a sailor for a time and then an NCIS agent for a special operation called Unit Ten, in which he was undercover in the Navy SEALs.

Undercover work in his unit wasn't like the undercover work that regular cops did. The closest type of undercover work he could think of was the DEA, because he wasn't just undercover. His life had never been the kind where he pretended to be something he wasn't for a short period until an investigation was complete. Widow had become an actual Navy SEAL. He had no choice.

The Navy SEALs are an elite operation, and there are only around two thousand members in the outfit. He couldn't just waltz in as a mysterious SEAL that had never been seen before. He had to live the life of a SEAL twenty-four hours a day, seven days a week, and fifty-two weeks a year. No getting around it.

Often he had to investigate other SEALs. In order to do this effectively, he had to take part in everything they did. Widow had to maintain a solid reputation. He had to train just as hard and deploy to the same far-off locations. He had to spend the same time at sea. Widow had to do more than just blend in. He had to live a double life. Now Widow was a drifter. Far from his old life.

Las Vegas hadn't been his destination initially, but that was where the road had taken him, and Widow was all about following where the road led, because that was life. Unless he had a target or a particular reason to go somewhere, in some specific direction, but he didn't. Not then. Las Vegas was a direction as good as any, and it was a place he had never been. And the more Widow thought about it, the more it seemed un-American to never go to the city of sin. Las Vegas was about as American as apple pie and guns and freedom of speech and crooked politicians.

Widow ended up getting out of the last guy's car on the freeway, and the reason for that wasn't hostile, unlike many experiences he had in the past and many more he'd have in the future.

It wasn't because the driver had enough of him, not totally. It was more of a mutual agreement. They had both had enough of each other. Two men stuck in a tight space was enough for any man to understand, but in particular, it had hit close to home for Widow because, from his Navy experience, he knew something about being in tight spaces with other people for long periods of time.

Widow had listened to as much of the guy's talking as he could handle, and the guy had said about as much as he could say. They had both listened to as much silence as they could stand as well. It was like one of those times when a guy is obligated to help someone out of the civilized concept of politeness. He helped Widow, but after the kindness had worn off and time passed and more time passed, the whole situation became a burden at first and then a nuisance and then unbearable.

For Widow, his time in the Ford Taurus with the middle-aged guy had come to that boiling point where he would either have to ask the guy to let him out, or he might have exploded on the guy and demanded he let him out. In all honesty, he was certain that the desert heat—which wasn't that bad, not at this part of his journey so far—had played a factor. The new Ford Taurus obviously had an air conditioner installed, but the guy wasn't using it. He was one of those drivers who liked the windows down, which was okay by Widow. He liked the wind in his face, rushing through his short hair, but it would have been a little more comfortable with the AC running instead. Thoughts like this made Widow realize that if he hadn't been complaining internally about the guy not using the AC, he would've been looking for something else to complain about. It was Widow's unrelenting need to not stay in one place. He was in a moving car, which was good. But he was in the same moving car for hours and hours, with the same company for hours and hours, and the same desert air rushing in.

He had enough.

So the guy let Widow out near an off-ramp exit that led to a large convenience store and a red-and-blue gas station, an Exxon Mobil that had been sold to a local, and now called something different but still with the same colors. It lay between the dusty border of Arizona and Utah. The 389 freeway snaked into southern Utah from the tip of northern Arizona, turned into the 15, and then dipped its way back down into Arizona for an expanse of road until it penetrated into Nevada.

Widow stood staring at the gas station off in the distance, beyond a huge sign that listed the prices of gas by the gallon, by the octane, and with the little nine at the end of each price to signal to the customer, "Hey, we round up from this penny." It was an old trick that gas stations all over the world used. Widow had seen it everywhere. It was a trick that never really fooled anybody, but no one cared enough about it to complain. It seemed like gas stations were the only market in the world that marked prices with that little nine-tenths of a penny. Oil companies would do anything to make a buck.

American capitalism was alive and well.

Widow stood at the bottom of the off-ramp, considering walking up the ramp and then down the long, winding service drive that led to the gas station, in order to buy a bottle of cold water for the road and maybe have a bite to eat. But his inner compass pointed him west, and his brain told him to keep on keeping on. Water was important, very important in the desert, but the 389 had enough car traffic. He didn't worry too much about being stranded for long. It was a busy roadway, not some deserted dirt road out in the desert. And it was a weekend. Surely he would have plenty of opportunities to get someone to stop and pick him up. Desert highways were a lot more conducive to getting rides than other spots. Maybe it was the heat, or the appearance of someone being stranded that made drivers more willing to take a risk.

Widow had gotten good at getting rides. Practice made perfect. Hitchhiking was like selling. It involved advertising and sales talk and closing the deal. He had to show drivers he needed a ride. He learned to use little white lies for this. Sales. American capitalism.

Widow had perfected a few different white lies about his life in order to get a driver to give him a lift. Not something he was proud of, but desperate times and all. He preferred not to lie, which he normally never did. Not in his personal life. Then again, he had no personal life. And the life he had known for sixteen years in the NCIS was all about lying.

Widow had been a double agent. He'd worked for the Naval Crime Investigative Service. Sixteen years. The NCIS was a police force that policed the Marines and the Navy.

The NCIS was about ninety-five percent civilian. Widow was a part of the other five percent. That five percent was enrolled in the military. Widow had spent most of his career undercover in the Navy SEALs.

So lying wasn't new to him. He didn't like it, but he was good at it. If he made up harmless scenarios in order to impress a driver into helping him out, then so what? It wasn't exactly perjury.

One of the common white lies Widow used was that he had broken down somewhere along the road. Often, he didn't have to tell this lie. Most drivers assumed it. They asked about it. And he would agree. Sometimes they expected to find a broken-down truck along the way. They'd assume the damn thing had stalled out on him like trucks do. Often he would nod along and say something like he had run out of gas, or the radiator blew, or a tire had blown, and it was his spare, and the car was getting towed.

Any of those were plausible and understandable and forgivable and even likely.

The best one to use was that he had run out of gas somewhere. This gave the driver the sense that all Widow really needed was to get to a service station and to a pay phone to get a ride back to his abandoned vehicle after he had purchased a gas can.

A driver felt a sense of pride in helping Widow out and a sense of safety because gas stations were everywhere in America. Therefore, the distance a driver would have to carry Widow was usually not too far. How often do you drive long distances and not come across a gas station? Maybe for an hour? Two at the most?

Widow left the exit ramp and headed west.

* * *

HE WALKED west for a long time. And no gas station. He regretted not getting a bottle of water when he had the chance. It had been forty-five minutes, and he was thirsty.

Luckily for him, and unluckily for the driver, he supposed, he witnessed a car breakdown.

He saw a lime-colored convertible with the top down and a long slipstream of golden hair barrel past him. It was like slow motion but only lasted for about a second, because right after the car flew by him, the back tire on the driver's side blew—straight into the air.

The lime-green convertible's rear end danced and flailed and whipped from side to side. The driver struggled to keep control of the car and wound up swerving and skidding in a complete one-eighty. It stopped safely on the shoulder, front end facing Widow, pointing east from about two football fields away.

The driver was very lucky. She had barely missed a brown Dodge Ram with California plates over in the right lane, which kept on driving even though the driver had to have seen the whole thing go down because he had started from behind her and then sped past her as she fishtailed.

The driver of the convertible was obviously a woman. Not that it mattered, but Widow was from the South, and in the South, boys are raised by strong mothers. "You always stop and help a lady" had been a common theme among men from that part of the country.

The broke-down woman appeared to be all of five feet two inches tall and might've weighed an entire ninety pounds soaking wet. She was in a kneeling position, her knees hovering about an inch from the ground, staring at her back tire. She wore white sandals with slightly raised heels, and she was tanned like she had spent the weekend at a lake or beach somewhere. She faced away from Widow as he walked up towards her.

Terrible situational awareness, he thought.

She wore a summer dress with an O neckline. It was short, not like a miniskirt, but above the knees

Widow neared the woman from the convertible, waited until he was about a dozen feet from her, and cleared his throat and stomped his feet as he approached to make himself known to her, like an announcement. He knew he wasn't the most sought-after stranger that a tiny woman would hope to stop and help her in the middle of the desert.

She spun around so fast she almost lost her balance, but she didn't because the fiberglass near the back corner of the car prevented her from falling when her backside scraped up against it.

Widow said, "You got a flat."

She stared up at him, automatically lifting her right hand up and over her eyes as a natural visor against the bright sun.

She said, "Yeah. I don't know how. It just blew."

"I saw it. I was walking back there."

"Did you break down too?"

The white lie came to Widow's mind, but he said, "No. Just hitching a ride."

"Oh," she said with that sound in her throat that Widow had heard a million times before. It was the sound of instinctive mistrust. An audible signal of danger like a scream, only less obvious. She said, "You walking out in this heat?"

"Not much choice. It's the only way to get to the next destination." Widow waited for her to respond, but she didn't. He asked, "Got a spare?"

"In the trunk. I think there's a doughnut tire. I never used it."

Widow stayed quiet and stood back. He gestured for her to open the trunk, moving his right hand slowly and steadily, making sure she could see that his movements were nonthreatening.

She rose and said, "I gotta grab the keys. I left them in the ignition."

"Just pop the trunk, and I'll pull the tire out."

She nodded.

"Don't worry. If you got a spare, then we're in business."

She nodded again, but he could still see hesitation in her eyes. Then he caught her glancing over his shoulder into the distance at oncoming traffic. Except at that moment, there was no traffic. The scene had gone from a car every thirty seconds to one every minute to none; there wasn't a single one. Not anywhere. Not even on the horizon.

It was like a horror movie where a stranger appeared out of nowhere, with the leading lady breaking down at the perfect spot. And Widow had appeared at the perfect moment, just when all the potential witnesses and all other signs of life had magically disappeared.

She said nothing, just stared at him like she was thinking the same thing.

Widow said, "Go ahead. Pop it." And then he paused a beat and said, "Don't worry. You don't have to give me a ride or anything. I'll help and then move on. No problem."

She faked a smile and clenched her hands together out in front of her like a nervous habit. With no other choice, she accepted his help. She walked back to the driver's side door and opened it and leaned in, jerked a lever, and popped the trunk.

Widow walked to the trunk and opened it. Inside, there was a bright-orange suitcase, a carry-on size with wheels and a pull-out handle. It was clean, with no visible nicks or scrapes or any other damage from traveling. Not brand new, but somewhat new.

He pulled it out and walked off of the gravel on the shoulder and set it on the last concrete part of the road, but still off the lane and well before the washed-out white line.

Widow walked back to the car and pulled up the carpet lining. He released the spare tire and the cheap jack from its screws and its plastic encasement. He lifted the tire up and closed the trunk.

"Make sure the parking brake is on."

"It is," she said.

"Pull the keys out."

She did and turned back to him.

Widow said, "Should only take a few minutes. No big deal."

She smiled and waited behind him with the keys clenched close to her body, the tips of them sticking out between her knuckles like a weapon, like a knuckle-duster. In case Widow tried anything less than gentlemanly, he assumed. It would've been simple to parry a strike from her with the makeshift weapon, and overpowering her would've been very easy, even if he hadn't been trained as a Navy SEAL. She was tiny, and he was huge—simple math. But if she had been trained well enough in mixed martial arts, then she could've put in a couple of paralyzing blows and made a run for it. Maybe.

He didn't react to her being on the defensive. He simply grabbed the tools and the tire and went to work. After nine minutes, the old tire was off and the spare was on. Widow lifted the rim with its flaccid tire and tossed it into the trunk. Then he walked over to the suitcase and rolled it to the back of the car.

He stopped and looked at her. She was still tense around him, even after he had changed the tire for her. *So much for earning trust*, he thought.

"Want me to toss this in the trunk, or in the back seat?" he asked.

"In the back seat. I don't want it rubbing up against the dirty old tire."

Widow shut the trunk on the remains of the old tire and the cheap car jack and set the suitcase down in the back seat. He laid it down on its side and tucked it nice and snug between the passenger seat and the rear bench.

Widow stayed about ten feet from her, giving her a safe distance.

He said, "Well, you should be on your way."

"Thank you so much," she said, pausing a beat.

Widow could see the wheels turning in her head like she was feeling guilty, wondering whether to offer him a ride.

Right then, Widow looked back over his left shoulder at the oncoming cars, which were sparse now. He saw a white truck with a big chrome grille on the front. It was one of those trucks with more than four tires. There were two in the front and several in the back. What was that called back in his home state of Mississippi? A dualie?

The truck's engine droned and whined and rattled. He figured that was normal because every one of those types of trucks he had ever been around had that same light rattling sound, like the engine inside breathed heavily.

Sunlight reflected off the windshield and into his face. He squinted his eyes. The truck slowed, and tires rolled over the blacktop and then over the gravel on the shoulder. It stopped about ten feet behind Widow.

"Who are these guys?" the driver of the convertible asked. She walked forward, closing that ten-foot safety gap, coming closer to Widow's side like she had suddenly accepted him as her protector.

Widow said, "Probably just want to help."

The truck stopped, and both the driver's side door and the passenger door creaked open. At first, two big guys stepped out, but then one more slumped out after.

They wore white painter overalls with white shoes, white hats, and white T-shirts. They all had paint stains on them. On their legs, on their torsos, and even on their arms.

Widow stepped two paces to the left and craned his head to the side. Down the side of the truck was a sign with big black letters. The first word he couldn't read, but the second and third were clearly "Brothers" and "Carpenters ."

Widow saw two different ladders attached to the back of the long bed of the truck. He imagined it was full of carpentry tools and big steel cans of paint and probably a variety of used and unused paintbrushes and those big roller brushes. Widow pictured that the cabin of the truck was full of old McDonald's or Arby's bags or whatever other fast food these guys liked. He pictured this because all three were heavy—and not in the slightly overweight kind of way, but like they were fighting a losing battle.

The two in the front moved along the sides of the truck, past the engine, and stopped just in front of the tires. The first passenger to step out stopped and leaned on the truck's hood in a gesture that said, "We're all friends here."

But somehow Widow doubted the gesture was genuine. He doubted it because he had been in similar situations. Sure, the world was full of Good Samaritans who might be concerned with a couple who broke down on the side of the road, the kind of good people who would stop and check, but something way back in

Widow's barbarian brain doubted these three guys were Good Samaritans. They looked like the definition of trouble. They looked like they'd been typecast by an out-of-touch Hollywood casting director to play the roles of three Arizona roughneck brothers who drank too much, smoked too much, and liked to force themselves on women. Especially women only a fraction of their size.

Widow tried to stay positive. He said, "Hey, guys. Thanks for stopping, but I just finished putting on the spare tire, and we're ready to go. I'm sorry, but you stopped for no reason."

The driver stopped walking at the tip of the truck's nose, right in front of the headlights. His belly hung out a good six inches from where it should be.

He asked, "So ya two don't need any help or a ride or nothin'?"

Widow shook his head, but the girl said, "Thank you for stopping, but my friend here already fixed me up. As you can see."

Better to let me do the talking, Widow thought.

At first, she didn't seem aware that these guys weren't interested in helping them or in their well-being, but it was obvious by her demeanor that she seemed to get on board with the realization of that danger pretty fast, about as fast as anyone Widow had ever seen before.

The driver asked, "Yer friend?" He looked at the second guy, and then he asked, "So ya two don't even know each other?"

Widow stayed quiet.

The woman walked up closer to Widow and leaned into him and placed her arm around his waist. Only she couldn't reach around it, but they got the idea.

She said, "Of course, we know each other. We're off to Las Vegas right now. We're gonna get married. You know, at one of those thirty-minute wedding chapels. "

The third guy had been inching toward the rear of the truck. Widow assumed his actions were intended to go unnoticed, but he was about as obvious as Hitler's mustache.

Widow kept his eyes forward between the front two guys, his hands down by his sides. In this situation, with a good ten feet between him and the two front guys and about fifteen from the last guy, his biggest concern was that the back guy was going for a gun, but that wasn't a reasonable fear because you don't keep a gun hidden in the bed of a truck. You keep it in the cabin. If these guys had been armed, they would've brought a gun out in the first few seconds.

The first guy said, "Ya from Vegas, little lady?"

She said, "Yeah."

The second guy said, "No shit! We can see yer plates say Nevada. And with that body and that fake rack ya got, well, ya must be from Vegas."

The first guy said, "Ya one of dem showgirls? The kind dat dance around on stage?"

Widow said, "Come on, guys. That's enough."

He craned his head again and watched as the third guy reached his hand into the back of the truck. His hand stayed down and hidden from view. Whatever he was reaching for, he had it already and was just keeping it out of sight until he needed it. Widow figured it was a blunt weapon because he could've pulled out a knife and concealed it quickly without Widow seeing it. Yes, he was sure the guy had a blunt object: a baseball bat or a shovel or even a big hammer.

The first guy said, "So ya two from Vegas. Then does that mean yer one of dem guys who dress like a woman?"

The second guy started laughing, and the third looked back at the road. And that's when Widow knew he had made a big mistake, because the third guy was checking to make sure that no one could see what he had in his hand. When he saw that the road was empty, he stepped away from the truck. Widow had been right about them not keeping a regular gun in the truck's bed, but he had been dead wrong in assuming two important details.

The first was that these guys were normal and had brains and acted like regular truck drivers, who kept their guns inside their trucks. But these guys weren't normal... they were dumb. That part he knew, but he had underestimated just how dumb.

The second mistake he had made was discounting hunting rifles. The kind that are hard to store inside a cabin when you have three fat guys riding in there already. And if the third guy sat in the back seat, he'd probably move to the center so that he could be a part of the conversation in the front seat. Therefore, he'd store a hunting rifle in the back on the bed. Perhaps he stored it hidden in a case or a toolbox. That way, if they got pulled over in a traffic stop, it wouldn't be out in the open to be seen by police officers. Maybe another reason they didn't store it inside the cabin was that they didn't want customers to see it on display. It might unsettle some people who'd called a random number from the internet to get their houses painted.

The third guy moved about as fast as he could and pulled out a Thompson/Center Encore Pro Hunter rifle, which is a scary-looking rifle. It looks like a Smith & Wesson 500 Magnum and a regular hunting rifle had a baby.

The third guy came forward so that the girl and Widow could clearly see the rifle, and he pointed it right at them, held down low at the hip.

The second guy said, "I sure hope ya are one of dem queers. 'Cause I ain't like my brothers. I ain't into those skinny type girls."

4

WIDOW STARED at the grisly rifle that was about ten feet from him now. It had a hammer, a scope attachment, and a stock that was built to last because this rifle had quite a kick to it. The stock was black, and the under-grip was customized with hunter camo colors. The rest was a chrome silver, like the grille on the front of the truck. This was not a gun that Widow wanted pointed at him because it was more than deadly. It was catastrophic. And right now, it was pointed about two inches south of his center mass, at his abdomen. Which was right up there among the last places he ever wanted to be shot. A round in the gut was never fun. It didn't matter what gun did the shooting. A gut shot wasn't guaranteed to be fatal, but it probably would be in his current circumstance, because he was on the 161 freeway out in the middle of nowhere and far from the next small town, which may not be equipped with a hospital that could handle a gunshot wound that caused the stomach and intestines to spill out. And he doubted they had a medical chopper on standby to pick him up.

Widow shifted his eyes from the gun barrel to the second guy, who was still talking. Only Widow stopped listening as soon as the guy started suggesting that he wanted to have his way with Widow. He stopped listening because this was not a serious threat, not because the guy wasn't serious. The guy was completely serious, but Widow didn't take it seriously simply because it wouldn't happen.

The first guy said, "Now, little lady. Why don't you be polite and toss your keys over here? Right at my feet will be fine. No need to throw dem at me."

The woman's grip on Widow's back tightened, and she pulled at him like a shield she wanted to hide behind.

The guy said, "Now don't ya make me repeat myself."

She looked down at her keys and then tossed them over to him. But they landed only halfway between that massive chrome grille and where she stood.

Widow said, "You intend to shoot both of us with that thing?"

The third guy said, "I'll shoot ya both."

"That's a center muzzleloader, right? I never fired one. Not like that. Not personally. But I know it only holds one round at a time."

"Yeah. So what?"

"So there's two of us. I'm sure you knew that because I'm sure you're just the best at math."

"I don't need no more than one bullet. I only need to shoot you."

"Is that right? Just me? And what makes you think that?"

The guy said, "'Cause she's a girl."

Widow said, "A girl that can kick your ass."

"Nah, she can't."

"Oh yes, she can."

The first guy said, "Shut up! Go stand over there!"

He pointed over to the side of the truck, which would block the two of them from the view of passing cars. If any cars were passing, but, at that moment, they were not.

Widow stayed where he was. He said, "No. We'll stay right here. Where cars passing by can see us."

The third guy kept the rifle pointed at Widow's midsection. He said, "You better do as he said, boy!"

Widow said, "You ever shoot that thing before?"

"Of course I has."

"You sure? Because it looks brand new."

"We clean it good. Dat's all."

"You know that thing has a hard kick."

"Yeah, I know. So what?"

Widow said, "So you're holding it down by the hip. You fire that thing, sure, it'll kill me. *If* you hit me. But it'll knock you on your ass."

The first guy interrupted and said, "Don't you worry about dat. You'll be dead. The kick'll be his problem. Now, get over there. By da truck."

The girl whispered into Widow's ear, "What the hell are you doing?"

Widow stayed quiet.

The first guy said, "I ain't going to ask twice. Billy here will shoot you where you stand."

Billy asked, "William, why did you tell him my name?"

Widow smiled and said, "Billy? And William? You guys are brothers?" He pointed at the second guy and asked, "So, what's your name? Willie?" He chuckled.

The second guy said, "It's Robert."

"Well, Bob, Billy, and Willie, we really gotta get going. So if we're done here, you heard the lady. We got plans in Vegas."

Widow backed away, with the girl behind his back. He knew that even though these guys were pretty stupid; they were bluffing. They wouldn't shoot them, not when at any moment a car could come sweeping over the hill and drive right by. Including a cop car or state trooper.

Billy said, "Stop, or I'll shoot ya!"

Widow paused a beat, stared him down, and then continued to back away. He shifted to the right and herded the girl out toward the road, figuring if he could get out in the open, it would force Billy to hide the rifle. No cars came at them from their side of 161, but he could hear a pack of them coming from behind him in the other direction.

He knew they would see the rifle if it came out from behind the truck, and certainly they would hear that thing if he fired it, which he wouldn't.

Widow calculated the seconds. Oncoming cars. Exposure. Twelve steps to get the girl in the car.

Billy said, "I'm warning ya! I'll shoot!"

Widow and the girl had moved over about three feet from the line to the road, and the next best thing that Widow wanted to happen, happened.

The best thing would've been for a state trooper to pull up and stop and ask if they were doing okay. But what happened was William tired of letting the situation get away from him, and without warning, he came charging at Widow.

William ran out toward Widow like a fat, lazy bull charging a stranger, but the guy was slow. It all felt rehearsed, like maybe these guys had done this before or planned different scenarios and acted them out, because another brother came running at Widow at the same time. Widow figured they had a playbook somewhere that they created to show the different moves they could do to put down the boyfriend in case he tried to play hero.

The second brother came faster than the first, and Widow figured in that split second that they'd reach him at about the same time.

Widow pushed off his toes and used his back to shove the girl backward. It was just enough to get her moving. Her legs reacted and carried her away from the charge. He didn't shove her hard, just used his body weight and her ninety pounds against her. She half slipped and half ran back toward the convertible. She ended up on the passenger side. Her two hands clutched the side mirror, and she stopped and balanced herself.

Widow used the slight momentum he had gained from moving backward to catapult himself forward in a violent rush like a two-hundred-fifty-pound football player rushing the quarterback, only with no one blocking him.

He rushed into the first brother with a sidestep to the right and a left elbow strike right into the throat—perfectly executed. The three brothers had rehearsed this scenario in every way they could think of, but they hadn't planned on a guy trained to fight by the US Navy SEALs. They hadn't planned on a guy who didn't have to rehearse because he wasn't the kind of guy who planned for things. Widow was the kind of guy who experienced things. He called audibles. For him, there was no need to plan for what might happen in combat. Fighting was all about acting and reacting. And when you'd been in as many street fights as Widow had, it was all natural.

The three brothers should've looked closer at him before they acted. If they had looked at him closer, they would've seen that his knuckles were covered in rough patches of skin that would never return to normal. They were rough and black and would stay that way. This was a guy who punched—a lot.

If these three brothers had a copy of Widow's Navy medical records, they'd see he'd had many of the bones in his body broken, cracked, fractured, or battered at one point or another, like a title holder in the MMA. Being an experienced fighter didn't come without a price. More than that, Widow had broken thousands of opponents' bones in the past.

If the three brothers had asked Widow to take off his shirt, they would've seen a nightmare. He was a naturally big guy, and his body was half covered in tattoos and knife wounds. There were three bullet scars on his back, arranged in a triangle. They were from when he was shot while undercover and left for dead. Widow had a long, dark past. But these three brothers had no way of knowing that. They had expected a run-of-the-mill boyfriend, and they had acted accordingly.

Two of the fat brothers ran at him, and he reacted.

Left elbow hard into William's neck. The front of the throat doesn't have much bone. All the bone is in the spinal column from the torso to the head, like a bridge between two major bodies of land. The rest of the neck is muscle, tendons, and ligaments. Widow had a lot of force and strength, and he was an expert at the elbow strike. For him, the trick was not to kill the guy, although in terms of self-defense, he figured he would've been well within his legal rights. But he was in Arizona and wasn't sure about the state's laws regarding murder and self-defense, and even though he would've been found innocent in a court of law, the American justice system still wasn't much of a picnic, even for the innocent. He had seen military law in action and up close and personal. And he regarded the military to be far more efficient over its civilian counterparts in most of its bureaucracies. Coming face-to-face with the Arizona justice system wasn't on the list of things he wanted to do.

Even when an innocent man gets arrested, he is still detained, imprisoned, and has to await trial if there are charges brought against him. How long would it be before he actually went to trial? Months? A year? No, thank you. Not for Widow. He had zero interest in seeing the inside of a courtroom or a jail cell or even a police cruiser. He had seen more than his fair share of the inside of cop cars.

He had given the guy a hard elbow to the front of the throat. Maybe enough to cause permanent voice damage, but not enough to kill him. The cracking sound that exploded from the guy's windpipe was a good sign he would at least never sing again, and he was out of the fight. But this guy wasn't much good at speaking, anyway. No real crime there. One down.

Robert, who might've been the fattest of the three brothers, whipped past Widow completely. Which was good because Widow needed to grab the guy from behind. Widow spun around to face the convertible and Robert's backside. He reached out and grabbed a big handful of the guy's carpenter overalls. He jerked him back, pivoted the two of them so that they now faced Billy and his Thompson rifle. Robert was now a huge human shield, and quite a good one, but only if Widow was strong enough to hold him upright, which he was.

Widow pulled the guy's shirt and overalls down hard from the back with his left hand, and the guy made choking sounds. Widow shoved his right hand into the guy's open mouth and fishhooked him hard to the right. The fat brother stumbled toward his pull. He didn't fight back, and he didn't try to escape Widow's grip. He simply gave up. Widow had expected some resistance, in which case he was prepared to punch the guy in the kidney hard enough to make him submit, but such a drastic attack hadn't been necessary.

Widow said, "Toss the gun!"

Billy said, "Let 'im go!" and moved the rifle up so the stock was deep in his shoulder, which was the only way to shoot that gun without breaking your wrists.

"Forget it! Drop the rifle!"

"No way! Ya let 'im go!"

"Billy, listen to your brother. William. Hear him?"

Billy stayed quiet, and Widow stayed quiet, but both of them could hear the Thompson rifle clatter a bit as Billy shook. He was nervous, which made Widow smile.

Billy said, "I don't hear nothin'!"

"Exactly. I hit your brother in his jugular."

Billy looked blank, like his fourth-grade teacher had just called on him to give his take on the Gettysburg address, and the only syllable he recognized from the question was *burg*, as in "burger."

Widow said, "His neck. I hit him hard in the neck." He pushed Robert toward his brother, slow and steady, trying to get closer to the gun. He said, "Do you know what's in your neck?"

"Of course, I know. Your throat's in there."

"Not exactly, but you're right. It's what we call the throat, but actually, the throat is higher. It's behind your mouth."

"So what?"

"So the neck's different. It's the place that's full of blood vessels and nerves and important stuff."

Billy's eyes flickered, and he looked at the side of the truck. Like he was trying to see his brother. Which he couldn't.

William was wriggling around on the ground and stomping his feet, but with little force. Each stomp got a little slower and a little slower, like a dimming light.

They had left their truck running, and the engine hummed, and the air conditioner quietly whirred through the internal pipes and vents as it pumped cold air into the cabin. The noises kept Billy from hearing his brother.

Billy said, "William? Are ya all right?"

Robert tried to speak, but Widow jerked his mouth hard to the right and pushed him harder to the front. His feet complied, and he moved closer to the barrel of the gun.

"He's not moving. He probably passed out already. Might be bleeding internally. You boys got health insurance?"

"Insurance? Course, we got insurance. State requirement for businesses. Ya see our uniforms, right? Ya see this is a company truck, right?"

"Insurance is good. Although I'm not sure it will cover a funeral for a fat tub of lard like your brother. I mean, you guys are criminals. And insurance companies always seem to find a way out of paying for funerals. You guys are just handing them a reason."

"What ya talking about, funeral? You da one gonna have a funeral! I'll shoot ya right here!"

"You shoot that thing, and your brother here is gonna be the one who will need a funeral. Then you'll be burying two brothers. Maybe the insurance company will pay in that case because one funeral for two people has to be cheaper than two separate funeral services."

Widow stepped closer and closer. He stayed snug behind his human shield, who still complied like a puppet. And he said, "Of course, maybe William will survive. Maybe he'll just be a human vegetable. You know? Hooked up to all those machines?"

"What ya talking 'bout?"

"Billy, I'm talking about William being a veggie. I'm talking about you showing your brother how much you love him. You do love him, right?"

"Of course, I love my brothers."

"That's good, because if William is a vegetable, he's going to need you to feed him and bathe him and change his diapers."

"What ya mean? Diapers?"

"Billy, he's not gonna be able to take a shit by himself. Who you think is gonna change his diapers and wash his ass for him?"

Billy said nothing.

"Have you ever seen your brother's privates?"

"You shut up!"

"Billy, you gotta think about these things. If we don't get William to a hospital, then you'll have to look at his privates and change his diapers and wash his ass. Are you ready for that?"

Widow was now about five feet from the barrel of the rifle. He said, "Then again, maybe we can wait longer, and he'll die. You got a family plot? Got a funeral parlor that your family has done business with over the generations of idiots that have made up your family tree?"

"What? We ain't got no such arrangement!"

Widow ignored him and said, "Bet they'll give you guys a break, like a discount. Two for one."

Just then, Widow stepped back away from Robert and then pushed off with his back feet and launched the fat brother into the other one, straight into the line of fire.

Billy reacted and fired the gun and screamed, all at the same time. The gun didn't fire. Lucky too, because then he really would've been burying his brother.

There were only two possibilities why it didn't fire. One, the rifle wasn't loaded. Widow wasn't sure that Billy would've even known because he had pulled the hammer back and pulled the trigger as if it would fire, meaning that he believed it would. Being a center muzzleloader, it was possible to miscalculate the weight. These guns only held one round, which wouldn't have been much difference in weight for him to have noticed.

The other possibility was that it could've jammed, which was a real risk with these rifles. It wasn't common that a center muzzleloader jammed, but it was far from unheard of.

Robert went tumbling into Billy like one big hippo falling into another. They fell back, off balance, and stumbled backward on top of each other.

Widow took the chance to make sure they stayed immobile. He jogged over to them, lifted his foot up, and stomped down on the back of Robert's head. One fat head slammed down into the other. A loud crack echoed off the side of the truck. It sounded like a cement block dropped out of a fourth-story window, crashing to a concrete street below, shattering into tiny little pieces.

Widow stepped back and reached down. He grabbed Robert's back collar and bunched it up. He rolled him off his brother, who was conscious and cupping his nose, which was inarguably broken.

Billy squirmed from side to side and turned and spit out his two front teeth. He said something that was mostly inaudible, but Widow guessed it was something about a broken nose or broken teeth or both.

The other brother was more of a concern because he wasn't moving at all. Widow rolled him over and tilted his head to the side, waiting to hear if the guy was breathing. He was. His chest moved up and down. His nose wasn't broken, but his eyebrows were already turning black and red.

Widow left him there and stepped on the rifle with his right foot. He bent down and picked it up, pulled the barrel down, and checked to see if it was loaded. It was.

He said, "Well, look at that. You're unlucky. Either that, or you don't clean the gun very well."

Billy said nothing.

Widow said, "Your brothers are alive, but William will need a hospital. Better get there soon."

Widow took the rifle and walked over toward the desert landscape and faced it. He raised the gun and aimed up at the sky and cocked the hammer and aimed at a cloud. He breathed in and held it and squeezed the trigger. The gun fired. The kick hammered the stock into his shoulder. A quick whip of white smoke ejected from the gun, and he pulled it away from his body.

"Fires just fine. You really are an unlucky tub of lard!"

Widow opened the rifle and pulled the brass out. He dropped it in the sand and stomped it down and down, burying it into the dirt.

He walked back to the vehicles and looked at the three brothers. The second one was now awake and was rubbing his forehead like he had the headache of a lifetime, which he probably did. All three brothers squirmed around like broken turtles.

He said, "You're all unlucky, but you're lucky too, because this is all you're gonna get."

The girl cautiously walked over and picked up her keys, then she returned to the driver's side door and said, "That's it? We're going to let them get away with this? They might've killed us!"

Widow said, "No. Not completely. We'll call the cops, but let's get on the road first. I don't want to waste time filling out paperwork and reports and so on."

"That's it?" she repeated.

Widow said, "Look. You can call them and do reports and all that stuff. I'd completely understand. And maybe you should. They might've done this before. They might do it again. I understand if you want to make sure that they get locked up."

She stared at him.

"A phone call from the road will do the same," he said. "The cops will come and arrest these guys and hold them. You can explain that you just wanted to leave as soon as possible. They'll get it. Believe me."

"What about you? What do I tell them about you?"

"Tell them the truth. I helped you. Tell them you don't know me and I vanished. Which is the truth. I'm not interested in helping the cops any more than I already have."

She nodded. She said, "I'm Scarlet."

"Widow."

She didn't comment on his name like he expected, but asked, "Do you want a ride?"

"Of course. Let's go."

Widow walked to the convertible. Then he stopped and turned and went back to the truck. He grabbed the door lever and jerked it, and opened the driver's side door. Widow grabbed the key and switched off the ignition and pulled the key out. He backed out of the truck and put the key in his pocket.

He leaned back in and pulled the lever to pop the hood. He walked around to it, lifted it open, and studied the engine for a moment. Then he ripped and pulled at things that looked important. He had never been a car expert or a mechanic, but he knew that cars and trucks couldn't run without wires and hoses and such. So he jerked and pulled and ripped everything that was loose. One thing he jerked out that he could identify was the distributor cap. That was one thing he was certain they couldn't drive without, even though he wasn't sure what the hell it did.

Widow took all the hoses and wires and the distributor cap. He opened the passenger door of the convertible and dumped himself down on the seat. He tossed the entanglement of hoses, wires, and distributor cap down into the passenger side footwell.

Widow looked over at Scarlet and said, "Come on. Let's hit the road."

"Okay," she said and opened the door and sat down. She cranked the car and reversed it so that she could turn the car around and head in the right direction, with the flow of traffic, which was only two oncoming cars, both of which slowed, the occupants leaning out and surveying the three guys on the ground. But neither of them stopped. Widow figured they felt it wasn't any of their business.

Ten seconds later, Widow and Scarlet were on the road and on their way to Las Vegas, on their way to getting to know each other, stopping for gas, stopping for coffee, and then continuing on their way to a motel off the Las Vegas Strip. They spent four days and three nights there, entangled in sheets, getting to know each other. The sheets were clean and fresh on the first day, but Widow had opened the door and slipped the *do not disturb* sign over the door's knob, and not once did any of the maids or the hotel manager come to knock. But on the third night, a security guard for the hotel came by and hammered an enormous fist on the door.

Widow and Scarlet were spent and had been lying there talking, which wasn't something that they had done much of.

"Who could that be?" she asked.

Widow said, "I'll get it."

Widow got up from the bed. He searched the floor and the tangle of bed comforters and sheets and clothes for his pants. It was unusual that he'd go so many days and nights without buying new clothes for himself. It just so happened that he hadn't needed clothes for a few days. Not his T-shirt. Not his shoes. Not his socks. And certainly not his pants.

He figured that even if he had never seen the Las Vegas Strip, which was the main reason a million people visited Las Vegas every week, then he'd still leave Las Vegas with a great impression of the city. The giant fist outside pounded on the door again.

Widow said, "Wait! I'm coming!"

Widow bent down and shifted the pile of clothes from one side to the other. He found his pants. He pulled them out of the pile and stood up straight. The legs were twisted together like a pretzel. He whipped the pants out in front of him. Once. Twice. Then he put them on and zipped up and buttoned. He walked to the door and unlocked the dead bolt and jolted the door open.

A heavy guy stood in the doorway, an older black man with a beard and a bald head, freshly shaved. The guy had the frame of a former bodybuilder who no longer put in the effort like he used to. He wore some kind of secondhand, store-bought security guard uniform. One of his hands was empty and down by his side. The other was out in front of him with a big flashlight. The beam was off.

He said, "Sorry to disturb you, sir. We've been getting noise complaints from the neighbors."

The guy leaned to his left and stared into the room. The lights were off, but the light from outside in the courtyard flooded enough of the room to light it up. He saw the bedding and clothes strewn across the floor, and then he saw Scarlet, who was naked but had covered her vital parts under a thin sheet.

The guard said, "Oh. So sorry to bother you, ma'am."

He nodded at Scarlet, and then he returned his eyes to Widow's face. The guy looked like not much scared him, but Widow's rugged face and massive torso gave him pause. Widow saw it on his face. It was a natural reaction he got often. The first part of his life had been filled with this kind of profiling, and it was annoying, but he was used to it now, and instead of huffing and puffing and making a big deal out of it, he often resorted to being as kind as he could to strangers while smiling. Smiling was key.

He shot the guy a big smile. All straight teeth. Widow had broken a lot of his bones on missions and in street fights, but he had always had good teeth. Never a cavity. His mother had been very insistent that he go to the dentist and take care of his teeth. She always said a woman likes a man with great teeth.

He said, "Well, we're certainly sorry for the noise. I guarantee there'll be no more noise tonight, and we check out in the morning. So no worries from now on."

The guy stayed in the doorway for longer than he should have, like he was trying to think of something else to say, but finally he said, "Good. You folks have a good night." And then he turned and walked away.

Widow shut the door behind him.

Scarlet said, "We were so loud they called security on us!"

"Yeah. You make too much noise."

Scarlet smiled and gestured for him to come over. She said, "Come back to bed. I have more noise to make."

Widow's smile turned to a smaller crooked one. His mother used to say it made him look like a little devil when he was a boy. She knew when he was up to no good because of that smile.

He unbuttoned his pants, unzipped them, pulled them off, and tossed them back to the pile of clothes and bedding. He stepped back to the bed, put one leg up and then the other, and crawled over to Scarlet.

She clawed her long fingernails across his back. She whispered in his ear, "This time, I'll be quieter. I don't want us to get kicked out."

She turned out to be lying, and Widow didn't mind one bit.

* * *

THE NEXT MORNING, Widow stepped out of the room, fully clothed, and went looking for coffee. He didn't lock the door behind him because he didn't plan to be gone long.

He went to the front desk in the lobby, where he expected they offered free coffee, like a lot of places do, but there was none. The girl behind the desk said their machine was broken. She said there was a Starbucks across the street. Widow smiled at her and said nothing else.

He left the hotel and crossed an intersection that was busy with cars carrying people headed to their jobs and their busy days. The street was called Sahara. Las Vegas was full of imaginative street names like Paradise and Sahara and Flamingo.

He went into the Starbucks and stood in a long line and waited for what seemed like forever for a simple pair of black coffees, which they didn't offer. They asked him questions like "What kind of roast?" and "What flavor?" and "What size?"

He said, "Coffee. Coffee. And regular."

The barista behind the counter was younger than he was, maybe even high school aged. She said, "What roast and flavor and size, sir?"

He thought he had answered those questions. But then she pointed at the menu board behind her. She said, "We've got different roasts for coffee. We've got a variety of flavors. And the sizes are short, tall, grande, and venti."

Widow saw behind her on a back counter a display of the coffee cups and their sizes. The venti was some kind of huge portion, but he liked it. To Widow, there was no such thing as too big, not when it came to coffee. But he didn't want to carry around a venti, and he needed to bring Scarlet a coffee too. That was the polite thing to do. He wondered if she even liked black coffee. She had a dancer's body, and she was a female, and she was working in Las Vegas. She probably drank one of those lattes or teas or something.

The barista said, "Sir?"

Widow shrugged and said, "Just give me two coffees, black. Two tall sizes."

"What about the flavor and roast?"

"You pick. Give me the most popular."

She nodded and told him the price, which was ridiculous for coffee, but he gave her his debit card and paid for it.

He walked down to the designated waiting zone for coffee, which was full of people.

Being idle wasn't something Widow enjoyed, but it was the price of a civilized society. We all wait for our turn.

While waiting, he started thinking. And a question popped into his head. He asked himself, if Scarlet lived in Las Vegas, then why were they at a hotel?

Then he decided it was better to not ask questions, and just enjoy himself.

* * *

WIDOW CARRIED the two dark roast coffees back to the hotel. He drank half of his on the way there. It wasn't too bad. He liked the flavor and decided that fighting battles against Starbucks was fruitless, since they didn't seem to go anywhere. He memorized the flavor and roast for future expediency.

Widow continued to contemplate the question of why they were at a hotel and not at Scarlet's place. Widow suspected he already knew the answer to this question. He hoped it was because she had an obnoxious roommate, or her place was being fumigated, or she lived with her parents, but somehow he doubted those reasons. Widow figured it was a live-in boyfriend. He didn't suspect a husband because Scarlet hadn't had a wedding ring on or a tan line from one, and she didn't strike him as the marrying kind. But he wasn't naïve. He suspected a husband was just as likely an answer as a live-in boyfriend.

Widow never got his answer, however, at least not exactly. He was left with the mystery of Scarlet's circumstances because when he returned to the hotel, her car was gone from the space it had been parked in for four days, and when he opened the door to their room, all that was left of her existence was the evidence that two people had three nights of incredible sex there. But there was no evidence of Scarlet. No clothes. No shoes. No female items left behind. The only thing she had left for him was a trace of her perfume, which had been in the air for days. Not that he minded it. It was a great scent.

He stood in the doorway and stared one last time at the room that was stored in his memory banks forever, classified under the heading of unforgettable nights.

On the pillow on his side of the bed, the one that he had slept on three nights in a row, she had left him a note on a piece of paper she'd ripped from the notepad on the nightstand next to the bed. He could see her scribbles from the doorway, and he could see the note was short. Three lines, maybe only two. He could see she had signed it not with a signature but with a kiss. An enormous pair of red lips rested at the bottom half of the page like she had put on lipstick and gently pressed down, using only her lips, to leave the impression of a kiss.

Widow didn't reenter the room. There was no reason to. He didn't need to know what the message said. He was sure it was something like "I had a great time," "I wish you luck," or "Under different circumstances..." and so on and so forth. It wouldn't say anything he needed to know, nothing he cared to know.

Widow turned and shut the door, drinking the rest of his coffee as he walked toward the street. He stopped at a trash can near the front office and tossed in the empty coffee cup. Holding the coffee that he had bought for Scarlet, he headed south along the road against the traffic. Widow thought about going to the Strip and at least walking it. Since he was already in Las Vegas, he might as well see the Strip. It made sense. Why waste the opportunity? He was essentially a tourist after all. But he was a little sad about Scarlet's abrupt departure and changed course to head into Texas and not wait. He'd spent enough time in Las Vegas.

5

THE KILL TEAM was smaller than the last one Glock had been a part of, but for their current assignment, it was way too large. Four team members for one target were three too many. He could locate and kill the target on his own. But this was the way the Principal wanted it. It was a waste of talent and money in his opinion, but then again, no one paid for his opinion. He was only paid to handle the dirty side of the business.

The Principal wasn't a man he feared, but he wasn't a man to be underestimated either. If the time came to get his hands dirty, the Principal would be there to do it. The Principal was a man with two faces. He was partners with Glock and also had another job. Everyone knew the Principal, everyone within a thousand-mile radius.

The kill team comprised four people—three men and one woman. One man was Hispanic. The Principal had probably thought he was valuable for his fluency in Spanish, but they could all understand and speak Spanish, including Glock. This was Texas, after all. A lot of white people understood Spanish.

Glock didn't have a problem with a Mexican on his team. He had worked in the SEALs and knew plenty of Mexican sailors. But he had a deep hatred for them. And like the Principal, he kept it a secret.

Each of the kill team members was experienced with Special Forces and counterintelligence. They were some of the best that money could buy, available on short notice. And the Principal had the money to spend. More money had been offered up by the Principal than Glock expected, but then again, they both wanted Hood dead—and fast.

Glock and the three other members of the kill team sat in his personal Chevy Tahoe on the street across from Claire Hood's El Paso apartment building. They'd been there for a few hours and realized her granddaughter had never come home from school. They had tapped Claire's phone line and had listened in the entire night, which had been easy since the old lady still used her house phone for most of her calls. And they weren't even sure she had a cell phone.

The woman on the team said, "He took the kid. We missed him."

Glock said, "No shit."

"What do we do now?" asked the oldest member of the team.

Glock sipped the last bit of his coffee, which he had brought in a big thermos, and he said, "I guess we split up."

"How?" asked the woman.

"Into two groups. You two stay on the old bird."

"But she's called about everyone she must know already. If she knew where Hood was with the little girl, she'd have gone there already. Right?"

Glock said, "Nah. She doesn't have a car. I looked before. She doesn't have a car registered in her name, and no driver's license either."

"Why didn't she call the cops?" the other guy asked.

"She can't call them. The kid is illegal. Like the mother."

The woman asked, "How's that? Hood looks white from his photo."

"Yeah, he is. Hood's not the actual father. He took in the little girl and her mother from Mexico. He brought them over illegal-like."

The older guy said, "I'm surprised the boss let you hire him. Didn't you guys vet him?"

"Just do your job!" Glock barked. It had been his mistake not to look closer at a new hire.

The woman asked, "So what do we do?"

"You two stay on her. If she goes anywhere, follow her."

"How the hell will she go anywhere without a car?"

Glock said, "Bus, maybe."

The woman nodded and asked, "What about you?"

"We're going to pay a visit to Mrs. Hood. His wife."

Silence fell over the SUV.

The other guy asked, "Isn't she dying?"

"Yeah. She's in the hospital."

"Are you guys going to kill her?"

Glock said, "We might kill them all. The Principal warned Hood two years ago. We told him what would happen if he caused problems for us. They all die."

"But we don't even know if he's told anyone," the other guy said.

Glock said, "We don't pay you to think. We pay you to follow orders. You got a problem killing a kid?"

"No."

"An old lady?"

"No."

"A dying woman?"

"No. Of course not."

Glock said, "Good."

The kill team didn't share Glock's motivations, but they liked money, and this was a well-paying job. That was all that mattered.

The woman said, "We need a vehicle."

"Let's go rent something. You stay here," Glock said to the other guy.

The other guy nodded and got out of the Tahoe. He walked over to a park across the street and sat on a bench and watched the apartment. Glock and the rest headed out to rent a second car.

* * *

WIDOW HAD BEEN BURNED in Las Vegas, like many of its visitors. Only he had been burned by a woman, which wasn't a big deal. It hadn't been the first time a woman had left him, and it wouldn't be the last time. That was the very nature of being a single man. Lovers would come and go, and they'd lie, and they'd have secrets, and they'd disappoint. That was a fact as old as time, and it wouldn't change soon. But the second time Widow got burned was when he was trying to get a lift out of Vegas.

He ended up getting a ride with a nice Asian couple in a tiny SUV. They came to Vegas as a live-together couple and left as a married couple, against the wishes of their parents. They told him an abbreviated version of their story, and when they asked him about himself, he had been honest with them. He had told them he was ex-military and was now a drifter and nothing more. But they must've not liked something about him because they traveled about twenty miles outside of Las Vegas and then stopped at a gas station. They gave him a ten-dollar bill and told him to grab them some bottles of water for the road, which he'd happily agreed to do. But as soon as he was at the register with three large bottles in hand, he'd looked out to the pump where they had been parked, and the car was gone.

He looked farther, tracing the service drive with his eyes, and saw them at the stop sign. He watched them turn right and speed off, back to the interstate. They had left him. Why? He didn't know. That was life. Some questions would always remain mysteries.

The kid at the register said, "Sir? You want to get those?"

Widow looked back at him and said, "Nah. Sorry, my mistake. I'll put them back."

"I can do it. Just leave 'em."

Widow put the bottled waters on the counter next to the register, and then he asked, "Where's the coffee?"

"We got some old stuff back there, but if you want the better coffee, we got a café. Over there."

Widow looked over at a tiny café attached to the gas station. He nodded and then asked, "You got any books or magazines here?"

As a kid, Widow had picked up a love of books from his mother. Being on the road so much gave him plenty of opportunities to read. But he hadn't had a book in his back pocket in quite some time.

"Sure. We got a few books back on the far wall. Near the oil and car stuff."

"Thanks."

Widow walked back down two aisles and turned on one, and found the book and magazine rack. On the rack was *USA Today*. No other paper of record to speak of, which he had expected. He saw on the cover of the *USA Today* an article about the building of a wall on the US-Mexican border. Then down on the front of the paper, some guy was mentioned as being attached to the proposal—Sheridan.

Widow picked up the paper and folded it. He might as well buy it. He also sifted through the books, which was easy because there were only ten of interest. The rest was that romance crap. A few

were authors he knew and liked. One was a ~~Grisham book he'd~~
read before but really liked.

He bought the book and the paper and headed over to the café
side and took a seat at an empty booth. After several minutes, the
same kid from behind the register came over and acted slightly
differently, like now he was wearing his waiter hat and not his gas
station attendant hat.

Whatever works, Widow thought.

* * *

THE KILL TEAM split up into two teams. Glock liked to think of
them as the A team and the B team—A being his team, the alpha
team, and B being the lesser team. Not that either team was less
suited for this assignment. James Hood was only one guy,
after all.

Right then, Glock and the Hispanic member were assigned to
watch the wife, which was a cake assignment because she was on
her deathbed in a hospital in El Paso. Glock didn't want to be
watching the wife, but the Principal figured Hood would attempt
contact with her before he ran. They knew the daughter had
already been taken. They'd missed the opportunity to grab Hood
before that happened. So now they figured he couldn't help but
see the wife before he left. So they waited for him.

He wasn't happy about having to kill a woman who was dying in a
hospital bed, but he wasn't upset about it either. Even when he
used to be a sailor, he never questioned what targets he was
supposed to kill. The way he figured it, there wasn't much difference between killing for money as a civilian contractor and killing
as a SEAL. Both were jobs.

The brass had booted him out. They'd shown their true colors.
But the way he saw it now was that he used to kill for them, and
they paid him. All that stuff about honor and brotherhood and
duty was just lies. The way he saw it, it all came down to money.
Everything was about money, and now he was getting paid a

whole hell of a lot more to maintain his own region in the Principal's network than he ever was as a Navy SEAL.

He looked down the hall at his teammate, who was a short guy. Older too. He didn't look like he was part of a kill team, which might've been why he was so good at it.

The teammate sat on a bench near the elevators and the vending machines. The hospital was a little busy today. Visitors walked up and down the corridors. It seemed there were as many visitors as there were hospital staff walking around. Then again, this was the oncology ward, and America had a lot of cancer patients.

Lucy Hood had no visitors at the moment. No one noticed him standing in front of her hospital room. He wasn't really there to kill her, but he might have to. And that was okay, too. Killing a dying woman in her bed was more about revenge than about killing her.

Glock was happy to kill whoever, to protect his interest in the Principal's organization.

* * *

WIDOW ORDERED a coffee and sat in a booth in a makeshift café, one of those generic things with stale muffins and day-old cakes and scones wrapped in plastic bags and two flavors of coffee —nothing fancy, just black—caffeinated, and decaffeinated, and that's it. And that was fine with him. He only drank black coffee. No sugar. No cream. No milk. None of those artificial sweeteners, not the pink ones or the blue ones or the yellow ones, and not even the ones with the tiny green leaf on the package that indicated to lesser minds, *Hey, use me. I'm natural. I got a leaf. I'm better for you than sugar*. Those sweeteners were worse for people than mountains of sugar. He had witnessed coffee drinkers shoveling it into their cups. The thought often made him grimace, but only a little, because Widow's opinion was basically live and let live. It was your life, your body, your choice, not his. So why judge?

He hadn't even cracked open the book he bought because he read the newspaper instead. He skipped over much of the political nonsense. One side was right and one side was wrong. And which was which depended on who you asked.

Widow stopped to read about this Texas senator named Sheridan.

John Sheridan—sounded like the hotel chain, only no connection —was a two-term Texas senator who used to work with the DEA and had quite an impressive rise there. Now he was a senator in Texas. The biggest takeaway about him was that he was the strongest advocate for the building of the border wall. In fact, the article traced the idea of the wall to his creation many years ago. It said that he was the one who had pushed the new presidential candidate on the idea. They were of the same party and were aligned on the entire issue of immigration—nothing surprising to Widow. Texas politicians had been screaming about illegal immigration for decades. The irony here was that most illegal immigration of undocumented people was from people traveling by air, not crossing the border. They simply came over with a visa and then overstayed. There was little enforcement of penalties for overstaying.

Things were different now than in previous decades because there was a real possibility of a wall. Widow didn't live in a border state, but he had been to Texas and had even crossed into Mexico before. The terrain was beautiful; he couldn't imagine sullying it with a big, monstrous wall. Then again, the Great Wall of China was pretty magnificent. Of course, that was apples and oranges. He couldn't imagine the same being true with a US-Mexico wall because the governments of today were all about saving money and cutting corners. Thousands of years ago, China was all about using the best materials to make a wall that was really impregnable. Which proved true because that wall was still standing and magnificent today. That's why it's called the *Great* Wall.

John Sheridan was an impressive guy to read about. He was wealthy, successful, and had a law enforcement background. He had gotten rich after leaving the DEA. The article didn't go into too much detail on how. It only said it happened through a series of investments and holdings, etcetera. Apparently, John Sheridan had aligned himself with all the right people in the public and private sectors.

Widow drank three cups of the generic but tolerable gas station coffee, then stood up from the booth and left five bucks in cash on the tabletop for the waiter who doubled as the gas station cashier. At first, Widow had felt bad for the guy as he'd watched him come over and serve him and then go back to the gas station to stock and rearrange the candy bar aisle. But on second thought, Widow's sympathy retreated because he thought maybe the guy had originally been a stock boy, making minimum wage, and the café gave him the opportunity to make tips on top of his wages. That didn't seem like such a bad gig. The guy looked like he should've been in high school instead of working at a gas station. Maybe he was eighteen, or maybe he had dropped out of school, or maybe both. Tips plus a decent wage wasn't bad money for an eighteen-year-old. Widow had worked for much less when he was this kid's age.

Widow guessed refills were free, as they always are for restaurant coffee, and he guessed at most that the coffee was two dollars plus tax, which was about eight percent. It was probably more like seven and some decimal points, but it was always better to round up. So eight percent seemed right. Five bucks meant the guy got a generous tip for serving only a coffee, even though it had been three trips.

Widow left the *USA Today* on the table and stuffed his new book into his back pocket. He walked out to the highway and started looking for a ride, which didn't take him long. He ended up getting into an old blue Buick with two women who weren't much younger than he was. They wore college-branded clothes— comfortable T-shirts with the same three Greek letters. They were obviously sorority sisters. Widow didn't recognize the letters or the name of the sorority because he had never been to a public university and had no interest in fraternities or sororities or what he had heard called the "Greek life."

The girls were half road-tripping and half on a mission. They explained to Widow that they had begun their trip to Amarillo about a week earlier. They had started as a trio who were best friends through all four years of college. The third friend was getting married in Las Vegas.

Now that school was fading into the past and one of them was getting married, they were going to be split up for the first time, something they were a little nervous about. Therefore, they had thought they should go out on one last adventure—one last road trip from Amarillo to Las Vegas to deliver their friend to her wedding, which they had done.

Widow rode with the two girls the rest of their trip back to Amarillo, which didn't feel as long as it actually was. Not at all, because he had a good time. He had met a lot of drivers on the road. Some talked, and some didn't. Normally, the ones who talked a lot rambled on and on. Widow would nod along and smile and try to listen in case he was quizzed afterward. He tried to memorize small tidbits of the conversation so that it seemed like he was interested, even though many times he wasn't. And sometimes it wasn't because the driver was boring or he wasn't interested, but because many times, different people had similar stories. These drivers were the ones who drove long stretches and were lonely and needed single-serving companionship, which Widow was happy to provide for the ride.

After the girls had accepted him into their fold, he felt for a brief time like he was part of their clique, like he was one of the girls, which made him smile because he was a large guy, a former Navy SEAL, and here he was, having girl talk. But Widow was never one to disrupt the flow. Sometimes going with it was the right course of action. So they talked, and he listened, and then he talked. He told them he was traveling the country like a tourist, and for no particular reason other than just to wander. Sometimes people needed a little more explanation, so he'd say he'd already seen the world. Why not see America?

They drove on I-40 east until they wound down into Amarillo. They stopped at a gas station to fill up and asked Widow where he wanted to be dropped off. He shrugged and told them they could leave him at the station if they wanted. But they refused this because they claimed to be new friends, and friends didn't abandon each other. They asked if he had ever taken the bus, and he told them he had ridden the bus before, but not that often. It was just one of those things. He enjoyed walking and following the road. When you buy a bus ticket, you have to choose a destination, and Widow didn't like to make choices or plans. He didn't mind hitching rides, but choosing a destination was like knowing where he wanted to be, and he wanted to be wherever life led him.

But in the end, he asked the girls to drop him off at a bus station, which they did, and they said their goodbyes and good lucks.

He walked up to a two-story building with red brick that looked orange. He glanced up at three oversized white letters painted high on the building that read "*Bus.*" Part of the building was painted white and wasn't two stories but was attached to the other section.

He walked through a set of double doors into the white part. Inside were maybe a dozen people waiting around for buses. He stepped up to a ticket counter, where a short guy with one lazy eye stood ready and smiling like he had the best job in the world—different people have different expectations. Widow smiled back because the guy had a warm smile and a glow about him. He might've been in his late thirties or early forties. When he spoke, he sounded a little slower than most, but not as dumb as many.

The guy asked, "You need a ticket?"

Widow said, "I do."

The guy asked, "Where to?"

And for the first time in a while, Widow froze. He had planned little further than walking up to the counter.

So he said, "I don't know."

The guy continued to smile and asked, "You don't know where you're going?"

Widow shook his head.

The guy said, "Well, that's like most people." And he chuckled a little at his own joke. Then he said, "Where would you like to go?"

Widow asked, "What are my choices?"

The guy said, "Well, you can go just about anywhere, but I'd suggest taking a direct bus, and that limits your choices by a lot."

Widow said, "Okay. Where's the next bus headed?"

The guy tapped his fingers on a keyboard. A first tap. A second tap. He could see the guy staring off to the right at a computer monitor.

And the guy said, "There's one in thirty minutes, south to Rough Creek."

Widow asked, "Rough Creek?"

"Yeah. It's a small town on the way to San Antonio."

"Why can't I just ride the bus to San Antonio?"

"It goes to San Antonio. But the ride from Rough Creek to San Antonio is full. There's one seat left, but you'll have to get off in Rough Creek."

Widow furrowed more than his brows; his whole forehead showed his displeasure.

The guy said, "You can buy a ticket to San Antonio from there. On another bus."

Widow thought for a moment and shrugged and said, "Fine. Give me a ticket to Rough Creek."

The guy clicked away on the keyboard some more, and then he said, "That's fifty-five dollars."

"Do you take debit?"

The guy said, "Of course, sir. We also have an ATM around the corner. Near the bathrooms. But it has a three-dollar fee for use that is automatically deducted from your bank account."

Widow handed the guy his debit card. The guy smiled and printed a ticket. Widow took the bus pass and stuffed it into his pocket.

Widow backed away from the counter and turned a corner in the lobby. He found the bathrooms and the ATM. Widow withdrew some cash from the ATM in case there was no ATM in Rough Creek, then stepped into the bathroom. He went to a urinal, which had a Power Ranger shoved in it on top of a bright green urinal screen. Widow decided he was having a good day so far—full of little bits of humor.

He did his business and zipped up and walked to the sink, which was the primary reason he had gone into the bathroom in the first place, because it was the middle of the summer, and he was in Texas. Texas wasn't a friendly state for summer temperatures. It wasn't as hot as it could've been, or even as it normally was, but it was still somewhere in the eighties. And Widow had been sweating from the moment he stepped out of the blue Buick. He felt the need to wash his face.

He stood over the sink, ran the water as cold as he could get it, and splashed it in huge handfuls onto his face. His hair had grown back out from the last time he had shaved his head. He debated on shaving it again, just because of the heat, but he wasn't planning to stay in Texas long. He considered the bus to Rough Creek and thought it sounded quaint, which was something he liked about small towns. Maybe he'd like it there. Maybe he'd stay a while.

After he got his face cold and wet, he didn't dry it. He walked out of the bus station and sat on a bench, waiting for the bus.

* * *

WIDOW RODE THE BUS, got off in the small town of Rough
Creek, and decided that after a nearly fifteen-hour day of riding,
he needed sleep. But first, he was hungry. It was already close to
midnight. He walked for a bit, stopped at a lounge playing live
jazz music, and ate cheese fries and had another coffee—black.
He sat at the bar and asked about the town. It turned out that
there really wasn't much to it other than the Native American
casinos. He wasn't a fan of casinos, nothing really against them
per se, just not big on them. So he called it a night and ended up
staying in a motel off the highway about a mile from the casinos.

He woke up the next morning to a hot, humid day with a relent-
less sun. This only added to the fact that he had no desire to stay
in Rough Creek any longer, or Texas. So he grabbed a quick
breakfast at a McDonald's and headed to the bus station. He
changed his mind about going to San Antonio. Widow's path was
like the changing wind. It went one direction and then the next.
He bought a ticket to Shreveport.

About thirty minutes after he'd sat down on a bench in a place far
from the other passengers, a little old lady walked over to the
benches across from him. She sat down like she had picked
Widow out of everyone else as the guy she wanted to be near. He
said nothing to her, but gave her a casual nod.

Another ten minutes passed, and the sun felt like it was getting
hotter. It fired hot rays down on the Texas terrain like it had a
personal grudge against the people in the Lone Star State.

Widow sat a little uncomfortably on a black bench that was half
rubber, half plastic, and completely worn out. He sat straight up
with his legs out, feet planted firmly on the cement, like tree
trunks that had grown up and burst through the pavement. His
knees went up higher than everyone else's who sat around him
because he was a big guy, six feet four inches tall. He ignored his
slight discomfort on the bench because he was more concerned
with the state of health of the woman who sat across from him.

She wore a short-sleeved, button-down black shirt with an
unstarched collar, like it had been pulled straight out of the

laundry and put on. She had a brown skirt on and different colored socks, one brown and one pink, which made no sense. He figured maybe she was color blind. She had a tiny purse, which rested neatly on her lap: a very proper woman, minus the pink sock.

She wore a ring, possibly a wedding ring, on her left hand. It looked ancient but well kept, polished to shine like it held memories of good times, and she wanted to preserve it as long as possible.

She wore little makeup, but what she had on looked like it was done by a seasoned professional.

The heat was becoming unbearable for Widow, and he was younger than she was and healthy. He could only imagine how it must've felt for her.

She kept looking at him, but every time he returned her gaze, she looked away. Besides the look of concern on her face, she also looked like she wanted to say something, but she stayed quiet.

Widow wasn't sure if he should speak first or just wait for her. He let this go on for a good while.

Finally, Widow looked at her. He straightened out his back and held his head high, which might've been the result of seeing an older lady who looked so proper. She reminded him of Mrs. Schneider, a teacher way back in his Sunday school days. She was the ruler-wielding type who barked orders like "Sit up straight" and "Eyes forward."

He asked, "Ma'am, are you okay? Maybe you should go sit inside where the air conditioner is blasting. Nice and cold. Get outta this heat."

She didn't speak.

Widow said, "I can come get you when your bus comes."

She stayed quiet.

"Ma'am, it's very hot. Why don't you step back inside? Let me come get you. I don't mind. Really."

The old lady looked at him, her watery eyes filled with a look like she was praying for him to help her. She said, "Oh, dear. No, I'm not worried about the heat."

Widow said, "Tell me. What's going on?"

She shook her head and said, "I shouldn't involve you."

"Maybe I can help you. Tell me what's going on."

The old lady clutched her purse tight and brought it up to her midsection. Her fingers strummed the strap in slow, nervous taps, like it was a musical instrument. She said, "I don't know where to start."

Widow said, "Why don't you just take a breath and start wherever?"

The old woman took a deep breath.

"Nice and slow."

She nodded and said, "It's my granddaughter."

She reached for her bag. She started with the long zipper, pulled it to the end of the track, and then she plunged her hand into the bag.

Widow expected her to pull out a cell phone to show him a photo of her granddaughter, like grandmothers do, but she didn't pull out a phone. Instead, she pulled out an actual photograph, a Polaroid. She leaned across the space between the benches.

A normal guy would've had to stand up and walk over to her. But Widow had long arms and a long reach. Widow leaned forward and took the photograph. He hadn't seen a Polaroid photograph in probably a decade, or maybe even two. He didn't know they still existed.

The Polaroid had a black backside and a thin, white trim around the photo on the front side.

He looked at it.

There were two females in the picture. The first was an older version of the other—obviously a mother and daughter.

The mother was attractive and Hispanic. She wasn't skinny, but far from having too much meat on her bones. The mother's hair was dyed—Widow thought the color was called platinum. She had brown eyes and a brilliant smile. There was a glow to her face. She was a naturally cheerful person. Widow could tell.

Then there was the little girl, who was around five years old in the photo. She also had a gigantic smile on her face and that same glow embedded deep in her face. She was laughing. It looked like she was being tickled by her mother. They both looked up and smiled at the same time. It had that look of real authenticity that people who created catalogs always wanted to capture and use as cover photos. Widow figured a professional photographer could've been behind it. Perhaps there were tricks of the trade that allowed him to capture such a joyously natural moment, but Widow doubted it. He believed that, more than likely, every moment with these two ladies was authentic. He doubted there were ever dull times.

He said, "They're beautiful ladies. You must be proud."

The old woman said, "She's seven. Almost seven."

"What happened to her?"

The old woman cried. She was a sweet old lady, but she didn't seem to be in a good frame of mind. She said, "I'm so sorry." And she reached up with her right hand, wiped a single tear off of her face.

Widow stayed quiet.

The old woman said, "My name is Claire Hood. And that's Jemma. And the older one is Lucy. Lucy's my daughter-in-law."

He repeated, "What happened to Jemma?"

Claire said, "It's my son."

She paused a beat and looked around. She said, "He's a mixed-up man. His name's James."

"What did he do to her?"

Claire's lip trembled and quiver. She looked like she was on the verge of more tears, and maybe she would've started gushing tears, but she also looked exhausted, like she'd been up for days.

Claire said, "It's... it's..."

"Go ahead, Claire. You can trust me."

"My daughter-in-law, Lucy, has cancer. You see?"

Widow nodded.

"It's terminal. Right now, as we speak, she's in a hospital. In El Paso."

She paused a long beat, and then she said, "She's not going to make it. She's in a coma."

Widow stood up and moved to the seat next to Claire. He put his free hand on top of hers and held the photo in his other like it was a sacred thing. He said, "Go ahead, Claire."

Claire Hood said, "Yesterday morning, James got out of prison."

"What did he do to Jemma?"

"James was never a bad man. But he's confused. And he's been mixed up with the wrong people." She turned to Widow and looked up in his face and said, "Bad people."

Widow asked, "How bad?"

"Bad."

"Where's Jemma?"

Claire's eyes again turned watery, and she said, "Jemma didn't come home from school yesterday. The same day James got out. He took her! He took my little Jemma!"

6

JEMMA LEFT her lunch pail back in the car. And now she was a little upset about it because the guy who looked like Daddy had ditched the car they had. He left it parked behind a busy gas station, and she'd left her pail inside it.

He had woken her up while she was still half asleep, so she had forgotten about it. But she didn't make a big fuss.

Her daddy took her to a car rental place.

For the first time in hours, he spoke. They walked into the lot, and he asked, "Pip, which car do you like?"

She covered her face in a shy way, and she smiled because she confirmed to herself it was her daddy. He had the same voice, and he called her Pip, which was short for Pipsqueak. That had been what he always called her before the police came and took him away one day.

She remembered that was when her mommy first got sick.

The policemen came to her house and put her daddy in handcuffs, just like she'd seen on TV.

He said, "Pip? Which car?"

She lunged at him and hugged him tightly.

He put his hand on her back and pulled her close.

"I missed you too. But, Pip, we gotta go. Which car?"

She pulled back and looked around. She still didn't speak, but she pointed at a silver Dodge truck.

He smiled and said, "That one?"

She nodded, and he said, "Okay. Let's get it."

They went inside to the rental place, and he rented the truck. Her daddy had to do all kinds of paperwork, and he told the guy behind the desk that his name was Jason instead of his real name, which she knew was James. He also gave a completely different last name. It sounded funny to her. It was Nikopovich, which was too big for her to spell. She thought it was strange that he didn't use his real name.

When they were finally done, she spoke. She said, "Daddy, I'm hungry."

"Of course, Pip. Let's get some food. You want to go to Burger King?"

She shook her head and said, "Grandma says that it's bad for me."

"Burger King used to be your favorite."

"But I'm not supposed to."

"Okay, Pip. Where you wanna go?"

She looked out of the truck's big window and watched for something she wanted to try. After ten minutes of driving through the town toward the interstate, she pointed at a restaurant.

She said, "Let's go there."

He looked at a tiny, generic restaurant called: *Ruth's Place* and said, "Okay, Pip. Let's do it."

He headed toward the restaurant.

* * *

WIDOW SAID, "TELL ME ABOUT IT."

Claire Hood said, "My little granddaughter went to the bus stop yesterday, and I thought that she'd gone to school, but she never came home."

"What did the cops say?"

Claire paused a long beat, and she said, "I didn't call them."

Widow said, "What? Why not?"

"I can't call them. They can't know."

"Why the hell not?"

Claire Hood looked around at the other people waiting. A bus came and pulled up to one of the other terminals in the distance. The voice of the guy from behind the ticket booth came over the intercom system, which was nearing the need to be replaced, and said, "The bus for Fort Worth is headed out in ten minutes."

Several people far from Widow and Claire rose and lined up and waited for the bus driver to load the bus.

Claire said, "I can't call them because Jemma is Mexican. Like her mother, she's an illegal. The police won't look for her, and even if they find her, she'll be deported. And her mother is undocumented. Where will she go for care? They'll send her back to Mexico. She'll be off of her treatments, and I'll lose them both."

Widow nodded. He understood. Claire was afraid that if she told the police, they might start asking questions about her citizenship.

Widow asked, "Claire, if her father is an American, even if he is an ex-con, then isn't Jemma automatically a citizen?"

"It doesn't work like that."

"I thought it did."

"No. See..."

She paused and let out a huff, which Widow wasn't sure was because she needed to pause or because of the heat, like she needed to take a breath.

She said, "Jemma isn't his real daughter. She's unofficially adopted."

Widow nodded, and then he thought for a second and asked, "Why didn't James just adopt her officially? Wouldn't that make her a legal citizen and protected?"

"Yes. It would, and he was thinking about it. But then he got arrested and sent to prison for ten years."

"Wait, if he was sent for ten years, why is he out now? Jemma's only six. The math doesn't add up. Did he get out for good behavior or something?"

"He's not supposed to be out. I don't know why he is. He only went in two years ago."

"Is it possible he escaped?"

"No way. Not likely. James isn't a criminal mastermind. No way he could have escaped."

Widow nodded.

"If he had escaped, they'd be coming to me first. No, he was released."

"I wonder why?"

"I don't know. All I know is that he took Jemma."

"Claire, how good is your relationship with him?"

"It's okay. But not great."

"Would he have told you he was getting out?"

She paused another long beat and fanned her face with her palm open. "No. I haven't spoken to him in over a year."

"I see."

"I just thought since he was in prison for ten years that maybe it was best not to expose Jemma to him, you know? I messed up with my son, but I wasn't about to let Jemma turn out like that. And then Lucy got worse, and I ended up with a full plate." She shook her head and then said, "I guess it was also for me too. I didn't want to see James in that place anymore."

"What did he do?"

"As I told you, he hung out with the wrong crowd. He was doing low-level jobs for this drug dealer from Mexico."

Widow stayed quiet.

"I could really use some help."

Widow said, "Claire, I think you should tell the police. They can do a lot more than I can. They'll be interested in finding James and recovering your granddaughter. I really think they won't even check far enough into her background to figure out she's not documented."

"I can't. But can you help me?"

"Where are they going? You must know since you're here."

"Romanth."

Widow asked, "Romanth?"

Claire showed him her ticket. "Romanth. It's a small nothing town on the border with Mexico."

"Is James trying to cross over with her?"

"I don't think so. I think Romanth is his destination."

"What makes you think that?"

"He talked about it once. He said it's a great forgotten town. The last time I spoke to him, he mentioned it. He talked about it like it was a mythical place."

"I see."

She repeated, "Will you help me?"

Widow looked into her eyes. A desperate grandmother who loves her granddaughter. Nothing wrong with that. He thought for a moment, even though he already knew his answer.

Then, right then, at that moment, Claire stood up from her seat. She wobbled a bit. Widow shot up and grabbed her arm gently to steady her. He said, "Are you okay?"

"I feel... I feel..."

Claire Hood never finished her sentence. Instead, she clutched her forehead with one hand and then gasped and tumbled into Widow's arms.

He shouted, "Help! Help!"

A security guard in her mid-thirties came running over. She asked, "What's wrong?"

"She collapsed."

"Oh, dear!"

Widow laid her down on the hot concrete and lifted her wrist. He tried to feel for a pulse. There was none.

He said, "Call 911! Now!"

"Okay!"

The security guard ran off, back toward the station hutch. That must've been her training by the bus company's corporate office, because surely she had a cell phone in her pocket. Widow was practically the only guy in America who didn't. But instead of pulling one out and dialing for emergency assistance, she ran back to the station, and probably back to a corporate telephone, one that the company pays for and tracks. That way, they can say they did their part to help someone in need—no disputing who called 911.

Widow leaned down and put his head near Claire's heart. He listened hard. He could hear a heartbeat.

He shouted back at the bystanders, "Call 911! Now!"

He hoped that maybe one of them would be faster with their cell phone.

He listened again. Claire's heartbeat was slow and faint. It sounded like the last drizzle of water squeezing out from a faucet before it ran empty.

He listened. He grabbed her hand and held it tight.

He said, "Don't you die! Jemma needs you!"

Widow felt a surge go through her body, and her hand squeezed his back. But it was weak. And then it went completely limp.

His military training had kicked in, and he attempted CPR. He checked her airway. It was clear, and he breathed into her mouth. He rotated between pumping her chest to get her heart beating and breathing air into her lungs. He repeated the cycle over and over.

More people were walking over and staring. He tried CPR for a long time, waiting for EMTs, with no luck.

He put his ear to her chest one last time and listened for her heartbeat, but there was nothing. Her eyes were wide open, staring blankly at the sky beyond.

Claire Hood was dead.

* * *

THE WOMAN from Kill Team B watched from the car, which was parked across the street, near a playground for kids from the nearby neighborhood. She looked at her partner and said, "It looks like she passed out... or may be dead."

He said, "What the hell are you talking about?"

"I think she's dead. She was talking to that big guy, and she just dropped dead."

"Are you serious?"

"Yeah. Take a look."

The guy from her team leaned forward in his seat and craned his head and looked past her. He watched for a moment as the stranger stood over the old bird and stared down at her.

She asked, "So now what the hell do we do?"

"Call the boss, I guess."

She nodded and pulled her phone out. She unlocked it and dialed the number. Their boss wasn't really a boss. He was the Principal.

She hit the last-dialed number and then put the phone to her ear and listened as the phone rang and rang. After several rings, a voice finally answered.

The voice said, "Yes?"

"We have some news."

"Wait. I'm not in a secure location."

She waited and looked back at what was happening with the stranger and Claire Hood. The stranger was trying to listen to her heartbeat. Other passengers were gathering around to help or to watch, and now the view was being obstructed.

The guy from Kill Team B said, "What's he saying?"

"Nothing. Yet."

Then the voice came back on and said, "Go ahead."

She said, "We've got a problem."

"What happened?"

"It looks like she passed out."

"Passed out?"

"Yeah. We followed her to a bus station back in El Paso, and we followed her bus. Now we're in Rough Creek."

"Rough Creek?"

"Yeah. I never heard of it either. It looks like she's on her way to the target."

"And she passed out?"

"Maybe."

"What do you mean, maybe? Did she pass out or not?"

"It looks like it may be worse than that."

"What do you mean?"

"I think she might be dead. There're sirens now. An ambulance is headed this way."

The voice said, "Damn it! We've got to know where she was going."

The woman said, "We were going to follow her bus."

"Now, what will you do?"

The woman said, "She was talking with this guy."

"What guy?"

"I don't know... some guy. Like a total stranger."

"What did she tell him?"

The woman said, "I don't know. But they talked for a long time."

"Is he a cop?"

She said, "I don't think so. But he's a big guy. He's got a look about him."

The voice asked, "What kind of look?"

"Like a do-gooder."

"I see. Wait for the ambulance and see what happens. Call me back." And the voice hung up the phone.

The woman slipped the phone back into her pocket and looked at her partner. She shrugged and said, "We wait."

* * *

A LOCAL COP showed up before the paramedics. He was a young guy on patrol by himself. He looked ex-military. Widow wasn't sure which branch, but he'd guess it was US Army. The guy was too muscular to be Air Force and had a look like he'd seen battle. And Marines usually hang on to that jarhead look. Although he could've been wrong on that account.

The cop tried CPR and had the same result. After a few more minutes, he reluctantly stopped and shook his head. Claire Hood was definitely dead.

The officer was nice, but thorough. He seemed to take the entire episode seriously. He asked the right questions. And he took witness statements. And he determined there was no foul play here and that Claire Hood had died from natural causes.

He told Widow to give his phone number in case his department needed to ask further questions. Widow didn't want to get into it, so he told another lie. He gave him the phone number for NCIS in Quantico, Virginia, which was an actual place and the home of NCIS training.

The other lies Widow had told the officer weren't things he was proud of, and he wasn't even sure lying was the right thing to do. He told the cop that all they did was talk small talk. She talked about her grandchildren like grandparents do, and he told her about his life in the military. They just shot the breeze and nothing else.

He wasn't sure he should tell lies to a police officer. What he should've done was told him the story she'd told and been on his way. But Widow wasn't the kind of guy to let wrongs go.

After the officer was done with him and the paramedics had taken Claire's body away, Widow was left alone on the same bench. He leaned forward with his eyes planted on the concrete.

"He took my Jemma," she had said.

"I can't tell the cops," she had said.

Jemma's mother was dying in a hospital back in El Paso. Cancer. Now who would get Jemma back? It was none of Widow's business, not really.

In the background, he heard the guy in the ticket booth's voice again, announcing another bus departing.

He said, "Last call for Shreveport, Louisiana."

Which was Widow's bus. He listened to the announcement one last time. He opened his hand and stared at Claire Hood's bus ticket. She had been headed to Laredo and then to Romanth, northwest on the border with Mexico.

Widow watched as the last passenger for his Shreveport bus boarded, and the driver closed the doors. The tired bus coughed as it reversed out of the terminal and then drove forward. He watched it drive off, past the service drive, and down to the highway.

About fifteen minutes later, he was boarding a bus to Laredo. His pass had the name Claire Hood written on it, but the bus driver didn't look too closely at the name on the stub. He just tore it and handed Widow the long end.

Widow stepped onto the bus and sat in the back. He closed his eyes and tried to get some sleep.

* * *

THE WOMAN from Kill Team B called the Principal and said, "The stranger got on the wrong bus."

"What do you mean?"

"I mean, the guy behind the counter said he bought a ticket to go to Louisiana."

"But he didn't get on that bus?"

The woman said, "No. He got on another one. He must've used the old lady's ticket."

"Follow him. He must know where the target is."

"We're already tailing the bus now. It's headed to Laredo."

The voice on the other end said, "Good. Stay with him."

Then there was a click, and dead air followed.

"So? What do we do?" asked her partner.

"We stay with the stranger. He'll lead us to the target."

7

WIDOW FELL asleep on the bus to Laredo about an hour after they had turned onto 83 South. He woke up three hours later when a loud gunshot sound rang through the cabin.

Widow's eyes darted open. He looked around, his primal senses on high alert, like he had been sleeping in his own bed and suddenly someone fired a gun in his house. But his alertness died down quickly at the realization that the sound hadn't been a gunshot because if it had, all the other passengers would've reacted and none of them had. Instead, they all appeared to be annoyed.

He sat up. He had planted himself in a seat next to the window— on the driver's side. No one sat in the seat next to him. The bus was only half full. Maybe a little more, but not much.

The bus skirted to the left, and the loud sound of scraping metal and the scrape of concrete blasted through the interior of the bus. Widow realized they had blown a tire.

He looked at the bus driver, who was a bald black guy with a blue ball cap. He seemed competent. Without looking over his shoulder, he shouted back to everyone, "Blown tire! It's okay!"

He pulled the bus over to the shoulder of a highway Widow
didn't know the name of. He hadn't been paying attention to the
drive, but it was definitely a highway and not an interstate. That
was obvious.

The bus driver struggled with the steering, and the bus skidded to
a stop on the shoulder. The remaining tires stopped hard, and the
brakes squealed, and dust rose from the sandy shoulder. The
driver put the gear into park and switched on the hazard lights.
He stood up and said, "Okay, everybody. Y'all stay put. I'm gonna
check out the damage, and I'll be back."

Widow looked around and saw that most of the passengers were
older people—not senior citizens—but most were over fifty. There
were some kids and two teenagers, both girls. No one else looked
like they could change a bus tire. So, being the guy he was, he
figured he'd better volunteer for the job. Widow reached his arms
up, extending them as far as he could, and stretched. He twisted
his torso to the left and then to the right to loosen himself up and
wake up his body. He scooted over the seat next to him and then
stood up in the aisle and walked to the front of the bus.

The other passengers watched him as he went.

Widow followed the aisle to the front and stepped off the bus. He
looked left and then right. The highway was basically in the
middle of nowhere, or at least that was how it appeared. The
landscape wasn't quite desert, but wasn't quite anything else
either. There were some patches of grass here and there, and
some trees off in the distance, but then there was also dry desert-
like land as well.

To the south, he saw a road sign that said there was a town called
Third Crossing seven miles away. It was the next exit. At least
there was a town nearby, in case he decided just to walk. Seven
miles wasn't that bad.

But he didn't want to get ahead of himself.

He walked around the front of the bus and heard the engine
humming. He stepped past it and onto the gravel on the shoulder

and saw that the driver was bent over, studying the blown tire. It was one of the back driver's side tires.

Widow approached and saw that it wasn't bad, because bad would show it had some chance of survival. This was worse.

The tire was completely shredded. It had been removed almost completely, like a shotgun had blown it off. There were fleshy strips of it left on the rim, but not much. And the rim looked entirely bent, probably because the bus was too heavy to be driving sixty miles an hour on it.

The driver had removed his ball cap and was rubbing his head.

Widow stepped five feet from him and stopped. He said, "It looks bad."

The driver turned and looked up at him. He stood up and said, "That's the understatement of the year."

Widow asked, "No chance of throwing on a spare?"

The driver shook his head from side to side in big movements. He said, "There's no way in hell."

Widow said, "Not even if I help you?"

The driver said, "No. Can't happen."

Widow said nothing.

The driver said, "I couldn't let ya—insurance thing. And I'm not supposed to because we're in Texas, and Texas has a union for us drivers. Ya see?"

Widow stayed quiet.

The driver said, "Ya see, it's a matter of the union. I ain't supposed to change tires this bad or do mechanical work on the bus while en route. In this situation, I gotta call it in."

Widow asked, "And then what?"

The driver said, "Then we wait. They send out a tow truck and another bus."

Widow asked, "How long will that take?"

The driver said, "Well, the tow truck will probably take an hour. But the other bus? I don't know. Could take all afternoon."

Widow nodded and looked up and down the highway again.

A car passed.

Widow said, "Well, then I don't think I'll hang out for that."

The driver said, "Ya can't leave. I ain't allowed to take your luggage out of the bus until the backup bus arrives."

Widow said, "I don't have luggage."

The driver said, "Well if you leave, you can't get a refund or transfer your ticket."

Widow hadn't paid for the pass. It was Claire's, and she was dead now. She didn't need a refund. Besides that, he didn't want to wait for hours and hours in the middle of Texas. That seemed like a heftier price to pay than the money. Widow viewed time as being like money because it could be spent, but there were no refunds on time. So he nodded at the bus driver and turned and headed south toward the sign for Third Crossing.

* * *

THEY DROVE the same highway as the bus the stranger had been on, and they had been along the side of the bus when the tire had blown out. They drove a white Dodge Charger, not an inconspicuous vehicle, but fast and reliable. And the Principal was footing the bill on the vehicle they rented.

The woman had picked out the car because she liked fast cars, but the other guy was the one who drove it.

They passed the broken-down bus and didn't stop to offer help because they didn't want the stranger to identify them.

"Now, what the hell do we do?"

"I guess we go to the next town and wait," the woman said.

"Wait for what?"

"I guess for them to replace the bus with a new one."

"That could take hours."

"So what?"

The guy asked, "What if he walks?"

She said nothing.

"What if he gets a ride? And we're in the next town? We'll lose him."

"I don't know. Should we just park off on the shoulder and watch him?"

"Look around. The land is flat and empty. He'll make us for sure."

The woman said, "Then I don't know. Where the hell do we go?"

"We go to the next town. We can get some gas and a couple of coffees. Then we come back and pass on the other lane."

"All right."

Kill Team B headed on to the next town.

* * *

TWO AND A HALF MILES LATER, Widow was again covered in sweat. The heat seemed to get hotter, and the air seemed to get drier, and the sun seemed to have gotten closer to the earth. His body was telling him the temperature was rising and rising, and maybe it was time to make better decisions instead of blindly following the path ahead. He reexamined his decision-making process. Maybe he should follow the weather instead of just picking something based on no established yardstick for deciding.

Widow wore a tight, black, long-sleeved shirt that was probably meant for yoga, which was okay by his standards. The shirt was cotton and thin. He had plenty of breathing room in it. He thought about taking it off, but he didn't know what kind of impression that would give to drivers who might give him a ride.

On the one hand, Widow had enjoyed good luck with women drivers in the past—he was young, and he knew he wasn't a bad-looking guy. He was far from pretty, but he was in good shape from all the walking, and he ate about as healthy as any American. Widow was blessed with good genes and was a big guy. He had naturally shredded abs like the side of a brick house. He had broad shoulders, and from the back, his shoulders and torso looked like an upside-down equilateral pyramid, the kind made from giant stones and decades of slave labor.

On the downside, Widow had tattoos. He discovered after leaving NCIS that he had quite an addiction to ink. He had started with a sleeve tattoo and learned that he really enjoyed getting them. Widow's chest and arms and shoulders were tattooed—no facial tattoos or neck tattoos or any of that nonsense. He believed you should be able to cover tattoos. Even though he didn't plan on having another professional career in his life, he still thought it was best not to have tattoos that might hinder his ability to get a job. Occasionally, he still had to do casual labor. You couldn't get around America these days without money.

He also had the three ugly scars from being shot in the upper back. Amazingly, he survived, and the bullets hadn't caused any irreversible damage because his ribcage had done exactly what it was designed to do—protect his vitals. Although it hurt like hell and he was hospitalized for a long period of time. He recalled the months and months of physical and psychological therapy required by the NCIS and Navy law that he had to endure.

Widow continued to walk south on the highway. He left his shirt on because the drivers who passed would most likely be men, and most men wouldn't pick up a hitchhiker who looked the way he looked with his shirt off.

He realized then that he was giving the whole premise of walking shirtless far too much thought. The heat must have been getting to him.

It was only five seconds later when he heard the sound that was the very best sound he could've heard at that moment. It was the sound of a car slowing behind him—tires over gravel, the calm hum of a car air conditioner, and the low whistle of good brakes.

Widow turned and saw a white Chevy Tahoe with green markings and letters on it. It was covered in dust and sand and had large tinted windows and four doors. On the top was a thick, low light bar, all one solid color. In the bright daylight, Widow couldn't tell the exact color, but a guesstimation told him it was all red because the vehicle was a United States Border Patrol SUV, and he didn't think they used blue in their light bars.

The US Border Patrol Tahoe stopped, and dust rose from the gravel on the shoulder. Sunlight reflected intensely off the tinted windshield, blinding Widow. He put his hands up over his eyes to block out the light. He tried to let his eyes adjust, and they squinted tight.

The driver's side door opened, slow like a gate, and a small figure stepped out and didn't shut the door. The driver just stepped slowly up toward the front tire.

A female voice spoke with a rather thick Texas accent. She said, "Need a lift?"

Widow's eyes adjusted as best they could with the bright sunlight in them, and he saw a woman of Hispanic heritage dressed in a United States Border Patrol officer's uniform. She was about five feet five inches tall—eleven inches shorter than he was. She looked to be a hundred twenty-five pounds, but that was probably way off because she undoubtedly wore a bulletproof vest under her uniform shirt, which Widow assumed was mandatory for Texas Border Patrol agents.

As he looked closer, he saw her shirt wasn't the standard uniform shirt, which he was sure was a green button-down thing with the Border Patrol's badge insignia on the upper left breast. This agent wore a black T-shirt instead, and there was no insignia on the left breast or the right breast or anywhere on the shirt. And Widow looked closely enough that he would've seen it. Her hair was

black and thick and long, but she had it pulled back tight underneath a hunter-green ball cap that had the badge insignia on it,
right smack in the center.

The agent wore a regular belt, not a department-issued cop belt
with attachments and a holster. She had a holster on her belt on
her left side.

Widow took a peek at her sidearm, which looked like a Heckler &
Koch P2000 SK. He assumed it was probably the standard-issue
weapon of the Border Patrol. He wasn't sure because he had had
little interaction with them.

The female agent asked again, "Do you need a lift?"

Widow said, "I'm sorry. I've been out in this heat for a few miles."

She said, "I figured. I saw the bus back there."

"I think the heat is scrambling my brain."

"It'll do that. Don't take Texas heat for granted. Many men have
gone crazy in it and even dropped dead thinking they were tough
and could handle it."

Widow nodded.

She asked, "You don't even have any water?"

He shook his head.

She said, "So get in. I got bottles."

Widow said, "Thank you."

He lowered his hand and walked around the hood to the
passenger side, opened the door, put one foot up on the step rail,
and dumped himself into the seat.

The agent followed and got in the driver seat. She looked over at
Widow and said, "You're supposed to sit in the back, but I guess
under the circumstances it's better this way, because Jake will
probably not take kindly to sharing."

Widow turned and looked back over the seat at what she was referring to. On the back seat was the biggest dog he had ever seen outside the Great Dane breed.

Jake was a massive Belgian shepherd with black and tan mixed into his fur, leaning more toward the black. His face was painted black, straight down his snout.

Although he didn't growl at Widow, he wasn't very warm and friendly either. He was on guard, but nonthreatening at the same time. Widow supposed Jake must've been trained to know that if a new rider wasn't in handcuffs and in the back, then he was a friendly. But there was a look of distrust in his eyes.

Good dog, Widow thought. He was a big fan of dogs.

The agent smiled and said, "Don't worry... he won't bite you. Unless you give him a reason, and believe me, you don't want him to."

"I can see that. He looks vicious."

She said, "Oh, he is! His bite is deadly."

"Really?"

"Oh, yes! He's killed a man in the line of duty before."

Widow asked, "Really? With you?"

She said, "No. He's a former Marine. A military service dog. He supposedly saved his master's life in combat by attacking an Afghani fighter. He bit the guy's jugular."

Widow paused a beat, and then he said, "I'll try not to give him a reason to kill me."

"Good. I would hate to do the extra paperwork."

Widow smiled. She had quite a good sense of humor, which Widow had found was an imperative part of good police work. A sense of humor was almost as important as a good sidearm because ninety percent of scars from police work came in the mental form and not the physical. And a good sense of humor could keep a police officer sharp.

Widow extended his hand and said, "My name is Widow."

"Donna Leon. United States Border Patrol."

And they shook hands.

"So, where are you headed, Widow?"

He said, "I'm headed to a place called Romanth."

Leon slid the gear into drive and hit the gas. The Tahoe jumped to life, probably like Jake would with the right instant command from Leon. And they were back on the road, headed south. She asked, "Romanth?"

"Ever heard of it?"

"Of course. It's a small border town. It's about a hundred feet from the Mexican border."

"Is that legal?"

"Not really. But it started as private property. Nothing wrong with that. It was a settlement, decades ago."

"What happened?"

"The original owners died, and it became a town. It's not big enough for anyone to challenge the legality of it. Or at least it's not worth it."

"How small are we talking?"

"Small. Like no one really goes there. It's not a major tourist destination or nothing."

"How many people live there?"

"Maybe a thousand or fifteen hundred."

Widow stayed quiet.

Leon said, "It's a registered municipality. It's got a school. A church. A sheriff. It even has a court. There's some brand name restaurants and stores, but not much else."

"How hard is it to get to?"

"Not hard, as long as you have four-wheel drive."

Widow changed the subject, and asked, "What happened to his handler?"

Leon asked, "Who?"

"Jake's master. You said he was a Marine in Afghanistan?"

"Yeah. He was. His master died."

"In the war?"

"No. He died from cancer, I think. It was natural causes. He died in a hospital bed here in Texas. Jake was donated to us after. The family thought he should be with a police force, I guess."

Widow looked at Jake, and then back toward the road. He said, "That's tough on a dog."

"Yeah. It was hard for him to adjust at first."

"I bet."

"He went through three other agents before landing on me. Don't know why, but he and I took together like we were old pals. He comes home with me every night and sleeps by my bed. We eat dinner together, and we fight bad guys together."

Widow said, "All every guy really needs is that one special woman to turn his life around."

Leon smiled again, another big smile, all teeth and glow.

"You've got a nice smile. If I may make such a comment."

Leon said, "Of course. Perfectly okay. Even a woman in uniform likes a compliment like that."

"Not sure how Jake feels about it."

Leon held the wheel steady, hands at the nine and three positions like she was being examined by a guy from the DMV. To Widow, she seemed like a by-the-books kind of officer. Nothing wrong with that.

She said, "He's fine with whatever I'm fine with. So don't worry. If I didn't like the compliment, you'd know it."

"You patrol out here alone often?"

"I'm not alone. I got him."

"Sure, but I mean with no other officers?"

"Agents. We're not officers."

"Sorry. Agents, I mean."

"Yeah. I come through here every Tuesday and Friday. It's my regular route."

"What level are you? Patrol? 'Cause you don't look like an average patrol agent to me."

She said, "I'm part of SOG."

"What's that stand for?"

"It's Special Operations Group. We've got K9 units and anti-smuggling units and even dirt bike units."

"Dirt bikes?"

Leon said, "Of course. Texas terrain toward the west is vast and rocky and mountainous and deserted. We've got a lot of ground to cover, and it's rough. Dirt bikes are great for that."

"Will I need a dirt bike to get to Romanth?"

"No, but you can't get there by bus. Not that I'm aware of. You never told me what's in Romanth."

"I'm looking for someone," he said. He didn't want to say any more than that. So he asked, "Where are you from?"

She shrugged and said, "I was born in Houston. I'm a Texas girl through and through."

Widow nodded.

"So tell me about yourself," she said.

Widow stayed quiet for a moment and debated about what to say because his story was a long one, but in the end, he shared the highlights, leaving out killing bad guys and helping people. Widow told her about his military career and that he used to be a cop. He left out the redacted information and the undercover part. Widow told her about his addiction to the drifter lifestyle. He told her all the things you tell a woman you just met and are attracted to and realize you will probably never see again.

* * *

KILL TEAM B was parked about a mile away. Its members stood on a slight hill and shared a pair of field glasses.

The man said, "He got picked up by a cop."

"It's not a cop. It's US Border Patrol," said the woman.

"What do we do now?"

"Nothing's changed. We follow him."

"We better tell Glock."

The woman said, "No. No reason. Nothing's changed."

"We can't follow a Border Patrol car."

"We won't have to. She'll drop him off in the next town. She's not going to drive him to wherever he's headed."

The man nodded.

"Let's go. We can wait for them down the road. Park at the first gas station."

They got into the Dodge Charger, fired up the engine, and headed south.

* * *

LEON SAID, "Sounds like you've lived quite a life, Widow."

Widow nodded and tilted in his seat. He felt the cold air blasting from the air conditioner on his neck and face. Which was nice, but it made the sweat on his torso sticky and his shirt clung to his skin. But he didn't complain. Being inside the SUV with Leon was much better than the alternative.

He said, "Yeah, it's been a ride. What about you? How long you been with the Border Patrol?"

"I've been with the agency for five years."

"Did you always want to be a Border Patrol agent?"

"Nah, I wanted to be a cop. But this actually pays better."

"Really? Is that true?"

"Nah. I don't know what cops make. I never tried out. This was more appealing. I actually want to be in the FBI, but it's pretty hard to get in. I got a degree and can speak Spanish, so this is where I ended up."

"You sound like you aren't thrilled with it."

"I do like it. There's just not a lot of moving up in the US Border Patrol. Not for a woman."

"It's like that?"

"It's not on the surface, but I see it. We have other women agents, but there aren't many in the upper echelons. There are a lot of old men. Still hanging on to their jobs."

Widow nodded and said, "Military used to be like that too. Change in America is a slow thing. You'll move up."

Leon said nothing and glanced in her side mirror for the third time in five minutes.

"What is it?"

"This car has been following us for a ways."

Widow craned his head and looked past Jake and over the back seat and past the cargo space and through the rear window. He saw a white Dodge Charger about ten car lengths behind them. He said, "It is a highway. There's only one direction to go."

"Yeah, but that's a sports car."

"So?"

"So normally people drive them fast. This is Texas. And they've been keeping their distance like that for miles."

"Maybe they don't want to get a speeding ticket. You got a light bar on the roof."

Leon gazed over at Widow and then back at the road ahead of her. She said, "I'm not a cop. I can't give tickets."

"Maybe they don't know that."

"Maybe."

Widow looked back one last time. Jake looked up at him, ears forward and eyes wide.

"Can I pet him?"

"Sure. Just do it slowly."

Widow put his palm out so the dog could smell it. Jake stretched his neck out like a turtle and buried his nose into Widow's hand and sniffed for a long second. Then Widow scratched the bottom of Jake's chin with his fingers. Within moments, he was ruffling the dog's head and ears. Jake complied like dogs often did when they felt comfortable with someone.

8

LEON AND WIDOW rode past the next town and didn't stop like Leon had said they would. Widow said, "You passed the town."

"I know."

Widow stayed quiet.

Leon said, "I'm actually headed down south. It's part of my route. I figure you seem like a nice guy, and being ex-military and all, the least I can do is take you part of the way."

Widow stared at her. He didn't know what to say.

She said, "Unless you want me to dump you out and let you take your chances with the buses. But that hasn't worked out for you today, has it?"

"No, it hasn't."

She smiled at him.

He said, "Thanks."

"Sure."

Leon flipped on the turn signal, and they cut over and turned onto the off-ramp for 55. She said, "I'm not going all the way, but we've reached Uvalde, and I can drop you off here."

"Sure. That sounds good."

Widow looked at the touchscreen interface in the center of the dash, and he checked the time. It was getting close to sundown. He hoped he could catch Hood and Jemma before they vanished. He hoped they were really going to Romanth.

Leon had told him it was a border town. He hoped James Hood didn't plan to take Jemma across the border. Then he might never find them.

"So, what are you? Like a private investigator? Or a bounty hunter?"

"Huh?"

"You said you were looking for someone. I figure a guy like you— military background and ex-cop and all—you must be hunting someone."

"I guess you can say that."

"Which is it? Private investigator or bounty hunter? You looking for a guy who skipped bail?"

"Nah, I'm looking for a deadbeat dad."

"What? He owes his wife alimony or something?"

Widow nodded and said, "Something like that." And then he changed the subject again. He didn't want to have to lie to her. Better to talk small talk, and not about Hood or Jemma. He said, "Sun's going down. You work at night?"

"Yeah. My shift ends at midnight."

"I see."

"You want to have dinner or something?"

Widow said, "I'd love to have dinner with you."

Leon shot him a look and then said, "Not with me. I work. I meant, are *you* getting hungry?"

Widow smiled, a little embarrassed, and then he said, "I could eat."

"You got to eat. Food is fuel."

"Right."

"You can grab a bite in Uvalde. I know a great little place."

"Sounds good. Do you want me to drive some ways?"

Leon said, "Pointless. We'll be there soon. Besides, it's against regulations to let a civilian drive. Come on, Widow, you know that."

"Giving drifters a ride is also not allowed."

"That's true. But you still can't drive."

Widow nodded. "Understood. Just thought I'd offer."

They both looked forward. The horizon grew closer, and the sun breathed its last breath.

* * *

JAKE KEPT his eyes open and on Widow, but he stayed with his head down and in a relaxed position like he was on standby. A well-trained dog, without a doubt.

Widow and Leon had driven the better part of four hours and had just about exhausted every piece of small talk on the menu for common American strangers.

The night had set in, and Widow was actually getting hungry.

In his mind, he had pulled up all the possibilities of what he had gotten himself into, and they all led back to the same answer—Claire Hood and Jemma Hood, and Lucy, who was dying somewhere in a hospital bed. Widow hoped that Claire's intel on Hood's destination proved to be correct. Otherwise, he was wasting his time—and time was running out for any kind of rescue for Jemma. The FBI said that if no rescue was made in the first forty-eight hours of an abduction, it was considered a homicide, and no longer looked at as a rescue. This meant that if forty-eight hours passed, he was most likely looking at a recovery of the body.

Widow hated to lose. Right then, he felt that way. Part of him wanted to tell Leon. Part of him was screaming at him to tell her now. They still could get an Amber Alert out there. But he remembered Claire Hood's words. Jemma and her mother were undocumented.

Where would Lucy go for care? Claire Hood had said.

Leon said, "Widow, what are you daydreaming about?"

"I'm just thinking."

"We're almost there."

"Got it."

Widow looked out the window at the city of Uvalde and was impressed to find it a much larger metropolitan area than he had imagined. It wasn't a major Texas city or anything, not like Dallas or Houston, but its size was respectable. Tall buildings lined the terrain, not skyscrapers or anything, but plenty of tall enough places.

Widow asked, "How far is Romanth from here?"

"If I were you, I'd get a hotel room for the night and then rent a vehicle tomorrow. Get a truck. I wasn't kidding around about the four-wheel drive. You'll need it to get there."

Leon turned the Tahoe toward the off-ramp on the cloverleaf, and they circled down with the flow of traffic and came off 55 and merged onto the highway below.

Jake shuffled around in the back seat, trying to stay comfortable and maintain his balance so he didn't roll off the seat.

Leon said, "Take 83 straight down toward Mexico and merge onto 35. When you get to Laredo, head north on Mines Road. Stay on it when it forks west. Somewhere along the way, you'll pass 255. Cross over it and keep going. The way ahead looks like a forgotten dirt track. I can't remember the name of the road, but it won't matter because it's not posted anywhere."

She paused a beat and flipped on the left turn signal, moving the Tahoe over to the fast lane and then into the turning lane.

"You'll be heading into the Rio Grande Valley. It's rocky at worst and hilly at best."

Widow nodded.

"Stay on course for about twenty miles, and eventually, you'll come to Romanth. It's the only thing on that road. We patrol it occasionally, but I doubt you'll see anyone else driving it."

Widow stayed quiet.

Leon drove him down one busy street, and then they turned past a Sheraton Hotel, which reminded Widow of the senator he'd read about. They pulled into the parking lot of a restaurant that looked expensive, not in the New York fifty-dollar-crab-legs sense of the phrase, but still out of Widow's budget.

Leon parked the Tahoe in a space far from the other cars and left the engine running. She said, "Here's as far as I go."

Widow said, "This is the restaurant? You must get paid better than I thought."

"Not this place, you numbskull. It's the diner over there."

She pointed to a tiny little store across the street. It had a big white door and a huge window with ugly green drapes.

Widow said, "Oh. It's hideous."

"Yeah, but it's great. It's a family business. Everyone from the cook to the busboy is a part of the same family."

Widow nodded.

"I guess this is goodbye."

"I guess so," Widow said and got out. He opened the door and hopped out, but he stopped before he shut the door and asked, "Hey, can I ask you something?"

"Sure."

"You're an accomplished woman of Latin descent—"

"Of Latin descent?" she interrupted.

Widow nodded.

"What is this, politically correct nation?"

Widow shrugged.

"I'm a Latina. It's okay to say it."

"Right. So my question is, what do you think about the wall?"

Leon stared at him. Her face registered she was processing the question. She leaned her head against her hands on the steering wheel. Then she said, "Truthfully, as a Border Patrol agent, I'm glad for any help we get from the government, but the wall will cost billions of dollars. That money is better spent on more agents —more equipment. Better programs. Better software and sensors. We could use more drones. I've heard the wall could cost over twenty-five billion dollars. That's a lot of manpower and equipment we could use. The wall won't do the same job we can do with a better budget."

Her response had been pretty much exactly what Widow had thought himself. He nodded again and leaned on one side, his left hand gripped around the top of the Tahoe, and his right gripped around the top of the door.

"As a Mexican-American woman, I'm appalled at the building of the wall."

"Really?"

"Yes! Absolutely! My job is to stop illegal immigration and to enforce the laws of our country. No question. When I catch illegals, I arrest them for breaking our laws. I round them up, and we ship them out. But as an American, it bothers me to waste my taxes on a big ugly wall. As a Latina, it offends me that so many of my American brothers and sisters are so afraid of Mexicans that they want to build a wall. Many people here want to blame Mexicans and blame everyone but themselves."

Widow said, "You feel that strongly about it?"

"Yes. It's outrageous that this is even a real issue."

Jake lifted his head and reared back on his hind legs like he was getting ready to launch at Widow.

Leon sat up straight and reached back and patted him on the butt. She gave a command in German. Widow had no idea what the words meant, but he could guess they were a command telling Jake to calm down and be at ease.

"Sorry to ask. I was just curious."

"Are you for it?"

"No way. I never even thought about something like that before."

Leon looked at him with a face that seemed to ask, "How dumb are you?"

"What?" he asked.

"You didn't know about the wall?"

"No."

"What have you been living under, a rock or something?"

"No rock. Just don't watch much TV."

"Maybe not a rock, but you may have your head in the sand," Leon said, and smiled.

Widow shrugged.

"You know it's an election year, right?"

He shrugged again.

"How the hell do you not know about the election?"

"I knew about it. I don't live under a rock. I just don't pay attention to stuff like that."

Leon returned to her upright position in the driver's seat. Widow could see the muscles in her arms twitching, and her breasts shudder just slightly underneath her body armor.

Leon said, "You're a strange man."

He said, "I know."

Leon said, "Good night, Widow. I hope you find the person you're looking for."

He nodded and said, "You be safe out there." And he stood back and shut the door, not slamming it but pushing it closed like he was thirteen years old again and trying to sneak out of his mother's house.

Widow stepped away from the Tahoe and over to the curb to the expensive restaurant and watched as Agent Leon and Jake pulled away and drove down the street. He watched until the Tahoe was gone from sight. And then he headed to the diner.

* * *

A WHITE DODGE Charger pulled into the parking lot of the expensive restaurant, and the two passengers watched as Widow walked to the small diner across the street.

9

WIDOW SAT at a table that was free, nearest the back wall. Behind him was a group of Texas teenagers—one girl and three boys. They sat and drank coffee and tea and laughed and horsed around. He tuned them out and gave his attention to his coffee and meal.

He ordered eggs and chicken, which seemed barbaric if one gave it too much thought, like eating a mother and her children. But he liked chicken and needed the protein because he really was starving. He ate everything naked, no ketchup or additives, and slid the plate to the side and gazed around the diner.

He saw a priest sitting in one corner. The guy wore a brown coat over his priest's attire. He had a white collar and black shirt and everything. The weather was hot outside, but he still wore that coat. In his defense, it was cold inside the diner. The family who owned it had the air conditioner running on full blast. Even Widow had to roll his sleeves down because it was like the Arctic in there.

Near the front door was an attractive woman who sat alone. She had been there as long as Widow had, came in right after he did. She had spent most of the time sifting through a day-old newspaper and the second half of the last hour playing on her phone.

Widow looked over to his right and saw an off-duty waitress. She was young and Mexican, just like the rest of the family. She had her waitress uniform on, but it was underneath a coat that was far too big for her, and she had a pack of cigarettes laid out in front of her, but she wasn't smoking. The place was nonsmoking, which was probably a city ordinance. Plenty of cities in America had done that, had made it illegal to smoke in restaurants. Widow figured if it was showing up in Texas, then it had gotten everywhere.

He didn't think one way or the other about it. He didn't agree with the government butting in about a person's right to smoke, but he didn't mind not having that smoky smell when he was eating food. Some social issues left him at an impasse as to what side he was on.

The thing that interested him about the off-duty waitress was that she was playing around on a tablet. He figured she must have Wi-Fi on it, and she must have the code.

He called over to his waitress, who looked like she was the other one's older sister. She came over and took his empty plate.

He said, "Is that your sister?"

"Cousin," the waitress said.

"Can you ask her a question for me?"

The waitress paused and gave him an accusatory look. She said, "She's underage, sir."

"What? No, no, I'm not like that."

The waitress said, "Oh. Sorry."

"I want you to ask her if I can borrow her tablet."

The waitress looked back at her cousin and then at Widow. She said, "What for?"

"Tell her I just want to look something up. Tell her I'll only be a moment."

"What's in it for her?"

Negotiation. A good sign. Strangers are funny with handing out their property to someone they don't know. Especially if that property is an expensive device, and they keep their own private information on it. It also doesn't help if the stranger looks like Widow.

He said, "Tell her I'll tip her for it. I'll tip you both. I only want five minutes."

"You'll tip us both?"

"You got it."

"How much?"

Widow thought for a moment, and then he said, "Five bucks. Each."

"Five? Each?"

"Yep."

"I'll ask her," she said, and she left with the empty dishes.

She went into the kitchen to drop the plates off at the dishwasher's station, and Widow wondered how they determined who got picked for that job. Maybe there was a younger brother who had to do it as a rite of passage, or maybe there was an uncle no one liked.

The waitress walked back into the dining room and passed by the teenagers, who were trying to flag her down. It looked as if they were finished and needed to pay their respective checks. The waitress weaved in and out of the tables and over to her cousin. She leaned down and whispered to her, and they looked over at Widow. He waved back at them.

A moment later, both waitresses walked over to him, and the cousin plopped herself down across from him in the seat.

"You want to use my tablet?"

"I do. It's important."

"For ten bucks? Five each?"

"Right."

"Okay. But I stay here with you."

"No problem. I only need a few minutes with it."

She nodded and handed it over to him, and the on-duty waitress returned to her job.

"You got the internet, right?"

"Of course."

Widow handed it back to her and said, "Why don't you do it? You know how to use that thing better than I do."

He was lying; in the Navy he had had extensive training and had to use electronic devices like a tablet. But he figured that to her, he was just an old guy, and he'd been out of the military life for some years now.

She took the tablet back and asked, "What are we looking up?"

"I need to find someone."

She said, "Oh, like a criminal? Or a missing person?"

He nodded.

"Are you a cop?"

He thought back to Leon's impression of him. He said, "Ex-cop. I'm a bounty hunter. Just trying to return a bail jumper back to court."

She nodded and accepted that claim. She said, "Okay. We can just google the name and see what pops up."

"Sounds good. Google James Hood."

She looked down at the touch screen and slid her finger across it, and then she typed on a keyboard on the screen.

Widow waited and sipped the last drop of his coffee.

She said, "If he's from Texas, then here he is."

She turned the device around and showed it to Widow. He leaned forward and saw the face of James Hood staring back at him.

* * *

THEY WERE LOOKING at Hood's Facebook profile, which was old. It had no activity for over two years.

"What do you want to look at?"

"Check out his photos. I need to see if he has a little girl."

"Is he a bad guy or something? He looks like a nice guy to me."

"I don't know if he's bad. We recover a lot of people who are good."

She nodded, turned the tablet back to herself, and jumped ahead, and sifted through his profile photos. She said, "Well, he doesn't have a lot of photos. Only three. And he's married, I think."

She flipped the tablet again like it was on a swivel, and she showed him full-screen photos. The first was Hood alone; the third was the same photo the grandmother had. It was Lucy and Jemma together. The way it should be.

Widow had to get her back.

He said, "That's the right guy. Thank you."

"That's it? You don't need to see anymore?"

"No. I just wanted to see his face."

"You don't have a photo of him?"

Widow shrugged and said, "I forgot it."

"Do you want me to send it to you? I can send it to your phone?"

"No thanks. I don't have a phone."

She said, "Oh, I guess that's why you needed to see my tablet." But she said it with a kind of snarky tone, like she really thought that Widow was ancient.

He had his sleeves pulled most of the way down, but his sleeve tattoos were exposed.

She studied them, as she had never seen them before on a man. And her snarkiness disappeared. She said, "Cool tattoos."

"Thanks."

"Do you have more?"

He nodded.

She remained quiet for a long moment, and then she asked, "Can I see them?"

Widow reached into his front pocket, felt past his passport, and jerked some folded cash-money out of his pocket. He pulled out a ten-dollar bill and handed it to her. He said, "Split that with your cousin."

She took it and said, "Thanks."

He calculated in his head and from memory the total amount he owed for the chicken breast, the scrambled eggs, and the two cups of coffee he drank, and he guessed what the state tax was. He rounded up to ten percent, which seemed high to him, but it might've been true. After all, Texas was one of the richer states. He put the money down on the table and added a tip to it.

He said, "Thank you for your help. Tell your family this is a great diner."

He got up from the table and walked out.

The young waitress remained seated and shrugged. She guessed he didn't want to talk about his tattoos.

* * *

WIDOW HEADED towards the Sheraton Hotel to book a room
for the night. Judging by Hood's photos and many other assump-
tions about fathers, he figured Jemma was in no immediate
danger. He suspected the chances were high that this was a situation of a father who'd gotten out of prison and stolen his own
daughter so they could start a new life together someplace else.

Widow wasn't certain, and he knew that, but he also had no
evidence that Hood intended to cause harm to his daughter. From
the look of things, the guy had done his time and gotten out of
prison. His wife was dying. Maybe he was concerned about his
daughter's well-being, and maybe he knew his mother would
never allow him to see her. Widow couldn't be sure about any
of it.

Then again, why didn't Hood try to make contact and simply ask?
Claire had made it seem like her son was just a guy who made a
lot of mistakes but wasn't evil. Still, Widow didn't know why he
would risk abducting his daughter and leaving so fast. The guy
was probably on parole, which meant he was under restrictions to
check in with his parole officers, and so on. Of course, the limita-
tion might've been for him to stay in the state of Texas, which was
a big place.

Maybe Hood had planned to call his mother when he reached
Romanth and tell her everything was fine and beg her forgiveness.
The whole situation could've been a simple fix. However, Claire
seemed adamant about trying to rescue Jemma. In fact, she had
died while trying to get her back. Therefore, Widow had to
rethink his earlier assumption, because it made no sense. There
must've been something dangerous about Hood having the girl,
because Claire felt it necessary to go after them on her own. She
didn't tell the cops, which Widow understood, but she also didn't
bring anyone with her. She came alone.

Widow turned a corner onto a four-lane road that was the next
block over from the Sheraton. The road was empty of moving
cars. He could see in both directions for a good six blocks and
several stoplights, and there was no traffic.

Just then, a pair of headlights pulled out from a street up ahead and turned toward him, slow. The lights pulled up close to him and stopped.

Widow's natural survival instincts set in because a pair of headlights stopping out in front of you on a dead street at night was almost always bad, or at least suspicious.

The car stopped twenty feet in front of him, and both of the front doors jacked open. Two people jumped out. First, the passenger jumped out. He was a big guy in a suit and tie about his size. Then, the driver got out. She was harder to see. The lights behind her shone around her silhouette. And that was how he determined it was a woman. She was small, but curvy enough to be unmistakably female.

The woman said, "Freeze!"

Widow couldn't see them in great detail because the headlights were on bright and blinding him, but he knew by their approach and stance, and of course, the word *freeze*, that they were holding guns and pointing them straight at him.

10

WIDOW LEARNED two important lessons years ago. First, never run from the police. Always obey them. Especially if they have a gun pointed at you. The second lesson was never to trust people who pointed guns at you.

He lifted his hands straight up into the air and said, "Guys, I'm frozen."

The woman said, "Good. Stay there."

The man approached at a steady speed but a little hesitantly, like he was approaching a tiger that had escaped from the zoo.

"Who are you guys?"

"FBI," said the woman.

"Badges?" Widow asked.

"We got the guns here!" the man said.

The woman said, "First, we need to restrain you and check for weapons."

"No one is restraining me. No way," Widow said. He didn't shout it or reply with severe rebellion in his voice. He simply stated it as fact, which it was. Widow had been arrested many times. He knew the procedure. He knew the players in this space. Widow understood what was real. These two had an air of deception about them. Which didn't mean they weren't law enforcement, but FBI? No way.

"We're giving the orders here!" the man said.

"We'll show you badges after," the woman said.

Widow stayed quiet. He waited.

The guy stepped closer. He moved into the glare of the headlights and stood about four feet from Widow. He shouted, "Turn around!"

Now Widow had more evidence that they weren't FBI. The guy had a Colt Anaconda, which was a big Dirty Harry gun, but not the same model. Old Clint used the Smith & Wesson Model 29, but both guns used big .44 Magnum cartridges. As far as power, they weren't much different. Only gun nuts would argue the differences. Both guns would take a man's head off, and Widow knew it. This wasn't a common weapon in law enforcement, and by "not common," Widow figured "not at all" was more accurate. The Colt Anaconda was a beast. It fired bullets that didn't just blow a hole through something—they removed that something. They made that something *not* something.

In fact, Widow couldn't imagine any department anywhere allowing someone to carry it. Widow knew it wasn't standard issue by the FBI. It was possible in some law enforcement agencies to use one's own firearm with approval, but Widow was fairly certain the FBI didn't have this policy. Of course, he could've been wrong, but he doubted it.

Widow pivoted like he was going to comply with the demand. He had been an undercover cop of sorts, and he knew how to deceive the enemy. Widow had learned all their methods and had even invented some. He slumped his shoulders in an "I surrender" pose and turned.

Looking visibly relaxed, he pivoted on his right foot, toes out, and then he swung out, hard. He jacked to the left, out of the line of fire, in one quick movement. ~~The guy~~ didn't fire, which told Widow he wasn't a cop and wanted him alive. A cop or FBI or whoever would have fired in self-defense.

Widow used the landing on his left foot and his momentum to execute a quick disarm move he'd learned in the SEALs.

The guy was right-handed and held the Colt Anaconda with both hands. His right-hand index finger was in the trigger housing. His left hand gripped lower. Which makes for a harder disarm, which is one reason professionals hold their gun with both hands. But there were still options available, and Widow knew them all. He expected the guy knew some as well.

Widow rocketed his left hand down from eye level and clamped his hand down on the back of the guy's hand, just below his wrist. He jerked the gun down and to his right. Widow stepped in and nailed the guy square in the face with a headbutt, not a deadly one, which he could've administered—easily. He wanted the guy stunned and disoriented, not dead or broken.

The big guy had been wearing a tie, what color Widow wasn't sure, but it was a regular tie and not a clip-on, another piece of evidence that the guy wasn't FBI. FBI agents and Secret Service agents and anyone else in a professional position that dealt with the criminal element knew to wear a clip-on tie. A guy who wore a regular tie and planned to be in a street fight had better be prepared to be disarmed and led around by his tie.

And that was exactly what Widow did. He gripped the guy's tie with his left hand and jerked it far back over the guy's shoulder. It was enough to choke him to death if Widow had wanted to.

Widow planted his feet, locked them into place like they were reinforced with solid concrete and rebar. He pulled the guy far down to the ten o'clock position and pointed the Colt Anaconda at the woman.

He said, "You freeze!" No yelling. No shouting. Just plain English.

* * *

THE WOMAN from Kill Team B had misjudged this drifter, and she knew it. He'd disarmed her colleague about as fast as she'd ever seen anyone do it. She wasn't even sure she could've done it that fast or gotten the drop on her partner.

She stared down the sights on her Sig Sauer and said, "Who the hell are you?"

"Who the hell are you?" the stranger replied.

"We're—" She started to say FBI, but Widow interrupted.

He said, "Don't give me that FBI crap!"

She said nothing.

The drifter said, "I saw you following me way back near Rough Creek."

She sidestepped back closer to the car. She wanted to shield half her body from him and possibly dive and retreat behind the car.

"Don't move! Stay where you are! Answer the damn question! Why're you following me?"

The woman didn't answer. She didn't know what to say. She was taking too long to come up with something, and she knew it.

The stranger didn't wait for her to answer. He jerked his gun hand—fast—and shot her partner in the back of the calf.

* * *

WIDOW FIRED THE COLT ANACONDA, and the muzzle flashed as one bullet rocketed out and blew away the big guy's calf muscle. The muscle and flesh exploded, and blood misted out, spraying across the front of Widow's pants.

The guy erupted in a scream unlike any Widow had heard in a long while. Widow jerked up on his tie, both to silence him and to keep him standing up and not toppled over.

He said, "Answer me, or ~~he gets another!~~"

The woman stayed quiet, but she gave Widow a confirmation that they were definitely bad guys, which he had been pretty positive to begin with. The woman confirmed his suspicions because she was looking around the streets. She was checking to see if anyone had heard the gunfire. She was looking for potential witnesses. Only bad guys look for witnesses. Everyone was subconsciously aware of the cell phone camera. Somebody fires a gun in an urban area, and twenty people show up with their cell phone cameras rolling. The modern smartphone made everyone a potential broadcaster.

But Widow wasn't worried about being filmed, nor was he worried about witnesses. He had done nothing wrong or illegal. At least not here tonight, he hadn't. But he noticed lights switching on at the top floors of a nearby building. Most of the other buildings were commercial and mostly office spaces. They were not in use at this hour, but one building had people inside it, and they were gathering at the windows to check out the gunshot.

And then the woman did something that shocked Widow.

The driver shot her partner. She jumped back behind the tire of the Dodge Charger and opened fire. She shot him three times in the chest. All good shots. She had real talent. The guy kicked back and into Widow. They both toppled backward.

Widow squirmed out from under him and blind-fired back. He heard the boom of the gunshots. He had fired three times. In the same second, he heard *Clang! Clang! Clang!* This meant that his return fire had climbed up the hood of the Charger.

The *clang* sound hadn't been the typical "bullets hitting metal" sound Widow had heard many times before. There was a deeper tone to it, like artillery shells hitting the side of a bridge. Then there was a whistling sound, and smoke rose from the engine. It was probably the radiator. Widow was surprised the engine was still running and hadn't completely shut down or choked or even caught fire.

Widow had always been trained to keep track of his surroundings, but it was a quiet and dark city street. He had forgotten, and he was cursing himself for it now. Luckily, city streets are not empty things, not even at night. There was a long, full bike rack. Widow scrambled toward it and dove behind several mountain bikes. A bicycle isn't the ideal hiding place to protect one from enemy fire, but twenty parked bikes come packed with a lot of steel and rubber. It wasn't ideal, but when you thought about a car nowadays, if you left out the engine, they were all fiberglass, which was no greater protection than thin metal.

The woman looked up over the hood and saw Widow. She jumped up and fired two rounds, and both clanged around in the metal of the parked bikes.

Widow shot out the nearest streetlight and then returned his aim to the woman. He waited for her to stick her head out. She didn't move. He kept shifting his focus from above the car to underneath the car. He stayed down low, but on his feet, not on his knees. Under the pressure of a gunfight, it was natural for people to duck behind cover and drop into a ball. But that was a bad idea because he needed to stay mobile and ready to bounce up out of cover.

He snapped his head to the right and to the left, fast. He saw that there was a short distance between himself and another parked car on the street. Looking in her direction again, he made a break for it. Better not to be where she was expecting him to be.

He darted fast, staying behind the bikes, and scrambled to the parked car.

Widow got up behind the trunk and hugged it tightly. He craned his head and looked back around the corner at the Dodge Charger. He could see the woman's outline. She stood up and looked back at the bike rack, gun extended, ready to fire, but she didn't fire. She saw he wasn't there.

Just then, they heard police sirens.

She looked around for him. She didn't see him, but they could hear voices in the distance. People were coming out of the office building and trying to see what was happening.

The woman scanned for Widow one last time, and then she holstered the Sig Sauer and stood up. Widow watched her get into the Charger and drive forward twenty feet. She leaped back out and scanned around for him once again, but he stayed hidden.

The driver scrambled around the front of the car and pulled the passenger door open. She grabbed her partner with both hands and dragged him a few feet and around the door. She hauled him up with all of her strength—and a little adrenaline, Widow figured. Then she shoved his body into the seat and slammed the door. The guy was dead. She had killed him, but she was recovering his body. She wasn't allowed to leave evidence behind. That told Widow she wasn't working for someone who allowed room for mistakes.

She returned to the driver's seat and hit the gas, heading in Widow's direction.

Widow waited until the Charger's front end was in line with the back end of the Volkswagen. And then he jumped out and took several large steps to the side so he was no longer standing dead-on in her path. He was now at an angle to where he could see the woman through the open driver's side window so he could avoid shattering the windshield. He took aim and squeezed the trigger. The whole thing didn't last even two seconds. Widow was certain the woman had seen him. They'd made eye contact. But he wasn't sure if she had tried to slam on the brakes or go for her Sig Sauer.

Widow fired once only—he wanted to wound, not kill. But firing in such a short span of time when a sports car with a lot of horsepower is gunning by and trying to hit the driver without killing her wasn't easy.

He squeezed the trigger. The muzzle flashed, and the gunshot boomed. The sound echoed in the street and bounced between the buildings until it died in the sky above.

The woman slumped back and then forward, and the Charger swerved to the right, and the horn blared. The car ran up onto the sidewalk and stopped.

Widow ran over to it. He jerked the driver door open, pulled her out. The police sirens were getting closer and closer. They were only blocks away now.

Blood seeped through the woman's blouse and covered her left shoulder and neck and chest in a wet blackness. Widow wasn't sure where he had hit her, but it looked like her shoulder, which was good. He needed her alive. He needed to ask her a few questions. She was semiconscious.

He pulled the door open, pulled her to the back seat, and dumped her on the back bench. She squirmed and cried out, but didn't fight him back.

He reached in and felt around where her gun had been holstered. Finding it, he jerked it out. He stepped back out and slammed the door. He tried to get into the driver seat but couldn't fit. The woman had pulled the seat all the way forward. He reached down and racked it all the way back. He dumped himself down and was amazed that the car was a stick. Then he was amazed the car stopped on the curb so easily. She had jammed the stick into neutral and her foot came off the clutch when he shot her.

He slammed the door and tossed both guns up onto the dash. He pushed in the clutch, shoved the gear into first, hit the gas and gunned it, and then made a quick shift to second.

Within moments, he was down the street and turning onto a busy highway. He turned a corner just after he saw two sets of police lights behind him slam to a stop where he had been just moments before.

11

THE WHITE DODGE Charger ran for another two miles and then stalled out just before Widow could pull onto the highway. He wasn't familiar with the city he was in, but the Charger had an onboard navigation system built into the dash. He punched the button for the map on the home screen, and then he hit a special emergency button and selected the "Nearest Hospital" feature.

Widow had shot the woman in self-defense, but he didn't want her to die. Widow still wasn't sure what was going on. He didn't know why they had been following him or why they had tried to take him alive, but Widow was far from dumb. He may not have been the smartest guy in the world, but dumb wasn't his style. Widow knew they weren't FBI, and he knew they didn't intend to take him alive and keep him alive. He also knew they had been following him, at least since he was in the SUV with Leon. When he parted ways with Leon, they hadn't continued following her. Therefore, they had been following him.

He looked back over the seat at the woman. In the streetlights that passed overhead, he could see her face clearly. Right now, she looked to be in great agony. A .44 Magnum through the shoulder was exactly that—through the shoulder. A .44 Magnum never diddled around in a person's body. It wasn't a stoppable bullet. It always went through someone. It was possible that much of her shoulder wasn't there anymore. Widow had no idea, because he hadn't looked.

His priority was to get away from the cops because he figured these two killers weren't after him for something he had done. And if they weren't after Agent Leon, then they must've followed him way back when he had met Claire Hood. Which, he could guess, meant they were after James Hood. And James Hood had possession of his six-year-old daughter, Jemma. And that concerned Widow.

Now that two professional killers had revealed themselves to Widow, he could safely assume that Jemma's and James's lives were in grave danger, and that was why James ran with her.

Widow looked back once more at the woman bleeding to death in the back seat, and he recognized her from the family-owned diner. She had been sitting there a few tables away from him. She was good. He hadn't made her like a tail.

Widow said, "I'm bringing you to a hospital. Just hang on."

He had had a plan. He would simply drop the car off near the emergency room and then walk away. On foot, he was good at disappearing. He knew that once the cops got hold of her, they'd try to get answers about what the hell was going on, but she wouldn't give any. Widow wasn't afraid of her giving an eyewitness account of him or telling the cops she was part of a kill team tracking a runaway ex-con, or that she had a boss. He wasn't afraid of her talking because whoever had hired her wasn't the kind of guy you snitch on. Widow knew that because the woman had killed her partner to achieve the mission. Once Widow had immobilized the big guy by shooting him, and there was no more use out of him, she had killed him.

That was when the Charger's engine had gone as far as it could. It spurted and coughed and groaned. Smoke burst out faster than a teapot. He veered the car over to the shoulder of a virtually deserted on-ramp and killed the engine so as not to allow it to catch fire.

He said, "Well, I guess this is as close as I get. Got a cell phone? I'll call you an ambulance."

He turned all the way around in his seat and looked down at her again. Blood was now everywhere—on her face, her neck. Her shirt was soaked in it. There was nothing left to prove she was a white woman—not a hint of skin that wasn't completely red.

She was dead. Widow didn't need to feel for her pulse to see that. She had that lifeless expression on her face. One he'd seen a thousand times, and that was probably not an inflated number.

He reached down and checked her pockets, looking for any information. He found nothing but her cell phone, which was a burner —a good quality iPhone burner, but a burner nonetheless. It didn't have a passcode on it, which meant she had either been sloppy or hadn't had the chance to lock it yet. Both scenarios seemed plausible to Widow. The big guy had been the sloppy one. He had carried that Colt Anaconda, a dead giveaway. And then he had let himself get taken down. The woman alone would've been a better opponent. If she had come on to Widow and made it seem natural, he might've fallen for it for a while. But that hadn't been the case. And now they were both dead, and the only answers Widow had were the easy ones.

He sifted through her phone for any information that might help him. Outside the Charger, cars passed, entering the highway. He could see the silhouettes of the occupants of each car look over at the Charger, but no one could see details of his face, and so far, no one had stopped to help. Good Samaritans were few and far between these days, which was good for Widow. He wouldn't harm an innocent civilian, not even to protect his own identity.

He continued to search through the phone and found two things of interest. The first was a photograph of James Hood. Which only confirmed what he had suspected—they were after Hood. The second thing of interest was actually two separate things— phone numbers. Only two numbers had been both called and received by her phone. He slipped the phone into his pocket. Then he checked the big guy. He found six more .44 Magnum bullets and another burner phone. His phone was a cheaper one. It was one of those old flip Nokias. There was nothing of interest in it. It looked as if he hadn't made or received a single call on it.

One thing the big guy had that the woman hadn't was a wallet. Widow checked it and found over a hundred bucks in cash-money and an Ohio driver's license. He really hadn't been the best money could buy. But he was a big guy, so Widow figured he must've been the muscle. Maybe he was used for heavy lifting and the intimidation factor.

The guy's real name had been Francis—Francis Mahoney. Which Widow heard himself pronounce in his head as Ma-*hunny*. That made him smile. Francis Ma-*hunny*. But Widow was certain the big guy had told everyone his name was Frank and not Francis. Too bad no one would call him either anymore.

Widow left the wallet and took the money. He took the .44 Magnum and the Sig Sauer, which turned out to be a Sig Sauer P227, a good and reliable weapon.

Widow stepped out of the car and looked both ways for oncoming cars or any other witnesses. Three cars were coming up the ramp and onto the highway. Widow turned casually, like he was going to look under the hood, and faced away so they couldn't see his face.

The cars passed.

He turned and looked back down the on-ramp. No one was coming. There were no headlights as far as he could see.

He went back to the driver's side door and opened it. He popped the trunk and went back to inspect it. Once there, he stopped cold. There were two black body bags. They looked like the kind he'd seen in Navy hospital morgues. Only these weren't stamped with any official labels as to whose property they were.

Not much riled Widow anymore because he had been all over the world on all seven continents—if you could count a cold three months in Antarctica investigating the crew of a nuclear subma-rine, where he had only stepped on land once. He had seen all kinds of atrocities man was capable of. He had experienced the worst kinds of treason and betrayal from being undercover with NCIS, but this was more unsettling than a lot of those things because the body bags were of two sizes. One adult. One child.

There was one for James Hood, and there was one for Jemma Hood.

12

WIDOW HAD FIGURED James Hood all wrong. Hood wasn't trying to abduct his daughter. He was trying to rescue her. Whatever he had gotten involved in, or whoever he'd gotten involved with, Widow could see the scenario now. Claire had said her son wasn't a bad guy. She had said he'd just been mixed up with the wrong people.

Hood had fallen in love with an illegal immigrant who had a young, illegal daughter. Widow recalled the photograph Claire had. It was the same one Hood had on his Facebook page. There was a glow in both Lucy and Jemma Hood. They were a true mother and daughter, like a dream family. Beautiful smiles. And then there was Claire Hood, James's incredibly brave mother. Widow could picture the guy feeling responsible for them and being desperate to provide for them, to protect them. Then he could picture Hood not being the brightest guy in the world and easy to take advantage of.

Maybe they were desperate for money. And Lucy was sick. Very sick, according to Claire. Widow recalled she had terminal cancer. Being responsible for feeding and clothing a six-year-old girl and her mother was one thing, but being responsible for the medical bills of a cancer patient in America was something entirely different.

Widow could imagine Hood doing what any good husband and
father would do. Hood sought other methods of making money.
And somehow he got involved with the wrong crew. And somebody in this outfit must have been the money man because these
guys were professional. Maybe not good enough to take him out,
but really, how often is it that a killing crew comes across a drifter
who has his experience?

Widow didn't know the details, but he felt he was right in his esti-
mation of the situation.

Now he had to find Hood and Jemma before more bad guys came
along. And he guessed there would be more, as soon as these two
didn't check in.

Widow checked the street again and saw no sign of oncoming
cars, just lights from the highway in the distance. He walked
around to the passenger door and grabbed the big guy, trying to
avoid getting blood on himself, and hauled him out of the car.
Deadweight was always hard to move. Moving dead bodies wasn't
what he had planned for his day, but here he was. He dragged the
guy all the way around and back to the trunk. One of the guy's
shoes fell off along the way.

Widow stopped at the trunk and made one quick glance back for
headlights. When he saw none, he heaved Francis up and
dumped him into the trunk on top of the body bags. He walked
back along the side of the car and picked up his shoe and tossed
it in.

Widow returned to the woman and pulled her out. She was
much, much easier than Francis had been. He lifted her up over
his shoulder and suddenly imagined a passerby coming up the
highway and seeing the silhouette of a giant hitchhiker carrying a
dead woman slumped over his shoulder. He smirked, and then
felt a little odd about it. Something he learned in the SEALs,
something actually taught to him in a serious class, was about
humor.

The instructors railed on the men to find humor in combat. Find
humor in the face of extreme odds because that old saying about

laughing in the face of danger had a ring of truth to it. He'd just killed two people, and that was never a good thing, but it was him or them. Well, technically, the woman killed the man, but that was splitting hairs. They were dead because of him. It was them or Jemma as far as he was concerned.

He dumped the woman down in the trunk on top of Francis and looked at them one last time. He tossed in Francis's wallet and locked the car up and walked away toward the highway.

He looked at himself in the car's passenger side window and saw he was unsuccessful in keeping blood off his clothes. He opened the door and leaned in and grabbed a water bottle the woman had left in the cupholder. She wouldn't need it.

He took off his shirt and cleaned it with the water. Most of the blood was on his skin. He cleaned himself off the best he could. He flipped his shirt inside out and put it back on that way to hide the bloodstains on the front.

He left the car and the dead bodies and walked away.

* * *

WIDOW GOT a ride from an off-duty firefighter, which wasn't good because he figured the guy would be well informed about the local news, and whenever the police popped that trunk, they'd find those bodies. Maybe there'd be a story on the news about it, and maybe the firefighter would remember the night he'd picked up a hitchhiker, practically in front of the car. The firefighter would remember Widow and possibly tell the cops.

Widow wasn't really too concerned about it because the police wouldn't pop the trunk. Not right away. That car would probably sit there for several hours. A patrolman would drive along and check it out. The windows were tinted, which was good because the cop wouldn't see the bloodstains on the back seat. But he would write a ticket and leave it on the window. And then several more hours would pass, and another cop would come by and see the previous ticket and slap a tow sticker on the window. Widow

had seen those stickers before on abandoned cars along the highway. Usually, they were bright pink or yellow. They were
signaling to the passing tow trucks to stop and pick up the car.

The Dodge Charger would get towed to a city impound, where it
would be forgotten for a while. No one would pay much attention
to it until the bodies decomposed and rotted and smelled terrible.
Then again, Widow hadn't thought about the giant .44 Magnum
bullet holes in the engine and the hood. So probably the car
would be towed to the impound, but only after the cops investigated the interior, found the blood, popped the trunk, and found
the bodies. In every scenario Widow's mind played out, he was
better off getting the hell out of there and on his way.

After the cops performed an investigation, they'd certainly find
his fingerprints. They would send them back to the department to
be analyzed, and then they would run them through the data-
bases. They'd run them through the FBI database first since it was
the biggest and most comprehensive. An hour or two would probably go by, and then their search would trigger a red flag in DC,
which would be referred to the Department of the Navy, and
then the search would be rerouted to Quantico, but not because
that was where the FBI trained its agents. It would be sent to
Quantico because that was the headquarters of the NCIS. They
would then see the search was marked as classified. The identity
of the fingerprints would be redacted and encrypted, and eventually, it would all trickle to Unit Ten, which was Widow's old unit.

Of course, they would deny information to the FBI and to the
cops as a matter of national security, and that would be the end.
But they would want answers.

Widow figured that all of this would really be a good thing
because now that things had changed for him, he could use the
help, which meant that eventually he would have to call his old
boss.

13

WIDOW SLEPT in a cheap motel off the highway, the kind that took cash and didn't ask questions about its occupants. Otherwise, it would have no occupants.

The room was filthy, and the neighbors were loud. The place was occupied by meth addicts and prostitutes. Widow had slept in worse places, but not in America. He had stayed in some less than reputable establishments in the US, but not like this one. This was like a bad episode of a cop show. Still, he had been exhausted and slept as well as a man could sleep on a mattress that was made with more spring than cushion. The noises hadn't bothered him because he could tune them out as easily as anything. He had slept on the cold metal floor of Air Force cargo planes. He had to sleep flying over the Atlantic to Germany more times than he could remember, and that didn't count all the times he flew in the same circumstances, only over the Pacific. Not to mention, he had had to sleep in situations of heavy gunfire.

A seedy motel in Texas wasn't a cakewalk, but it was the Hilton compared to some places he'd slept in.

Widow had scrubbed his bloody clothes in the sink, then filled the bathtub with soapy water and let them soak for forty-five minutes before he took them out, rinsed and wrung them all out, and left them hanging up overnight to dry.

He woke up at first light and decided it was best to hit the road. His clothes were dry by then, but a new change of clothes wouldn't hurt. First thing, he needed to shower.

He had to admit that even though the motel was far from stellar; the shower was pretty good. Hot water the way he liked it and tremendous water pressure—all good things.

Widow showered and toweled off with a thin white towel and dried his hair with a smaller one. Then he slipped his clothes back on and left the shady motel, never to think of it again.

Widow walked a quarter of a mile, toward the busier and more modern areas of the city. He found his way past a McDonald's and a Target, which wasn't open yet. He walked on, looking for a twenty-four-hour store or a department store that opened early. Widow found a small surf shop that had a sign out front that read, "Going Out of Business Sale."

An attractive bleached blonde was sitting on a lawn chair out front with some racks of jeans displayed. She wore sunglasses and cut-off jean shorts.

She said in a fantastic Texas accent, "Hey, how ya doin'? Up early today?"

Widow said, "Going out of business. Why?"

"This little store just didn't make it."

"Bad location?"

"Yeah. I mean, there's a bunch of box-retails around here. There's a Target down the street. We just couldn't compete."

"You going to be all right?"

"Sure. This is my first store, but I got two others. Tough times is all."

Widow nodded.

"So, you need some clothes?"

He nodded and stood behind the rack, out of her sight to avoid being too memorable in case the cops tracked him this far.

She said, "Okay. Well, today, everything is half off."

"You got a big-and-tall section?"

"We don't got any dress clothes for a guy your size. But there's plenty to pick from in the t-shirts. Most of what we got is extra-large."

"What about pants?"

"Try the jeans. They're in the back of the store. Right side."

"Can I try them on?"

"Sure, honey. The fitting room is in the back, past the counter."

Widow nodded and asked, "Aren't you worried about me stealing?"

"Nah, honey. I'm aiming to sell all this stuff by the end of business. There ain't no room for it at my other stores. If you don't buy it, then it all gets donated. Besides, you look trustworthy enough."

He didn't respond. He shimmied past the racks of girls' pants and accessories and into the store. First, he grabbed a black T-shirt, just because it was the first XL he saw, and then he hurried over to the jeans and studied them for his size and grabbed a dark blue pair.

He took them back to the fitting room and undressed and then dressed again in the new clothes. Everything fit well.

Normally, he would've thrown away his old clothes at the store, but even though they were clean, crime forensics was an impressive field. He didn't want to chance it. It was best to take them with him and throw them into a dumpster.

Widow came out of the store and held out the tags from the jeans and the shirt. He handed her two twenties from Francis's cash.

He said, "This should cover the price, with the discount. Keep the change."

The bleach blonde store owner opened her hand and took the cash. She stayed seated and said, "Sure thing. You want anything else?"

"No," he said and then stopped and asked, "Which way to the bus station?"

"Greyhound is about three miles down that road. Just head straight and turn right near the Waffle House. It's across from the police station."

Great, he thought and repeated the words *police station* in his head.

* * *

EVERYONE GETS a little intimidated from time to time. When you're guilty of murder, you get a little more so than the average person. Especially when you're waiting for a bus and sitting right across from the police station.

Widow had walked from the clothing shop that was going out of business and passed by a closed restaurant. He dumped his old clothes in a dumpster there, as well as the Colt Anaconda, after wiping it down. Tossing it made him a little sad because it was such a beautiful weapon. But he didn't see the practicality in taking it with him. It was huge and bulky and not a weapon he could conceal in just jeans and a T-shirt. He kept the Sig Sauer, which was much more practical. The only thing about it was that the woman hadn't brought extra rounds. So he had to settle for having only five left.

Tossing the Colt Anaconda wasn't the end of his sadness because he still had the bullets to deal with. He had unloaded the remaining bullets and the brass, and then he had the extra ones from Francis's pocket. He didn't want to toss them into the dumpster with the gun, so he walked over two blocks and found a sewage drain and dumped them down the grate.

Widow walked to the bus station and bought a ticket. Then he spent the next forty-five minutes waiting for his bus to Laredo. He waited on the bench farthest from the police station's line of sight. He knew there was no real chance of anyone pinning him as a suspect for shooting two people only the night before. Despite that, he was going to feel a lot more comfortable when he was far from the city.

Widow had the bus ticket in his back pocket. It was flattened out in his latest paperback book. He felt a little restless and a little hungry. He was ready to get on the road. Widow got up to walk around the station for a few minutes and stretch his legs. He walked around to the other side of the station's hutch and stopped by a water fountain. Widow took a swig and then looked above the fountain at a map of the roads of South Texas. He studied it and recalled in his head the conversation with Leon.

She had said that to reach Romanth, he would need something with four-wheel drive.

Widow had an idea. He looked down the street and saw one of those old mechanic shops that had been open for decades—a dying breed. He forgot about taking the bus and walked across the street to the mechanic. The sign out front said "Torrocel's." Widow walked in, and a bell above the door chimed his arrival.

He waited in front of a counter for someone to come out of the back. Behind the counter was a bookshelf with used auto parts books. He could see pages torn and folded, and spines creased. A long moment passed, and he thought about calling out, but then a little old man came from out of the shadows. He wore a green collared shirt and a pair of gray slacks. He was wiping his hands, which were greased up from working on a car, Widow figured. The guy must've been a pretty good mechanic because his clothes were clean. Then again, maybe he was just the front desk guy or the owner, and someone else lower down the food chain was the one who did the actual labor.

The guy reached into his front shirt pocket and pulled out a pair of thick-rimmed glasses and slipped them on. He said, "Yes? Can I help you?"

Widow said, "How are you today?"

"Fine. Doing fine."

"That's good. I need to inquire about your lot."

"What do you mean?"

"I saw around the back that you got a lot of cars back there."

The guy said, "Yeah. What of it?"

"Are they all customers' cars?"

"Not all. Two of them are employees. What's this about, son?"

"See, I'm in desperate need of wheels."

"Yeah?"

"I'm wondering if you got any old trucks lying around that you wouldn't mind parting with?"

The guy cocked his head up and stared at Widow's face. He said, "This isn't a car dealership."

"I realize that, sir. But I figured a bunch of those junkier rides were yours."

The guy continued to stare into Widow's face.

Widow said, "I figure you use them for spare parts."

The guy said, "Well, if I use them for spare parts, don't you think that none of them would work right?"

"Isn't there something back there that runs?"

"So let me get this straight. You want to buy one of my old junk vehicles?"

"That's right. I need a truck. With four-wheel drive. Nothing fancy. Just reliable."

The guy paused a long moment, and then he said, "You don't care about any luxuries?" Widow stayed quiet, and the guy came back with, "What I mean is, it don't need AC?"

Widow said, "I don't care if it has doors on it."

The guy nodded and said, "Wait right here." And he removed his glasses, turned, and walked back through a door into the shadows.

Widow stood near the counter and waited. He looked at the clock on the wall and recalled the map from the bus station in his head. He had about a two-hour drive down to Laredo, and then another hour northwest.

The guy returned without his glasses and had an employee following behind him.

He wore mechanic's overalls and was covered in grease—a real mechanic.

The guy said, "Yes, sir. You looking to buy something with four-wheel drive?"

Widow nodded.

"You got cash?"

"I got a debit card."

The guy thought for a moment, and he turned to the old man, who must've been the owner, Torrocel, and whispered something to him. They spoke in low voices, and then he turned back and said, "Good enough. Come on back."

Widow followed the two of them through the shadows and out a door. They walked into a small three-slot garage. All three slots were occupied with cars up on the lifts. There was another guy there, all greased up and working underneath one car.

Widow followed the mechanic past the work area and out through one of the open garages. They walked into a small parking lot that was jam-packed with cars. They walked beyond what Widow assumed were customers' cars waiting to be worked on and then through some cars that looked more like scrap metal and then over to a wooded area where three vehicles were parked.

The guy walked up to a 1990s Jeep Wrangler. It was lifted with big tires, and painted Army green. The Wrangler might as well have had an Army star slapped on the side door. It had no top on it, and no visible top anywhere. There were half doors, and a winch on the front, and a spare tire on the back. It was well kept, but there wasn't much to say about the exterior. It looked like the bones of a daily driver, as a work in progress.

The guy said, "I got this Jeep. I need to sell it. It runs good. The wife is having our second, and I need to get rid of it."

Widow looked it over and asked, "Any engine problems?"

"What you think?"

Widow stayed quiet.

"I work in a garage. I keep it running good. Solid engine."

"The four-wheel-drive work?"

"You know it does. That's the whole reason to have one. Take it for a drive if you want and try it out."

Widow said, "Nah. No need. I trust you. How much you want for it?"

The guy said, "How much you want to pay?"

Widow asked, "What's the value?"

"The book value on these things is around six thousand."

Widow said, "Steep. I'll give you four."

The guy was silent, and then he looked at his boss and back to Widow. He said, "Make it forty-five hundred."

Widow thought for a moment and said, "Done."

They shook hands and returned to the shop. The mechanic had convinced his boss to sell the Jeep as if it were a part of his own inventory to Widow. Which meant Widow paid the boss, and the boss gave the mechanic straight cash-money. They followed this procedure so that they could swipe Widow's debit card.

After swiping Widow's card, they made Widow watch as the boss counted $4,500 out of a safe. He wasn't sure why they made him watch. Finally, the mechanic reached into his pocket and pulled out a key ring with over a dozen different keys on it. He slipped out the Jeep key and handed it to Widow.

He said, "I need to run home to get the title."

"Just hold on to it. I'll come back for it," Widow lied. He didn't intend to keep the vehicle. And in the event of it getting impounded, it would be better not to have any paperwork trace back to him.

The guy didn't seem to bat an eye at this. He said, "It's got a full tank. Take good care of her. She's been with me for years."

Widow nodded and checked the clock one last time as he walked out the door. He figured he could get Jemma back by nightfall if he was lucky.

14

DRIVING DOWN 35, Widow put the Wrangler in fifth gear and decided he had to recalculate the time it would take him to get to Romanth, because it turned out that the older Jeep wasn't built for speed. It topped out at fifty-five miles per hour as long as he stayed flat and not going up hills. It was not a fast-moving vehicle.

He drove for over an hour and guessed he would be in Romanth within two-and-a-half hours. He enjoyed driving with the top gone. It was nice, even though the hot sun beat down on him. He figured the best-case scenario was being at risk of getting a farmer's tan, and the worst-case scenario was getting burned.

The Wrangler drove well, just like the mechanic had said. The tires were balanced and straight. Widow felt every rock on the road underneath, but it was in a good way. He was really impressed with his new Jeep. He was even considering keeping it. Widow liked the life he had chosen of owning nothing and wandering the landscape, free of possessions. But there was something tantalizing about riding in a Jeep. He imagined it was the same for guys who rode hogs across the country. He could understand the motorcycle appeal, the life of a rebel.

Just then, the cell phone he had taken from the woman vibrated and buzzed and made a dinging sound he had heard from other people's phones before. It was the latest iPhone sound. It was weak and said, *Hello. You have a text.* It wasn't a sound he would choose for a phone—if he owned a phone. It was too soft.

He reached down and picked the iPhone off of the passenger seat and checked it. There was a text from one of the numbers programmed into the phone.

It read, "Where r u? Y haven't you checked in?"

Widow thought about responding, but what for? He could've called both numbers and talked to the bad guys on the other line, but what was the good in that? He had the advantage.

The two people who had been following him were trying to find out where he was going. That's why they had been following him. They didn't know where Hood was, and they didn't know where he was headed, and he wanted to keep it that way. Once he had Jemma safe and sound, then he could ask Hood about what was going on. Then he could deal with Hood's trouble.

* * *

JOHN GLOCK CALLED the Principal and said, "I can't get hold of them."

Silence fell over the line, and a nervous voice came on and said, "Have you called?"

"No."

"Why the hell not?"

"I texted. We don't call on the phone. They were supposed to check in, and they didn't. So I texted."

The Principal sounded nervous. He asked, "And?"

"And nothing. They didn't respond."

Silence fell over the line, then the Principal came on and said, "You know what's at stake here?"

"I know."

"I've spent the last fifteen months preparing for this. We've invested millions."

Glock said, "I know."

"We can't have Hood out there. We need to know what he told the Feds."

Glock said, "If he told them anything."

"You don't think he did?"

"I think if he had spoken to them, they'd have come down on us already."

"So why the hell is he out?"

"I think he told them something, but I don't think he gave them proof."

The Principal said, "So they let him out as a sign of good faith?"

Glock said, "Exactly. Maybe to go and say goodbye to his family. Or maybe they let him out, and he ditched them. Whatever happened, I guarantee they aren't on to us. We'd have seen them already."

The Principal said, "So what do we do?"

Glock asked, "Where are you?"

"I'm in Austin."

"Campaigning?"

"Yes."

"Is our candidate there?"

"No. He left. He's got a debate coming up."

Glock asked, "How did it go for him?"

"The crowd loved him."

"What about the negotiation?"

The Principal said, "Don't worry about that. It's not time yet."

"You know we have to get those contracts!"

"Your job is cleanup. Don't tell me how to do mine. Now find Hood and put a bullet in him!"

"What about the family? You still want them dead?"

The line was silent for a long moment again, and Glock could hear the Principal breathing heavily on the other end of the line.

Glock had no intention of letting anyone in the Hood family live. The dying wife. The girl. They were all going to die. That was how he operated. But he wanted to make sure the Principal had the stomach for it.

The Principal said, "Do it."

Glock smiled.

"Ask him what they know first."

"Don't worry. I'll have a good conversation with him before I put him down."

The Principal asked, "Where's the last place you heard from the others?"

"South Texas. Don't worry—I'll find out what's going on."

"Call them. I don't care about protocol."

Glock said, "I'm going to when we hang up."

The Principal said, "Good."

"This may take until nighttime. Where you gonna be?"

"I'll be home after five."

"Good. I'll call you when it's done," Glock said and hung up the phone. He looked at his watch and then at his phone. He called a number for his contact at the Jericho Men.

The phone rang, and then he heard a click, and a voice came on.

Glock said, "Danny, it's me."

The voice on the other line said, "What's up?"

"I need you to track a phone."

There was a short moment of silence on the other line, and then the guy named Danny said, "What's the number?"

Glock relayed the number to him and said, "It's one of our burners. We lost an asset."

Danny said, "No explanation required. But I'll need them to answer the phone so I can get a ping on it."

"Understood. How long do I need to talk with them?"

"There's no minimum. Just get them to turn it on. Once it's on, then I can track it."

"I'm going to call them now," Glock said, and clicked off the phone. He searched his phone for the woman's name. Glock found it and hit the Call button. He waited for it to ring.

* * *

WIDOW DROVE the Wrangler and had no problems. The engine ran well. Wind blew in hard as he barreled down the highway. It was hard to hear the woman's phone when it rang, but he had it in the cup holder and saw it light up.

Widow pulled over to the side of the road, slow. The tires spit gravel up in the air, and the dust settled around him. He put the gear into neutral and jerked up the emergency brake. It clicked.

He picked up the phone and hit the button to answer. He put the receiver up to his ear and said nothing, just listened.

A horrible voice that sounded like a guy trying to swallow a whole pigeon said, "Hello. Where are you?"

Widow stayed quiet.

The voice said, "Jane? Answer! Where are you?"

"Wrong person. Jane won't be coming to the phone. Ever again."

The voice on the other end said, "Who the hell is this?"

"I'm the guy who killed your friends."

"They're dead?"

"As doornails."

"Who are you?"

"I'm nobody."

"You're the stranger. The guy who talked to the old bird before she croaked."

"And you're the asshole who hired two amateurs to follow a poor defenseless old lady."

Glock said, "They weren't amateurs. They were experienced professionals."

Widow said, "Whatever. They're dead now."

"You must be good to have killed them both."

"I didn't kill them both. Your friend Jane killed the other guy."

"I'm sure you gave her no choice."

Widow said, "What are you? The boss?"

"Something like that."

"What the hell's wrong with your voice? Did you bite your tongue off?"

There was a pause on the line, and then Glock said, "I was stabbed. In prison."

Widow waited a long second and then said, "Is that supposed to scare me?"

Glock said nothing back.

Widow asked, "Somebody tried to kill you?"

"And they failed."

"Too bad. You better hope nothing happens to Hood and that little girl. Or I'll finish the job."

Widow hung the phone up. No reason to continue. Nothing left to say. He tossed the iPhone back onto the seat next to him and looked back at the oncoming cars. Widow waited for an opening and threw the gear into first and released the emergency brake. He hit the gas, the Wrangler bounced, the tires kicked up dirt, and he was back on the road.

* * *

GLOCK CALLED Danny again and said, "Tell me you located the phone."

"Of course. No problem. He's headed south on 35 toward Laredo. Is he coming to us?"

"No. This isn't one of our guys. This is a meddler. A guy sticking his nose where it don't belong."

"I see. You want me to get the boys together? We can cut him off."

"No. I'll handle it personally. Get everyone in. Stay at the compound."

Danny asked, "What's this about?"

"We have a situation. A guy we worked with once before got himself arrested. He got ten years."

"Who is it?"

"James Hood."

No recognition came from Danny.

Glock said, "Doesn't matter. It was before your boys came on board. This guy got ten years. We let him live because he has family. People we can hurt."

"I understand."

"He got out yesterday, only did two years. Didn't tell us. We want to know why."

"You think he talked to the cops?"

"Probably."

"Now you need him silenced?"

Glock said, "Right."

Danny asked, "This guy we're tracking. Where do you think he's going? Think he wants to cross the border?"

"No. This guy is after Hood. He thinks he can stop us from getting to him first."

"So, he knows where this Hood guy is?"

Glock said, "Yeah. Keep an eye on his phone. Tell me where he stops."

"No problem."

"And Danny?"

"Yeah?"

"Better gear up. We might need your guys tonight. This guy's already killed two of my guys."

Danny said, "Got it."

Glock hung up. He was already in his Tahoe and headed south. He was only a few hours behind this stranger.

15

THE SUN SET over huge rock formations and rock shelves. Fiery reds swarmed across the sky. The last ten miles were rough on the long, winding dirt track that led to the town of Romanth. Red clay and empty river beds filled the landscape. The whole scene was majestic.

Widow drove on until the road turned into blacktop. The tires bounced up onto the road, and the ride smoothed out. Widow turned a sharp curve and came to a sign that said, "Barclay," but the word was crossed out. Written over it was the word *Romanth*.

After the sign, Widow saw the town cemetery. *That's weird*, he thought.

His first introduction to the town was the graveyard. It was small and had less than fifty plots. There was a black wrought-iron fence posted around it, and the tombstones looked over a hundred years old. They were cracked and overgrown with weeds and some remaining grass. Someone must've started out watering here, but stopped. Outside of the fence was nothing but red clay and dirt.

Widow continued along the road and entered the town.

There was a tall water tower. A huge brick church appeared out of place because it looked like it could hold hundreds of people, but Widow would've been surprised if there were more than a thousand people living here.

The town was booming with life and improvements. Widow saw families walking to dinner and teenagers hanging out in front of storefronts. He saw two school buses that were parked in the local school lot. It was a good size campus, but he imagined it was K through twelve and not separated like most of America's schools.

There was no hospital in sight, but there was a two-story medical center with a sign that listed the many services they provided. It was not a twenty-four-hour establishment.

He followed the town's main drag and noticed immediately that everyone stopped and stared at him.

Look at the stranger.

Widow drove on. He turned off the main street and onto another one. He followed it to a dead end. The street must've been where the adults headed after hours because it had two bars, both country bars—the kind with live music and cold beer, his kind of bar.

Widow circled around and returned to the main street. He looked over the locals, who were staring at him. There were young men in cowboy hats and blue jeans and cowboy boots. Widow saw slender young women in summer dresses. He saw the older men who carried slightly more stomach than their younger counterparts. He saw the older women with slightly wider hips, but who still held their own in the attractiveness department.

Then he noticed something that wasn't really strange. He couldn't help but make a mental note of it. Almost everyone looked Mexican. There were a few white people peppered here and there, but most of the town seemed to comprise Hispanic people. Which he guessed wasn't that unusual. It was South Texas, and he was pretty close to the border. This was Romanth, a small Texas town with a small population. Now he needed to find Hood and Jemma. He looked at the iPhone and clicked on the screen. It was about dinner time. He thought to himself, where would Hood take Jemma to dinner? Then he turned another corner and found a few restaurants and the town's only hotel so far.

He figured that would be as good a place as any to start. Unless Hood had a friend here, then he and Jemma would stay in the hotel.

Widow pulled into the parking lot of the little hotel with no name and parked. He left the Jeep near the road and walked to the office. Inside, he saw two people. One was an older lady, and the other was a young guy about Widow's height and build. He looked tough. He had buzz-cut hair with a long razor mark down the right side of his head that could've been a scar, but Widow wasn't sure. Even though he looked tough, he gave Widow a friendly smile and said, "Welcome."

The old lady repeated, "Welcome. Do you need a room, sir?"

Widow said, "I do."

"No problem."

The lobby was half office and half where they lived. And suddenly, Widow was reminded of that old Hitchcock movie *Psycho*.

A momma loves her boy.

"You're lucky today because we have a first-floor room available."

Widow nodded and said, "Perfect."

They went through all the procedures and asked for his identification and a credit card to use for incidentals. Widow used his debit card. They had him sign two forms, and they made a copy of his passport. After everything had transpired, they told him his room number and gave him a plastic key card. The mother started to explain how to use it, but Widow reassured her he had used them before.

He pulled out the cell phone that belonged to the dead woman, and he opened it and found the photo of Hood. He said, "By any chance, have you seen this guy?"

The old lady said, "Sorry, sir, but we can't give information about other guests who may or may not be here."

Which gave Widow the impression that the answer was yes.

He nodded. He thought about trying to bribe them, but didn't feel it would've gotten him anywhere. Bribing someone for information normally only works when the person is alone, like a lonely clerk at midnight—underpaid and overworked. In his experience, those were the guys who were the easiest to buy information from. But not a mother trying to raise her son and run a business. It wasn't likely she would take Widow's money right in front of her son.

Widow left and turned the corner and headed to his room, but outside he heard a voice call to him.

"Sir? Sir?"

He turned and saw the son following behind him. He waited for the son to catch up.

The guy said, "This guy you're looking for? What's it worth to you?"

Ah, the perfect question.

Widow smiled and said, "I can pay money for it."

The guy said, "A hundred bucks. I can tell you."

Widow thought for a moment and then reached into his pocket and pulled out the rest of the dead bad guy's cash-money. He glanced over the amount. It was less than a hundred bucks.

He said, "I'll give you sixty-five."

The son looked displeased, and he huffed and sighed and saw that it was all the cash Widow had. In the end, he agreed and took the money. He said, "He's here. He checked in to the room on the end."

Jackpot. Widow smiled.

He asked, "Was there a little girl with him?"

The son nodded.

16

WIDOW'S HOTEL room was the cliché of every motel and hotel room he'd ever seen. It was better than some, and worse than others. The AC wall unit was turned off, and the room was musty and hot. No one had stayed in it for a while—he was sure about that—even though the mother had made a big deal about him being lucky enough to get one when they weren't all sold out. Right now, Widow doubted they were ever booked solid.

He had nothing to leave in the room, no luggage. The only extra things he was carrying were the keys to the Jeep. He wanted to wash his face and use the bathroom. And he could use a nap, but he had a head start over the guy he had spoken to on the phone earlier, and he had caught up to Hood. He wanted to keep it that way. So he used the toilet and washed his hands and then his face.

Widow pocketed the key card and left the room.

He walked down to Hood's room and looked through the window. He saw no movement. No lights. He knocked on the door. No answer. He knocked again. No answer.

He knocked harder and said, "Mr. Hood? I'm a friend."

He leaned in close and listened to hear something on the other
side. There was nothing. No sound. No movement. No sudden
jump from the intrusion—and there would've been.

He turned and inspected the parking lot. Surely Hood would
park close to his hotel room. The lot wasn't full, but not
completely empty either. In front of Hood's room, there were
trucks of different models and makes. Some new. Some old. No
way to know which was which. Two of them were Hertz rentals.
They had the stickers on the windshield. Widow guessed it was
probably one of these two vehicles, but it was only a guess.

He gave up and looked in the next logical place, a restaurant.

* * *

WIDOW SAT, back to the wall, at a table for four people. The
restaurant was full. It was an Applebee's, which wasn't his first
choice of a place to have dinner. There were two perfectly good
local establishments on the same street, but in the end, he decided
Hood would take Jemma to a more corporate kind of place.
Applebee's and Chili's and all those kinds of American chain
restaurants had larger crowds, and they normally offered a child's
menu. Some of them might even offer a kids-eat-free deal. Widow
wasn't sure because he had no kids, and he hadn't been a kid in
decades. But it seemed logical.

The waitress had offered him a happy-hour deal and asked him to
try a plate of this and to add on that. She did everything she was
supposed to do. She tried to upsell items from the menu before he
even ordered anything. The hostess had handed him three
different menus. One was for the bar, one was entrees, and the
other was for specials. To come into one of these American chain
restaurants nowadays reminded him of trying to go to a government office and get something done. Between a glass of water and
dessert, there was more red tape than the United States Department of Veterans Affairs.

The waitress was a twenty-something brunette—slim and tall.
She must've figured Widow was alone—and he wore no wedding

ring—so she saw him as a target to do a little flirting to get extra tips. Widow knew it from the first word to the end of the meal. But when you're a drifter in your mid-thirties and a young woman wants to flirt with you, you take advantage of the situation. So instead of ordering a black coffee, which he normally would've done, he ordered a domestic beer. By the end of the meal, he'd drunk two cold Buds. As for the other menu items she wanted to serve him, he had said no to them.

He ordered a grilled chicken sandwich and fries. Simple.

He ate and drank and paid his check. He waited a little longer and drank the rest of his last beer. There was no sign of Hood or Jemma.

Widow said goodbye to the waitress, and walked back to the hotel.

Before he returned, he looked around the town. It didn't take long. He discovered in less than forty-five minutes that he had seen everything the town offered on his way in. The downtown area was small. It was everything required for a municipality and nothing else. There were two small areas to the west of the town, all subdivisions—suburban America. Nothing unusual. But he realized again how many Hispanic Americans he saw. It was like they had gotten together and built a town.

He walked on and cut through a minuscule park. The playground equipment was unlike anything he'd ever seen. It was all steel and painted blue. The only things he recognized were the swings and a slide. Parks had changed since he was a kid.

Widow walked through it and back down a street toward his hotel. He had had no luck finding Hood. He knew they were staying in the hotel. It was best to wait there.

* * *

BACK AT THE HOTEL, Widow waited in his room with the lights off, but he left the window open so he could hear Hood and Jemma returning. He was only three doors down from them.

Widow waited on the bed with the Sig Sauer still loaded with the
five rounds he had remaining. He lay back and stared at the ceiling. He tried not to think, just keep his ears open and alert and
sensitive to cars starting up or pulling into the lot or engines shut-
ting off or doors opening or voices talking.

What he hadn't expected was that the hotel room bed was a little
more comfortable than he had thought and that the silent night
would rush by without a disturbance. He fell asleep, not a long-
deserved deep sleep but a nap. It wasn't a power nap, too long for
that, but too short for proper sleep.

Widow jumped up, instinctively checked for the Sig Sauer,
which was exactly as he had left it. He glanced out the window.
Everything was quiet. He checked over his shoulder at a desk
clock with huge red block numbers. The night had moved into
the prime-time hours. He had slept for two hours.

He still had his shoes on, laced up. He got up and stuffed the gun
into his jeans, at the small of his back, and puffed out his T-shirt
to conceal it. Then he left the room.

He walked down three doors and looked again at the window to
the room that Hood was supposed to be in, but there was still no
activity. Nothing to be heard from the door.

Widow didn't bother to knock. He turned and looked over at his
Jeep and then walked back toward the office where he had
checked in. Before he entered, he stopped and turned back to the
lot. He scanned it. Before, there were two vehicles with Hertz
stickers in the window, and now there was only one. He closed
his eyes and tried to picture them. Two trucks. One was a silver
Dodge. It was gone.

He entered the office and looked for the son. He wasn't there.

The old lady was seated behind a desk, and there was a flat-
screen TV. She had it on one of those twenty-four-hour news
channels.

Widow said, "Sorry to bother you, ma'am."

The old woman said, "Can I help you?"

"Is your son around?"

"What for? You need something fixed?"

"No, ma'am. I just need to speak to him."

"Is there a problem with the room?"

"No, ma'am. The room is fine. The bed is especially comfortable."

"That's good. So what do you need my son for?"

Widow said, "I just need to ask him a question."

"Any question you need to ask him, you can ask me."

Widow thought for a moment. He didn't want to ask her about Hood and potentially get her son in trouble, because he may not give him an answer later. So, he said, "Well, ma'am. I'm a lonely traveler."

She nodded.

Widow said, "I'm interested in where to go to find some..."

She nodded again and leaned up in her chair.

"I want to find some female company."

"Oh, gosh," the old lady said. She slumped back in her chair and said, "He's a good boy."

"I didn't mean to suggest he's not, ma'am."

"He's out back, taking out the trash. Go around the front of the building and around the corner."

Widow nodded and said, "Thanks, ma'am." And he left her where she was. He walked out of the office and followed her instructions. Widow circled past a group of soda machines and an ice maker. He walked around to the back of the building, where he found the son, only he wasn't taking out the trash.

The son saw him and coughed and spewed a little. He was leaning up against the back wall, smoking pot. He said, "Whoa! You scared me."

"Sorry about that."

"I thought you were the sheriff."

"No. It's just me."

"If you got a leaky toilet, then you'll have to wait. I'm gonna smoke the rest of this bud."

Widow said, "That's not it."

"What ya want? You want a puff?"

Widow waved it away and said, "The guy I showed you. Is he still here?"

"Man, sorry about that. He left right after you came asking about him."

Widow said, "He checked out?"

The guy nodded and said, "Yeah, man. I tried to knock on your door, but there was no answer."

"What time? How long ago?"

"Over three hours."

Widow shook his head. Hood had left right when he went to dinner.

The guy said, "I'm not giving your money back, man."

Widow said, "Keep it." He stopped for a moment, and he asked, "Did he still have the little girl with him?"

The son took another puff of his pot, and then he answered, "Yeah, man. There was a little girl."

Widow nodded and turned to walk back to his Jeep with no idea of where to go next. He got to the corner and heard the son speak again. He said, "Wanna know where they went?"

Widow stopped and turned back to him. He asked, "Where?"

"They went camping."

"Camping?"

"Yeah. They had camping gear in the back of their truck. So they must've gone camping."

Widow asked, "Do you know where?"

"Sure," he said, and he pointed south. He said, "They went up to Miner's Rock. That's where everyone goes. There's a road that leads up past the rock shelf, and there's some really cool spots out there. You can see the stars really great."

Widow said, "Thanks. How do I get there?"

"You can follow the signs, man."

"Thanks," Widow said again, and he half walked and half ran back to the Jeep. He still had a big advantage over the people who were after Hood, but the truth was he didn't know how many more there would be. He knew that eight hours ago, they didn't know where they could find Hood, but that could've changed.

Widow got to his Jeep and jerked open the half door and dumped himself down in the driver's seat. He fired up the engine and took off the emergency brake. He shifted it into first gear and hit the gas and headed up to Miner's Rock.

* * *

ACCORDING TO GOOGLE MAPS, the route to Romanth is best taken down I-35 toward Laredo. But Glock had been down there many times. He had never stayed in Romanth, but he knew it was there. It wasn't far from their compound, less than an hour's drive. So Glock knew that the fastest way to get down there was to take the less traveled roads and stay in the desert.

He accelerated the Chevy Tahoe, and the tires bounced. The engine hummed a good healthy sound. He checked the clock on the dash, just above the full-screen map that showed him the route through the desert.

He had his phone synced in with the Tahoe's onboard computer. Chevy has a state-of-the-art computer system installed in the expensive models of the Tahoe. One of the key features is hands-free talking and commands. This didn't matter to Glock because the talk features for the computer were programmed for human voices, and his was virtually inhuman. Instead of trying to order it to call Danny, he simply picked up his phone and clicked the buttons. He kept the phone hooked up to the onboard computer and heard Danny's voice come over the speakers.

Danny said, "What's up?"

"Danny. Get the boys ready. I'll be there soon."

"You're coming here?"

"Yeah. Any more movement on the phone?"

"It's in Romanth," he said. He had texted Glock earlier and told him the location.

"I got the text."

Danny said, "We can narrow it down to a precise radius."

"Good enough. Get ready. I'll be there soon."

Glock hung up the phone.

* * *

WIDOW DROVE about a mile and a half south of Romanth and found the sign to Miner's Rock. He followed the rocky road, passing twists and turns, up through the rocks, and into the gloom. Suddenly, the desert landscape merged with more green pastures. There were low trees and grassy lands. The stars were out, and the night was breezy. Texas temperatures. Long, hot days and short, cold nights.

The Jeep had big square lights on the front that rested behind a big chrome grille. But the beams were low and not bright. Widow switched on the high beams, which didn't help, but then again, there was nothing to see that he couldn't see with the lights off because of how bright the stars were. For a moment, he considered switching them off completely.

He drove until he came to a circle that was high on the rock shelf. The circle was the last stop for campers before they took to hiking. He parked the Jeep behind Hood's rented truck and hopped out. There were four vehicles in total—his Jeep, Hood's Dodge, and two SUVs.

Widow grabbed the Sig Sauer and looked around. There was no one there. He knew that the woman had fired the Sig Sauer at him, but Widow was a firm believer in testing your own firearms. So he ejected the magazine and the chambered bullet and reinserted it back into the magazine. He aimed the gun over the valley and dry-fired it. It worked like a dream. He reinserted the magazine and chambered the round.

He slipped it back into his jeans at the small of his back and walked over to the Dodge. He felt the hood. It was cold. The door was locked.

He looked around for signs of which direction they had gone. He saw that there were basically two paths. One headed down into the valley and the other headed up to a ridge. He scanned the horizon, down in the valley, and saw two campfires. He looked up at the ridge and saw one. If Hood was using any kind of brainpower, he'd know that higher ground was always better. Widow headed up the path toward the higher ground.

17

JAMES HOOD WAS A SLIM MAN. He used to weigh more, but two years in prison had... done things to him. He was an ex-con who had quite an experience being incarcerated. It was not an experience he cared to repeat. No way in hell was he ever going back. He had been released early, and he ran the first chance he got.

His daughter sat next to him, staring up at the stars. He had stolen some camping equipment out of another truck, back in town. He wasn't proud of it, but the equipment was the least of his concerns. In the last twenty-four hours, he had abducted his daughter, stolen two different vehicles, and stolen money from an old friend back in El Paso. Of course, the friend had thought he was merely borrowing it, but surely by now, he knew Hood wasn't coming back with it. It was only five hundred bucks, of which he had two hundred left. Soon he would have to commit more crimes just to keep him and Jemma safe and eating.

He needed a better plan, but everything had happened so fast.

They had a fire going, finally, and Jemma was cuddled up next to him.

She said, "Daddy, how many stars are there?"

He looked down at her and smiled. He said, "Millions."

"Millions?"

He nodded.

She asked, "How many is that?"

"It's a whole lot."

"Daddy?"

"Yeah, Pip?"

"When is Mommy coming?"

Hood paused a long beat. He wasn't ready to explain it to her yet. He wasn't ready to tell her that her mom wasn't coming. In fact, he wasn't sure she'd live much longer. The FBI agents had told him she was on her deathbed.

Just then, out of the darkness, the silhouette of a bear emerged from out of the brush. At first, Hood thought it was a grizzly, but he wasn't sure if there were any grizzlies in Texas. He didn't see why not? Then again, it could've been a black bear. That's when the thought occurred to him it didn't matter what kind of bear it was. Anything short of a teddy bear wasn't a bear he wanted to see in the dark. Another thought hit him in that short second— weren't bears afraid of fire? This one certainly wasn't.

Jemma saw it about one second after he had because she sat up straight as a board and grabbed his arm tight. She said, "Daddy! Daddy!"

"I see it. Stay still, Pip!" he said. Truthfully, he wasn't sure what kind of advice to follow for avoiding being mauled by a bear.

A voice came from the bear. It said, "Relax. I'm not going to hurt you."

It wasn't a bear, but a man—a big guy. He came up to the camp slowly. He held his hands out so they were clearly visible and nonthreatening.

* * *

WIDOW HAD the Sig Sauer in his right-hand back pocket. He had taken it out of his jeans and shoved it into his back pocket. Too many times, he had seen undercover officers in the Navy try to draw their weapons from a pancake holster in the back, and the weapon got caught on clothes. No amount of oil could compare to a loose gun ready to grab. He didn't expect that Hood would shoot him, but you never know. A desperate man on the run trying to protect his daughter might have shot his own mother in the dark first and then asked questions.

Hood said, "We ain't got no money here!"

Widow made no reply. He was surveying the situation, making mental notes of all the visible equipment and looking for weapons.

James Hood had made a fire, and a good one at that, not his first time camping. There was a bright red tent with zippers in front and back. The flap was open. The wind blew and punched at it like a sail on the sea. Widow could see that inside, there were two rolled-up sleeping bags.

They sat on two small lawn chairs, the kind that were low to the ground.

What he didn't see anywhere was a chest or ice cooler. There were no cans of food. No bags. Nothing. They had no food.

Jemma was dressed like she was going to school. She had a little blue skirt and clean shoes with big white socks. Her hair was pulled up and styled. She wasn't dressed for camping, but she had a man's jacket on. Widow figured it was Hood's because he wore a white thermal shirt and blue jeans. No jacket.

Widow looked at Jemma and tipped an invisible ball cap. He said, "Ma'am."

"I said we ain't got any money!" Hood said in a voice that must've registered in his head as firm, but by the time it released from his mouth, it was full of fear and regret, like he regretted saying it.

Widow said, "Relax. I'm not here for money."

"Yeah, what you want?"

"I'm a passerby. I'm just passing by."

"Yeah?"

"Yeah. Can I sit with you guys? By the fire?"

Hood looked skeptical, but Jemma was excited. She said, "It's warmest over on this side."

Widow said, "Is that right?"

"Yeah. The wind blows the flames this way."

"That's a great observation," he said, and he walked over to them. He walked up to the fire and stopped in the light. He stayed quiet for a moment and let Hood size him up. Hood's eyes looked from top to bottom and bottom to top. It took a moment because Widow was harder to take completely in when he was close.

Hood said, "I guess it's okay."

Widow said, "Thank you. I promise I have only good intentions." And he reached back quick with his right hand and shoved the Sig Sauer back—deep in his pocket. The last thing he wanted to happen was for it to fall out of his pocket as he sat down.

He walked around the fire and stared down at Jemma.

She said, "Do you want my seat?" She jumped out of it and offered it to him.

"No thanks, ma'am."

She said, "It's comfortable."

"I'm sure it's very comfortable, but I'm afraid I wouldn't fit in it. It's too small for me."

She had her head and neck cocked all the way back just so she could look up at him.

Hood said, "Pip, ~~take your seat.~~ Sir, we have sleeping bags. You can sit on one of them while it's rolled up."

"That's not necessary. I can squat," Widow said, and he popped a squat next to Jemma. He asked, "Did I hear right? Your name is Pip?"

"No," Jemma said and leaned forward in her chair. She was full of energy.

"It's a nickname," Hood said.

Widow nodded.

Hood said, "Like Pipsqueak."

"My name is Jemma."

Widow nodded and said, "Mine is Widow."

Jemma took a deep breath, her face very animated, and she asked, "What kinda name is dat?"

Widow paused a moment, and then he said, "What kind of name is Jemma?"

She fell back in her seat and waited for her dad to look at the stranger. Then she stuck her tongue out—fast, like a gunslinger.

Hood said, "We're just passing through as well."

Right, Widow thought.

Hood stuck his hand out and said, "John Smith."

Widow took his hand and nearly rolled his eyes at the man's terrible choice in fake names. He said, "Jack Widow." And they shook hands.

Widow moved back near Jemma, but not too close. He figured Hood was already jumpy, and he still wasn't sure whether Hood had a gun or not. He doubted it, but there was no being certain. So he squatted down and stayed that way for a few moments, and then he decided just to plop his butt down and take a seat in the grass.

Jemma said, "Huh! Your jeans are going to be filthy."

"No. See, the grass is dry. Which means I'll be able just to brush the back off."

The one thing Widow had to ignore was the Sig Sauer jamming into his ass.

Hood broke the ice and said, "So, Mr. Widow, what are you doing out here?"

Widow thought for a moment. He wanted to be honest, but he didn't want to tell Jemma her grandmother was dead. Plus, he didn't even know if Hood would believe him. So, he said, "Like I said, I'm just passing through."

"What, like a drifter?"

"You got it. That's right," he said, and it was. That's almost always what he was doing, traveling from one ocean to the next and back again. On the one hand, Widow was all about going forward, and on the other, his journey was a loop. It went to one edge of the country and then back to the other.

"What are you, like ex-Army?"

"Navy, actually."

Hood was quiet for a moment, and Jemma said, "Are you a soldier?"

"I was. But we prefer sailor."

Jemma's face turned curious, and she asked, "Were you in a war?"

Widow wasn't sure she even had a grasp of what a war was. He figured if she was six, then she must be in the first or second grade. He hadn't been in those grades in over twenty years. Widow couldn't remember what they were teaching back then. He thought it was probably spelling and reading, but hell, he couldn't remember.

He said, "I saw some combat."

Hood stayed quiet. Widow could see his suspicions diminishing, but Jemma's curiosity was intensifying. She said, "The Navy. Does that mean you were on a ship?"

"I've been on ships."

"One of those big ones? Like in *Battleship*?"

"I was on carriers more often than battleships, but they aren't much different."

She struggled with the word for a moment and said, "Carry on?"

"Carrier. As in an aircraft carrier. They're really big ships. Airplanes land on them."

She looked amazed. "Airplanes land on them?"

"And take off. Mostly fighter jets."

She asked, "Fighter jets? Like the Angels?"

"Angels?"

"You know, the blue ones?"

Widow nodded and said, "You mean the Blue Angels. No, they don't go out on aircraft carriers. They're stationed in Pensacola and El Centro."

She looked perplexed, and she grunted in a low voice and said, "El... el..."

"El Centro. It's a base in California."

She nodded like she understood, but he could see she was probably more confused.

Widow said, "So what grade are you in?"

Hood interrupted and said, "She's homeschooled."

Widow nodded and decided not to push it.

Jemma pressed on with a different question. She asked, "How tall are you?"

Hood interrupted and said, "Pip, that's enough questions."

She nodded and slumped back in her chair, and they sat in silence.

Widow looked around the horizon and figured they were about as safe out here as they were anywhere. He couldn't foresee any way the guys who were after Hood could find them out in the middle of nowhere.

* * *

LESS THAN AN HOUR PASSED, and two vehicles pulled into Romanth from the west. They didn't belong to locals. The front vehicle was a black Ford Explorer, a new SUV with all the bells and whistles, except this one had after-factory qualities not normal to the Explorer. It was lifted on big tires built for off-road driving. A blip of dust and dirt rose behind it as it passed the first suburb and made its way onto the blacktop. Following behind it, not close but close enough to see the dust in the dark, was Glock's Chevy Tahoe. He followed behind with three passengers in tow.

The passenger in Glock's front seat was a big guy who looked like he had grown up in Nebraska and had been corn-fed his whole life. He had red cheeks and pale skin. Glock wasn't sure about his age because he had gray hair, but his face was young. The other passengers were similar in description. They were all big white guys. They ranged in age from the late twenties to late forties. Then there was Danny, who drove the Explorer. Danny was their leader, and he was the oldest and the only one with a college degree. Glock didn't interfere with Danny's hiring processes, so he really didn't know who had gone to college and who hadn't. He was making an educated guess because most of them had volunteered for this kind of work.

Working with Danny meant they were aware of Glock, and working for John Glock meant you were a certain type of person. Not the kind of guy who went to college and graduated top of the class and then went on to a career in the military. No—these guys

either had nowhere else to go, or they loved the idea of killing
Mexicans who crossed the border.

The Jericho Men weren't the usual type of gun nuts who joined
together to protect America from illegal aliens crossing the
borders. These were mercenary wannabes. They didn't arrest
people and turn them over to the Border Patrol, like some of the
other militias did. Danny's guys did the work themselves.

In Danny's SUV, there were four more guys, including Danny.
Between the eight of them, they had sidearms and five AR-15s
and two riot guns. They had brought the hardware.

18

IT WAS AFTER MIDNIGHT. Widow wasn't sure of the exact time, but he figured it was zero dark thirty, a time he always naturally knew. In the SEALs, he had plenty of missions that took place at zero dark thirty. It was the preferred time for SEALs to infiltrate. In his experience, he had found that any time between midnight and five was a good time. Most people were asleep, and people in a dead sleep were a lot less likely to retaliate in full force. In his experience, hitting enemies in those hours and finding them ready meant his team had been betrayed somewhere along the chain.

Jemma had fallen asleep and was curled up in her father's lap. Her head rested on his thigh, and her hands were shoved into the pockets of her jacket.

The firelight was still burning, but it had died down to a small fire, which was still good enough to keep them warm.

Hood said in a hushed voice, "I don't mean to sound rude, but I think it's time for you to move on. We need to get to sleep. You understand?"

Widow stared up at the stars for a moment, and then he said, "They're beautiful out here."

Hood stayed quiet.

Widow said, "Listen, James. I gotta come clean with you."

Hood's eyes perked up as he realized Widow had called him James and not John. He asked, "What's this?"

"Sorry, James. I didn't want to lie to you, but I needed to speak to you."

"I don't understand. What about?"

"I needed to know a little more about you."

"Like what?" Hood said. He trembled. His fingers clenched tightly on Jemma's shoulders.

"Take it easy," Widow said. "Take it easy. I'm not here to hurt you. I promise."

"Who are you, mister?"

"I told you. I'm just a guy. But James, I have some terrible news for you."

"What?"

"Your mom is dead." Hood looked right in Widow's eyes. He still looked confused and untrusting. So Widow continued, "I'm just a drifter. I didn't lie about that." He paused and said, "I met your mom at a bus stop in El Paso."

"What was she doing there?"

"She was coming after you. She was coming here to Romanth."

Hood stared down at the fire and said, "She remembered it."

"Yeah. She said you told her about it once. Said she figured you'd come here."

"How did she die?"

"She was an old lady. It was very hot. She just passed on."

Hood was quiet for a long, long moment. He stared at the fire and then said, "Oh God! Oh God! She died coming after me!"

Widow stayed quiet.

"It's my fault!"

Widow said, "She only wanted to find you and Jemma. I don't think she knew what was going on. I don't think she knew why you ran."

Hood broke out in steady tears, but not a waterfall of them like Widow had seen before in men a lot bigger and a whole hell of a lot tougher. They were the tears of a man who had lost his mother. Next would come the guilt and, possibly, paralysis, which was something that needed to be avoided until Widow could get them out of danger.

Widow said, "James, I know this hurts, but I need to know what's going on. I can help."

Hood lowered his voice back to a hush and asked, "What do you know?"

"I know there's some bad people after you."

He nodded and said, "Very bad people."

Widow nodded. He said, "I already encountered two of them."

"Two of them?"

Widow stayed still.

"Oh man! Did they threaten you? How did you escape?"

"I wouldn't worry about them."

"Why?"

"They're dead."

"You killed them?"

"They brought it on themselves."

Hood said, "Who was it? I mean, what did they look like?"

"They were professionals. They weren't run-of-the-mill thugs. These were killers—paid killers."

"Was it a guy? A guy with a messed-up voice? Big scar on his neck?"

"No. This was a man and a woman."

"A woman?"

Widow nodded.

"I never saw her."

"I told you. She was professional. These two were hired killers. They'd be too expensive for regular muscle."

"How did you...?" He started to ask for details about their deaths, but then he switched gears and said, "I'm glad you took care of them."

"I need some info. You gotta tell me what's going on."

"I don't know everything."

"Tell me what you got."

Hood said, "I was hired two years ago. On the spot. Like a temp. They needed someone to help with a situation. They wanted to show strength in numbers. Their usual guy wasn't available."

Widow nodded, encouraging him to continue. He folded his arms and straightened his posture, accidentally cracking his back.

Hood said, "It went bad, and I got caught."

"What were you doing? Muscle for what?"

"It was persuasion. That's all. No one was supposed to get hurt."

"Who got hurt? Who were you supposed to be persuading?"

"It was just this guy who worked on the city council. No big deal. Some politician. He was blocking contracts."

"Contracts? What contracts?"

"From what I got from the exchange, it was heavy equipment purchases or transport or something."

Widow paused and asked, "Heavy equipment?"

"Yeah. You know. Like construction equipment."

A wolf or a coyote or a wild dog howled far off in the distance, and Hood shot a look in that direction. After the howl died down and the night silence returned, he looked back at Widow, who asked, "Who hired you?"

"His name's Glock."

Widow said, "Glock? Like the gun manufacturer?"

"Right. No relation to the gun. Just John Glock."

"What else?"

"He works for someone bigger. With money. A lot of money. A corporation."

"What corporation?"

"Auckland Enterprises."

"What's that?"

"It's a huge corporation. It's behind all kinds of major projects. All over the world. Under-the-radar kinds of things. I don't know specifics."

"Why do they want you dead?"

"After I got arrested, they threatened me."

Widow asked, "Why?"

"'Cause I overheard enough of their conversation to know the name of the company, I guess."

Widow said, "So you got hired, things went bad, and you got ten years? Then what?"

"They told me if I ever talked..." He stopped mid-sentence and looked down at Jemma. "They said they'd kill my family."

"So you took your daughter and ran? But what about your mother and wife?"

A look that ~~Widow had seen before in some~~ criminals came across Hood's face. He said, "I didn't think. My mom is an old lady, and my wife is dying. I guess I thought they wouldn't bother with them."

"I think you're wrong."

"But they didn't kill my mom. You said she died of natural causes."

Widow said, "That's true, but the two I killed were following her. You put all of their lives in danger."

"I know. I'm sorry. What could I have done?"

Widow almost said he should've told the FBI, but then he remembered Jemma and Lucy were illegal. He remembered Claire Hood begging him not to involve the police.

Widow said, "What about Lucy?"

"You don't think they'd hurt her? She doesn't even know anything. She's about to die," he said, and whispered the last word —*die*. He didn't want Jemma to overhear.

Widow said, "James, you don't know the first thing about these guys."

"And you do?" he said with a bit of defensiveness and humiliation in his voice, all like he knew he had made a huge error but felt stubborn about it.

Widow said, "I've known guys like this all my life."

"From being in the Navy? But don't you guys just sit out on a boat all the time?"

"Ship."

"What?"

"They're ships, not boats. And I wasn't that kind of sailor."

"What kind were you?"

"Actually, I wasn't—not for very long, anyway. I was an NCIS agent for most of my career."

"NCIS? Like the TV show?"

Widow said, "I wouldn't know anything about a TV show. I never saw it. But I'm sure it's inaccurate. NCIS is like the FBI for the military."

"So, you were like a cop?"

"I wasn't like a cop. I was a cop. I worked undercover with the SEALs."

"Like the Navy SEALs?"

Widow nodded.

"You guys do all that black-op stuff?"

Widow shrugged and said, "Sometimes."

"So you were undercover. Does that mean you investigated other sailors?"

"Unfortunately, that was one aspect of the job. But many times, when I was sent in to investigate crimes, the bad guys were just as likely to be foreign."

"That means you're some kind of top-rank cop?"

Widow said, "I'm just a normal guy who did a job. That's all."

"What was your rank?"

"James. Focus. I know these types of people, and they're dangerous. If they said they'll kill your family, then that's what they'll do."

Hood's face flashed a deep sense of horror. Maybe he realized that not only was he responsible for his mother's death, but he had left his wife behind. Widow knew they would kill her whether she was on her deathbed or not. They would execute her just because that was the kind of business they were in.

He said, "These kinds of people aren't joking around. I saw two of them. They're the real deal. And if you say this corporation is connected to them, that means they've probably had ties to criminals all over the state. If they're trying to strong-arm city politicians, that also means they're the worst enemies to have."

Hood stared at Widow's face and said nothing.

Widow asked, "Do you know who the top guy is?"

Hood shook his head and said, "I don't know. All I know is Glock."

Nothing was said between them for a long while. Hood petted Jemma's head, and Widow saw real love there. Hood wasn't a bad guy, mixed-up maybe, but good. He was like his mom had said—a father trying to do right by his family, only not the best at making decisions.

Finally, Hood said, "What now? We got to get to Lucy. If what you say is right, we have to warn her. Maybe call hospital security."

"What about the FBI? They let you out, right?"

Hood shook his head and said, "No. No. Not possible. I can't trust them. They let me out but under supervision. I escaped them. They can't protect us."

Widow believed that involving the FBI was the right thing to do, but he wasn't going to argue. If Hood said they couldn't be trusted, then they couldn't be trusted. Besides, if the guys behind the kill team were a part of the criminal arm of a corporation, who was to say that they couldn't infiltrate law enforcement? Easy as anything. Widow had seen it before.

Widow said, "I say we circle the wagons."

"What do you mean?"

"You can't run. They'll find you. If what you say is true, they'll catch up to you one day."

Hood said, "I can hide. We can go to Mexico. The border is right there." And he pointed out over the horizon to the south.

Widow said, "Mexico is more corrupt than here. How long do you think it would take them to find you?"

"But Lucy has family there. They can protect Jemma. I can bring her to them and come back for Lucy. I can come back and then call the FBI."

Widow shook his head and said, "No way. They'll kill you. Somehow. I've seen it before. She's already lost her grandmother. Her mom's about to die. I can't let her lose her father too."

"So what do we do?" he asked.

And right then, his question was answered for him—nothing. Nothing, because they heard rustling in the bushes from all sides. First, it came from the west and then from the north and the east. In less than five seconds, they were engulfed in bright flashlight beams and loud military voices.

The first things Widow saw were the muzzles of the AR-15s and the two riot guns. His first impression was that this was a military force because they had swept in hard and fast and snuck right up on him. He didn't even hear them until it was too late, which told him either he was getting very, very rusty, or these guys had competent training. But then he saw some of them.

Hood jumped up from his seat and stuck his hands straight up in the air, like he probably had many times before. And Widow imagined his first instinct was that these guys were police or FBI. He must've assumed they were SWAT coming for him.

Widow knew better. He knew better because several of the guys were fat—not slightly overweight, not husky, but fat. They wouldn't have passed even the smallest town's most modest fitness requirements to be a member of a SWAT team. Therefore, these guys were civilians with military pasts or civilians with far too much time on their hands. The one thing Widow was absolutely certain about was that they were private citizens. Other than a few of them being overweight, they had no consistent uniform. ~~Two of them wore black Kevlar vests~~ that looked expensive, like what police officers are provided with. Another two had cheap, secondhand vests in desert colors. Some guys wore all black, and others wore desert camo or casual clothes.

Law enforcement and military and other agencies all have similar dress attire. Some don't require uniforms, but they require certain professional standards in their agents' appearances. These guys had no style, no code, and nothing else that might show they were law enforcement.

Only one of them, obviously the leader, had a professionalism about him.

The reason Widow knew he was the leader was because the guy said, "Well. Here we are."

The guy's voice was disturbing. It was harsher than an explosion over the speakers of a car stereo. He sounded like a creature from another planet, like he spoke with one of those synthesizers popular with DJs.

When he spoke, he stepped out in front of the flashlight beams and looked directly at Widow, not Hood and not Jemma, just Widow.

19

JEMMA WOKE UP SCREAMING. She saw the guns and the flashlight beams and the guy with the creature's voice.

Glock said, "Shut her up, James!"

Hood said, "Calm down, Pip. It's going to be okay."

Jemma grabbed at his leg and shivered. She wanted to be picked up. She was afraid, which Widow understood.

"You must be Glock," said Widow.

"And you must be the stranger," Glock answered.

"You found us."

"Yeah, imagine that."

Widow thought for a moment. *How did he find them?* Then he closed his eyes and cursed himself. *The phone.* They tracked the phone he stole from the woman. Widow knew about phones. He had plenty of training in modern technology. And of course, in the field, he had to use computers and phones and so forth, but even he made dumb mistakes. They must've traced the phone.

Stupid!

Glock seemed to know what he was thinking because he said, "Yeah, the iPhone. Did you not know that anyone can track it? As long as you leave it on and it has cell service, we can see where it is online."

Widow said, "Sorry, James."

Hood had put his hands up, but Widow had not. He still had the Sig Sauer in his jeans, but he only had five rounds, and there were eight of them. There were three at his six o'clock, plus the other four circled around them, plus Glock. Every sector of the clock-face was spoken for. No way would he have been able to draw, aim, and fire at them. His mind had already clocked the three without vests on, including Glock, but even if he could outgun them all and kill three, there would still be five remaining, and they had AR-15s.

Widow wasn't going to shoot his way out of this. That left his first best weapon, his mouth. He said, "I don't suppose you're upset about me killing your girlfriend?"

Glock said, "That's not going to work. I don't care any more about her than I do you. And I want to kill you."

So much for that, Widow thought.

In his next breath, Glock said, "Toss the gun. Slow."

Widow nodded, slow and defeated. Glock wasn't stupid. He didn't even ask Hood for a weapon. Maybe he knew Hood wouldn't have one or that he wouldn't have the guts to use it. But he knew Widow would.

Widow reached back, slowly as he was instructed, and pulled at the Sig with his thumb and his index finger. He pinched the butt and dropped it on the ground near the dying fire. And he knew he was done.

* * *

JEMMA STARTED CRYING.

Hood lowered his hands slowly, staring at the guy with the closest gun. He said nothing, but he kept his eye contact with the guy as he picked up Jemma and held her close to his chest.

Widow's primal brain scanned the faces, the guns, the exits, but the only way they were getting out of this alive was by talking their way out. He said, "You won't kill us here. There are other campers. They'll hear the gunfire."

Glock laughed, but his laugh sounded more inhuman than his voice. It reminded Widow of the sound a wood chipper makes when a bunch of rocks are thrown into it, which was something he had done once at his friend's uncle's farm in Nebraska.

Glock said, "This is Texas. No one here is going to come running because of gunshots."

Widow shrugged at this point. He was only trying to stall until he thought of a plan, but Glock would not give him much more time.

He looked at John Glock. He was around six feet tall and lean, like a lot of guys Widow had known in the Navy. And Glock had arm tattoos as well. One of them was a frog skeleton holding a trident.

Widow asked, "You a SEAL?"

"What of it?"

"I know something about it."

"Yeah, what you know?"

"I know you must've gotten kicked out. No way would they keep a piece of shit like you."

Glock smirked and said nothing.

"Couldn't hack it, I'd bet," Widow said.

Glock said, "You don't know the first thing about me."

Widow was about to say more, but then Glock glanced at one of the other guys, the one who was holding a riot gun and had no flashlight, and said, "~~Enough talking. Do it.~~" He motioned his head to the guy to step up.

They say your life flashes before your eyes before the moment you die, like a movie of all of your greatest hits. And for most people, this might've been true, but Widow had been near death many, many times before.

His life didn't flash, but the riot gun's muzzle did.

The guy had aimed it from less than fifteen feet and straight at Widow's center mass. He smirked and squeezed the trigger. The muzzle climbed, but the short distance provided the bullet with a chest target.

The sound cracked through the air and echoed off the trees and the rocks. The bullet flew true and nailed Widow in his right pectoral muscle and upper chest.

The bullet hit Widow's chest, and the air was knocked out of him, and he fell back on the ground. And he might've had a broken rib. He wasn't sure, but his chest hurt.

The bullet that hit him wasn't a lethal round. It was a rubber shell. It hurt like nothing he could remember, and he was sure he'd have a huge bruise. Otherwise, he was alive.

He sank down into the grass and rolled back and forth, holding his chest, trying to breathe.

Glock stood over him and looked at one of the other guys. He said, "Hit him."

Widow's head filled with rage. He didn't want to get hit again by one of those bullets, and not at close range. But the guy who stepped up from behind Glock wasn't the one holding the riot gun. It was a thin guy, kind of squirrely and nervous. He had an AR-15 slung back over his shoulder on a strap.

He came out with a strange handgun with a bolt action on it. Widow had never seen one like it before.

The guy pulled back the bolt and loaded it with what looked like a tranquilizer round—and it was.

The guy aimed at Widow's thigh, but Glock said, "Wait!"

He walked between them and stared down at Widow, who was coughing violently, still trying to catch his breath.

Glock knelt down and said, "We are going to shoot you with a tranquilizer. We're not going to kill you, not yet." Glock's lizard voice sounded terrifying up close. He said, "But we will enjoy killing them. Maybe I'll take the girl with me. You know they pay top dollar in some parts of the world for a girl that age?"

Widow continued to cough and gag.

The guy loaded the tranquilizer gun and shot Widow in the thigh. The pain was immediate, but the effect from the round took another few minutes. Several minutes later, Widow was out cold.

20

WIDOW WOKE up with what felt like a head full of rattling bullet casings.

His head hurt.

He shook it and stared ahead. His vision was blurry, and trickles of light prismed around in his sight. His equilibrium was compromised. He couldn't tell where he was. At first, he wasn't even sure whether he was seated or standing. He waited a few moments and just concentrated on breathing.

He leaned forward, only to have the pain in his head and chest push him back like a gut shot from a hunting rifle. His chest throbbed, and his head pounded—even his knuckles hurt, like he'd been pounding on a punching bag all night, or rather, the punching bag had been pounding on him. He could hardly move his fingers. He moved the ones on his right hand first and heard the joints crack. His vision was still blurry, but he stared at his hand. It reminded him of that scene in *The Terminator* where Arnold flexes his metal robot fingers in front of people.

He remembered being shot with a rubber bullet and a tranquilizer dart and wondered what the hell had been in that dart. Whatever it was had some serious side effects. He wasn't a doctor or a pharmacist, but he knew a couple of them were disorientation, blurred vision, and grogginess—no doubt about it.

He heard muffled voices. He couldn't tell what they were saying, not because they were whispering, but because they weren't close enough. They were off in the distance somewhere.

He waited a few more long, long moments for his brain to reset. Then he shook his head and squinted his eyes and could see images, which manifested into tangible objects. First, he saw a steering wheel and gauges and a windshield with a crack in it that had spider-webbed over time to become a serious problem for the vehicle's owner.

Widow blinked his eyes—a lot—and tried to focus on the rest of the vehicle's interior. He saw a long stick shifter and saw the floor was metal with small holes in it. He looked up at the sky and realized he was in the Jeep.

He looked to the rearview mirror and saw his reflection. His face was okay. His eyes were still blue, and his features still rough like an old barn door. He opened his mouth and heard his jawbones crack like his fingers had, and he added dry mouth to the list of side effects.

Nothing was wrong with his face, other than the things he had always thought were wrong.

His face, being untouched, made him wonder what the hell Glock had done to him. Surely, they wouldn't have shot him with a tranquilizer and left him alive and unharmed? He inspected the rest of his body—no broken bones. No wounds anywhere. No blood. Not at first. Then he noticed the back of his hands, precisely his knuckles, and his jeans.

There was blood—a lot of blood. It was on his T-shirt as well, but the black hid it better than his blue jeans. There was none on the palms of his hands. They were clean, except for the usual wear and tear and grime from him being outside all day.

Then he adjusted the rearview mirror and scanned behind him. He saw the source of the voices. It was two couples—an older one

and one barely out of high school. They stayed a long distance
from the Jeep, but they were talking about him. No doubt. They
were nervous and anxious and jittery, like they were afraid of
him, which made him wonder why they just didn't get into their
vehicles and leave. He looked ahead and saw that their trucks
were close to the Jeep, and he realized they were afraid to pass
by him.

He didn't have his seat belt on, which was no surprise because he
had been put in his Jeep by Glock and his men. Why? He still
didn't understand.

Why not just shoot him? They could've shot him easy as
anything.

Widow sat up straight and grabbed the steering wheel, turned,
and jacked the door open. He shuffled out and onto his feet.

Dizziness hit him square in the face as soon as his shoes touched
the ground.

The sun had been bright when he was in the Jeep, and it had no
roof. But as soon as he got out of the Jeep and was standing beside
it, the sun's brightness went up several notches. At first, he
thought it was rising faster than he believed possible, but then he
realized it wasn't rising. It was already out. He had been in the
shadow of a low, flat peak and some trees. The sun was still low in
the sky, so the morning hours were still young.

Widow took two steps away from the Jeep and yawned, which
was unexpected—another side effect from the dart.

He looked back at the people. They were standing behind some
trees, like that was going to hide them from him.

He looked at them and yelled, "What?"

They didn't respond. He looked back at the Jeep and then over at
the vehicles. Hood's truck was still there. It hadn't moved.

He headed back to the path and up to where their campfire had
been. But he didn't make it past the Wrangler because that was
when he saw the body.

Widow circled around the front of the Jeep and stopped dead in his tracks in front of the big chrome grille. He saw a pair of legs, sprawled out like broken scissor blades near the passenger side front tire. He walked slowly around to see whose they were.

It was James Hood, and the only reason he knew that was because it was a man wearing the same clothes Hood had been wearing. Other than that, there was no way to identify him because his face had been beaten to a pulp. He looked like a tomato that had been pulverized by a sledgehammer.

Widow saw jagged white bone jammed through bloody skin. The eyeballs were jostled back into their sockets. The skull had been completely caved. There was a huge sinkhole on the top of Hood's head. Parts of brain matter had burst through the cracks, and ran down Hood's face like a cracked egg.

There was no sign of his nose. It had been beaten in so hard that Widow couldn't tell it from any of the other destroyed parts that commingled with the dried blood on Hood's face.

Widow had seen many people murdered in his life, some of them simply gunshot wounds or stabbings. He had seen some brutal murders, but he had never seen someone beaten to death quite like this. Widow had investigated dead bodies before, but he wasn't an expert. He wasn't a medical examiner, but he would guess that there had been no weapon used in this murder.

Hood had been beaten to death by hands. He had been killed by someone with big fists.

Widow looked down at his own fists and gasped. He looked at his knuckles. They were big. And they were covered in blood.

21

IT WAS arid up on the ridge. Widow returned to the Hoods' camp and examined it. Their sleeping bags were untouched. The fire had burned out. The tent was still up.

Widow rifled through everything, which didn't take long, because all they had brought with them were the sleeping bags, the tent, and a bag of pretzels, which was rolled down to the bottom.

Widow thought about what he remembered. He remembered everything that had happened until the part where they shot him with the dart, which they had removed and probably taken with them, because there was no sign of it anywhere. He looked around the camp and saw plenty of evidence of their tracks, but that meant nothing. They were scattered and crisscrossed over each other. He was decent at tracking people through landscapes, but he was no expert. Navy SEALs were good, but they weren't magical shamans from ancient Native American tribes.

Then he thought about the iPhone he had taken from the dead woman. He jammed his hand into the pocket where he had kept it, and it was gone. He searched his other pockets—nothing but his passport and his latest foldable toothbrush. The Sig Sauer was gone. Even his paperback was gone. His Jeep keys were gone too, or they were back in the ignition. Maybe the phone was there too.

Maybe it was on the seat or in the cup holder, although he doubted it. He didn't think they would leave it behind. Glock wasn't an idiot.

The good news was that there was no sign of a child's dead body, which was what he had feared. They had killed Hood, but not Jemma—not yet, anyway. She was probably still with them.

He had no watch and had no idea of the correct time, but he knew they had come after midnight, and now it was early morning. They had put him to sleep with a dart, carried him down the ridge, down the path, and put him in the Jeep. He knew that because he had long legs, and there would've been a trail left behind if they had dragged him. So they carried him. Which meant they'd probably forced Hood to follow, carrying Jemma.

Widow returned down the path and through the trees, and headed toward the parked vehicles. The people who had been there several minutes earlier were gone. They had taken off, which was fine with Widow, but meant he had little time until they told the sheriff. His hands were the ones covered in blood, and in a small town with a small-town sheriff, that meant he was guilty as sin.

He came to the clearing with the parked Hertz truck and his Jeep and the dead body of James Hood. Just as he had thought, the people had left in their trucks. The dust was still floating in the air from them peeling out and hurrying away.

Widow rushed over to Hood's rented truck first and tried the handles, but the doors were locked. He peered in through the window, looked over the seats, into the cup holders, and on the top of the dash. There was nothing in there. No phone. No weapons. Nothing personal.

He dashed over to Hood's body.

Widow checked Hood's pockets, looking for a phone. He found nothing on him, either. Hood's keys were gone. His wallet was gone, if he had one. Also his phone, if he had one.

~~Widow knelt facing him, trying to think of what to do. But one~~ question kept eating at him. *Why did they kill Hood but leave me alive?*

Thirty-five seconds later, he got his answer as a big white truck with old, Big Gulp–size lights on top. They didn't start sounding or lighting until he was in sight.

Widow turned and locked eyes with the driver, only the driver didn't show his eyes. They were hidden behind a pair of reflective aviator sunglasses, the kind he'd seen on small-town cops all over the country.

22

THE SHERIFF'S truck was only a single bench with no console, apparently, because there were three people in the front seat. The driver was the sheriff, Widow guessed, and the other two were deputies. All three were white guys, unlike most of the population, from what Widow had seen.

The truck came skidding to a dramatic stop, kicking up dirt and dust like they had been wanting to make a big action movie entrance.

They stopped twenty feet away from Widow. The two doors shot open, and two of them emerged from the passenger side. Then the driver came out with a Glock in his hand. He had his arms locked out over the big hood of the truck. His sunglasses were still on, but he had one side cocked down so he could aim straight at Widow.

The driver wore a brown cowboy hat, and Widow imagined there were probably cowboy boots beneath his line of sight that matched the hat.

The deputies took out their guns as well. They might've been personal weapons, because both were different. One was a black Beretta M9, which Widow was very familiar with. It was standard-issue for a lot of the world's military. The other deputy had a silver 1911, but from this distance, Widow couldn't tell which manufacturer. The most popular was the Colt version, but that was on the pricey side. Many people settled for the cheaper versions.

The deputies might've been full time or half time or simply civilian deputies—Widow wasn't sure. They didn't wear uniforms like the sheriff. He wore the cowboy hat and the sunglasses, but everything else was standard sheriff uniform—green button-down shirt with long sleeves and a big, shiny badge on the left side of the breast.

The deputies wore all black—black T-shirts with gold stars sewn in and black jeans. Neither wore cowboy boots. They both had regular black leather shoes, cheaply made.

The sheriff screamed in a cop voice, "Hold it!"

Not *"Freeze!"* Which was what Widow was expecting, since everything else they had done seemed like it was stolen out of a bad movie.

Widow said, "It's not how it looks." Which he realized was exactly what the character from a bad movie—the character supposed to be him—would say.

"I said, hold it!"

Widow didn't move. He stayed quiet and still.

"Slow like! I mean, slow! Stand up!"

Widow frowned at the thought that for the second time in a short few hours, John Glock had gotten him exactly how he wanted him. They didn't kill him because they didn't want to bury the body and hide the truck and get rid of the trail of evidence that was left behind.

Glock had beaten Hood to death and smeared blood all over Widow's clothes and knuckles to frame him for the murder. Which may not have held up in the long run, but that probably didn't matter to Glock.

James Hood was the one who knew too much. He had made a deal with the FBI and probably could've given more names. Glock was probably a ghost on paper. That probably wasn't even his real name. But somewhere there was a guy who was higher up, and he needed to silence Hood. But Widow was a nobody. So for now, he'd do as a patsy. By the time anyone would believe him, Glock would be long gone, and his trail would be colder than arctic ice.

Widow stood up slowly, like he was told.

"Put your hands out!"

Widow did.

"Open them!"

Widow did that as well.

"Now turn around! Face away!"

Widow pivoted as he was told and faced away. He closed his eyes and cursed himself because he knew this part all too well. There must've been some kind of world record out there regarding who had been handcuffed the most. Widow was certain he'd win the title, hands down. No competition.

Widow felt and heard the deputies approaching him from behind. He heard one of them, the one on his left, holster his gun. He expected to hear the clanging of cuffs, but he was wrong. There were no cuffs. Instead, he felt plastic and heard the clicks and felt the pressure of tightening zip ties.

The other deputy holstered his weapon, and they both put their hands on his forearms and closed their grips, tight. Neither of them could reach all the way around Widow's wrists.

One of them said, "Damn, boy. You're a big fella."

Widow stayed quiet.

The sheriff said, "Chris, get him in the truck."

~~Which Widow thought meant they were going to take him right~~ back to the station in town. They didn't.

They still had the body to deal with and a crime scene to investigate.

The deputy on the left opened the passenger side door and said, "Sit your ass down! And don't move! Don't even breathe funny!"

Widow put one foot up on the step bar and then dumped his butt down in the seat.

"Keep your legs out."

Widow kept his legs out, and the deputy left the door wide open. He stepped back and stared at Widow. He kept his gun holster unbuckled and his left hand on the butt of the gun as if saying, *Give me a reason to shoot you.* And he would have too. Widow had no doubt about it.

He figured the guy had been itching to shoot him, itching to shoot someone in the line of duty. A quiet town like this doesn't get a lot of action.

Widow was actually a little afraid of getting shot by mistake. He almost told the deputy to keep calm, but he didn't want to agitate him.

The sheriff and the other deputy went over to look at Hood's body. On closer inspection, the deputy puked. He just retched right there, got some on Hood's shoes.

The sheriff said, "Damn it, Rick! Go back over by the truck!"

Rick said nothing. He just wiped his mouth and returned to where Widow and the other deputy were.

The sheriff spent a long time over by the body. Widow just kept thinking about Jemma. He kept thinking about how he was going to get out of this and save her.

How the hell am I going to track them down?

After several more minutes—or it could've been forty, because Widow had lost track—the sheriff walked back away from the body and pulled out his cell phone. He called for paramedics or whatever their equivalent was. He said they needed a van to get out here and take away the body.

Then he hung up the phone and put it back into his pocket. He returned to the truck and said, "Rick, can you get over there and take photos? Don't puke on it."

He said *"it,"* which irritated Widow because he had known Hood —briefly, but he'd known him. And he liked the guy. Hood was flawed, but not a bad person.

Rick said, "Sure."

"And stay with it. Watch it. Don't let the buzzards or any other critters get it."

"Where you going?"

"We gotta take him in."

"You gonna leave me out here?"

"You'll be fine."

"What if he wasn't alone?"

The sheriff looked at Widow and said, "He was alone. Look at him. He's probably always alone."

Widow wasn't offended, not because he agreed with it, but because he didn't care what this guy thought. He wasn't the type to care about what strangers thought about him.

The other deputy said, "Where's he gonna ride?"

The sheriff said, "Better put him in the back."

"But he could jump out."

"Cuff him to the bar," the sheriff said, and pulled out a pair of handcuffs.

Widow smiled. He knew he couldn't get through the day without being fully cuffed.

They left the zip tie on him and cuffed him over one tie and cuffed the other end to the rail. He was locked in place.

23

ROMANTH'S POLICE station looked like it was carved out of an old residential house. It must've been because it had a porch, green shutters, and clean wood floorboards that squeaked. The rest of the place was painted white. A large wooden sign was hammered into the front yard with the sheriff's name plastered on it—Sheriff Ron Harks. It wasn't a name Widow had heard before, but then again, his own name was unusual.

The inside of the station was just like an old Western, only with modern office machines. There were two desks facing the jail, which was one big cell. Widow guessed that the people they rounded up for crimes were supposed to share it. Right now, it was empty.

The sheriff told the other deputy to throw him in the cell. The deputy tried to walk Widow over to the cell, but he didn't budge.

"Come on! Move!" the deputy said.

Harks said, "What's the problem! Now, you giving us a hard time? I can have him tase you! You're going in that cell!"

"Phone call," Widow said. He couldn't think of anything else. Nothing was going to get him out of this situation fast enough. He needed some help.

"What?" Harks asked. He was standing behind the desk. He took off his hat and laid it flat on the desktop next to a dirt-covered keyboard that looked like it belonged in a mechanic's shop instead of a police station.

Widow said, "I want my phone call."

"Well, you'll get that when I say so. Now get in that cell."

Harks plopped himself down in a high-backed office chair. He looked at Widow with disgust on his face. He was playing a power game with Widow. Harks was trying to show him who was in charge, like a warden does with a new inmate or like his old Recruit Division Commanders had done, but as with the Recruit Division Commanders, this game wouldn't be won by the sheriff.

Widow said, "No! Phone call first!"

Harks stood back up and shoved his finger in Widow's face and said, "Listen here! You beat that boy to death out there, and you are going into that cell! I don't care about your rights!"

Widow sighed in defeat and said, "Look, I'll go in the cell. I won't give you any problems. If you give me a phone call."

But Harks wasn't budging on his power trip, so he said, "I told you; you're getting in that cell. I'll give you your phone call when I decide to give it to you."

"When will that be?"

"In this state, I have to provide it to you within twenty-four hours after your arrest."

Silence fell between them.

Harks said, "You probably noticed that this is a tiny little speck of a town. We ain't got no prison here. We ain't got no courthouse. You know what that means?"

Widow stayed quiet.

"That means we ain't got no judge. Out here, I am it. So tomor-row, the state police will send someone from Laredo or San Antonio or wherever, and they will take you far, far away."

Harks sat back down and tried to pull his seat forward. It didn't have wheels, which he seemed to forget, because then he scooted it forward. He clicked on the keyboard and ignored Widow. Conversation over.

Widow closed his eyes, imagined Jemma all tied up somewhere. She'd be scared. Jemma had probably watched her father get murdered, and she had to be scared. She probably knew she was going to die.

He could still find her. She was probably still alive. Glock had mentioned selling her to a friend who dealt in sex slaves. That might've just been a scare tactic, but Widow had been around the world. He'd been undercover in some of the most unbelievable environments, many, many times. He knew it had as much chance of being true as it did of being a lie.

She must be alive.

Desperate, Widow paused a breath and said, "If you let me make my call now, I'll give a full confession."

This seemed to interest Harks because his eyebrows arched, and he looked up.

"You could be the hero here. Why should those state boys take the credit?"

Harks said, "You'll confess?"

"Yes."

"Sign the papers?"

"Yes. Right here."

Harks said, "Sign it first."

"After. Phone call first. Then I'll sign it."

Harks thought for a moment.

Widow said, "It'll be a short call."

"One minute."

"That's all I'll need."

Harks looked at the other deputy and back at Widow. He said, "You keep the zip tie on."

Widow smiled and said, "I wouldn't have it any other way."

Sheriff Harks stood up again and pulled out his cell phone, which was one of those old ones with only buttons and a black-and-green screen like a calculator.

Harks walked around the desk and sat on the edge. The other deputy took a strong grip on Widow's wrist and jerked him into a position so the sheriff could hold the phone up to his ear, which wasn't quite legal, because these phone calls were confidential if he had been calling his lawyer. But he wasn't calling a lawyer, and he didn't care how they did it.

"What's the number? Who we calling?"

"It's a government number. You'll have to ask for a woman named Cameron."

Harks said, "Government?"

Widow nodded and said, "Yeah. My old unit. They'll send a lawyer."

"What're you? Military?"

"Former."

Harks asked no more questions. He just nodded and asked for the number. Widow gave it to him, and he dialed. It was answered by an automated voice, which asked him for an identification code. Widow gave it to him, and he said it out loud and waited.

A male voice answered, and he asked for Cameron.

The male voice asked, "What is this regarding?"

Widow said, "Tell him my name."

Harks stared at him, and Widow realized they had patted him down but took nothing from his pockets. His passport was still in his pocket.

"Tell him Jack Widow is calling for Cameron."

Harks told the guy, and the male voice told him to wait a second. Harks looked at Widow and moved the phone from his lips. He said, "Jack Widow?"

Widow nodded.

Harks was about to make some remark, but a voice came over the line, and Harks said, "No, ma'am. This is Sheriff Ron Harks."

The voice on the other line asked another question.

Harks said, "Texas. Romanth."

The voice said something else, and the sheriff pulled away from the phone and put it up against Widow's head. He leaned into it and said, "It's me."

NCIS Special Agent Rachel Cameron was Widow's old boss and still commander of Unit Ten, an off-the-books division of the Naval Criminal Investigative Service. She was one of the few members of NCIS who knew his real name. She had been the voice in his ear for sixteen years.

Cameron was older than him, but not by much. He had never known her age. And he had asked many times. She'd never tell. But he guessed she was probably about forty now. If she still looked the same as the day he'd left, she was still a lean and muscular woman. When he had last seen her, she had long blonde hair with short bangs. She didn't look like a special agent in charge, but that was part of what made her dangerous. Widow had never seen her in action, but he had heard stories of her taking down men twice her size. Easily.

Cameron said, "Widow, I've been here all night and was just about to leave. So tell me... what the hell is going on? Are you under arrest?"

"Yeah. You could say that."

"What for?"

"Murder."

Cameron sighed over the phone and asked, "Who did you kill?"

"Nobody. Not yet, anyway."

"So, what's going on?"

"Listen, I don't have time to explain, but I will. Right now, I need some information, and I need it fast."

"What is it?"

"I need to know about a company called Auckland Enterprises."

It sounded like Cameron wasn't writing it down, but was typing it into a computer. He heard keystrokes, and he imagined her sitting in a dark office, typing on a state-of-the-art computer.

"I also need you to look up a guy named John Glock."

"Glock? Like the gun?"

"Yeah. Could be an alias. But maybe not."

"Anything else?"

"Yeah. Get on the phone with Border Patrol and find the cell number of an agent named Donna Leon. She'll be near here somewhere. Tell her my name. Tell her she gave me a ride yesterday. Tell her I need her to call me ASAP."

Cameron typed some more. She paused a beat, and then she asked, "What number does she call?"

Widow looked at the sheriff, and he said, "This one. Tell her to call this one."

"What about you? You're in jail now?"

"Yes. I'm in cuffs. Well, those cable ties actually."

"Do you need me to get you out?"

"No. That'll take time. Even for you."

Cameron asked, "What's the rush? Something time sensitive?"

"Yeah, a little girl's life."

Cameron said nothing to that. She didn't need to. She didn't need to ask Widow questions. Cameron understood. He'd get free. She had known him for a long time.

He said, "I'll call you back in a half hour."

Harks shook his head and pulled the phone away. He said, "No, you won't, son. You'll be behind those bars over there for the rest of the morning."

Harks pulled the phone up to his head and was about to ask who the woman was that he was speaking to, but there was nothing on the line but dead air. She had hung up on him. He clicked off and said, "Now, we had a deal. You're gonna sign a confession."

Widow didn't wait. There wouldn't be a better chance.

In a quick one-two movement, he whipped his head back like a turtle and launched it forward. One of his favorite strikes was the headbutt, a move that often got the job done. He had killed a guy once with a headbutt. But he didn't want to kill Harks. The man was only doing his job.

He landed a solid headbutt. The front of his forehead broke the sheriff's nose. Harks flung backward off his feet and tumbled violently over the desk. He dragged the filthy keyboard with him, and the wires dragged the monitor along the desktop. He landed on the other side.

Before the deputy could react, Widow ran backward at him for almost ten feet, and then he slammed him into the wall. Widow stepped away and turned. The deputy was still standing, but stunned. Widow kicked him square in the nuts—hard enough to kick a football out of the stadium.

The deputy clamped his balls and toppled over like a glass pyramid stood up straight on its point. He puked right after.

Two deputies had puked in one morning.

Widow didn't wait for a victory lap. He kicked off his shoes—fast, like he was back at his mother's house as a teenager. Then he dropped to the ground, on his back, and lifted his legs to pull his zip-tied arms past the back of his knees and over his socks. He jumped back to his feet and shot his hands out straight in front of him as fast as he could, and then, even faster, he stabbed them back into his center mass as hard as he could.

In the SEALs, they had taught Widow many, many tricks of the trade, or tradecraft as they called it. And one was how to escape from zip ties. The trick was to use force plus speed to rip them apart. He had seen a guy wearing twenty zip ties use this move to escape.

As he stabbed them toward his midsection, he pulled apart in both directions, away from his body. By the time the zip ties touched his abdomen, they were shredded to pieces. He was free.

The deputy was still on the ground. His face was blistering red, and he had one hand still clamped on his groin. But in his other hand, he held out his Beretta M9. He should've fired it, but he didn't. Widow kicked it away and stomped down on his hand and groin—hard again.

The deputy winced forward and heaved, but didn't puke. He was all out of ammunition to puke with.

Widow reached down and twisted the deputy so he could grab the weapon he wanted from the moaning man.

He ripped a stun gun from the deputy's belt. It was a smaller version of the ones he had seen before. It didn't have a holster, but was clipped onto the belt. That made it easy to draw it quickly, but what the manufacturer had added for convenience, Widow figured it had sacrificed in power.

Widow spun around and saw that the sheriff was just getting up over the desk. He didn't have his Glock out, not yet. Maybe it was because he was too shocked, or maybe it was because his nose had bloodied his entire lower face. He was probably having extreme problems breathing.

Either way, Widow put him down. He aimed the stun gun and fired and watched the cable whip out behind the prongs. The sharp prongs stabbed into Harks's chest, right below his badge, and Widow squeezed the shock trigger. Electric current jolted through the cables and shocked the sheriff. For a long moment, he shivered violently, and then Widow released the current. He didn't want to kill or severely injure the sheriff.

Harks fell back to the ground. Widow scrambled over to him and took his Glock. Hours ago, he had a Sig Sauer with only five rounds, and now he had both a Glock and an M9. He slid both guns into his pockets. He knelt down over the sheriff and patted him down. He found the cell phone and the keys to his truck.

Harks writhed around and took in deep breaths, trying to regain his senses.

Widow said, "Sorry about this."

He stood back up and checked the deputy. He was still on the ground.

Both men were done.

Widow waited and gave them five minutes to recover and get their bearings. Harks took only the five minutes and looked like he was ready for more, but the deputy wasn't even close.

Widow took everything from their pockets and told them both to get into the cell. He locked them in.

Before leaving the station, he jerked out the cords of all the phones and computers and the fax machine and anything else that looked like it was capable of communication, either through the phone lines or the internet. He ripped them all apart. He didn't destroy the phone or computer or any other machine. They could all be repaired with a trip to RadioShack for some new wires.

He closed all the blinds and took their keys and locked the doors
behind him.

Widow jumped into Harks's truck and fired it up and sped off.
He wanted to get outside town. He drove north and found no way
out, so he turned around and headed west.

24

WIDOW DROVE past dirt and rock and sporadic tree lines. In the distance, the rocky terrain settled into yellow and green grass, bushes, some trees that were bursting with life, and others that were wilting away. As he ventured west, the Rio Grande Valley moved farther south. Morning clouds scattered the sky, with no signs of bad weather.

He checked his rearview mirror, which wasn't the best way to view what was behind him because the back window of the truck had a rifle rack. But there was nothing following him. He was safe.

Two guns were attached to the rack. They were locked by a key lock. The bottom weapon wasn't a rifle. It was a Browning tactical shotgun with a pistol grip. Above that was a Winchester Model 73 with lever action and a short barrel, a weapon that Widow had never fired before. Being in Texas, he felt a craving to fire it, and he imagined he would.

Widow checked his radius in a complete three-sixty and saw no one. He pulled the truck over to the side of the road, which wasn't very wide. He left the engine running and stepped out. First, he checked his weapons. He dry-fired the Glock and then the M9. Both worked well, but he didn't need both of them. He opened the glove box and tossed the Mg in. Before he shut it, he found ammunition for the rifle and the shotgun. An ammo box had five rounds left for the Winchester rifle. There were only three shells for the shotgun—disappointing—but what made him smile was that they were Magnum shells. The downside was that it had only three uses. The upside was that anyone standing in the path of just one wouldn't be standing anymore, because the Magnum shells would remove him from his legs as if he'd been hit by a speeding locomotive. Widow had seen guys hit with these shells before, three or four times. And he could remember at least one of them being blown out of his shoes.

He had full magazines for both handguns, but he picked the Glock simply because it had been the sheriff's weapon of choice. And he figured that Harks was more likely to have a reliable weapon. The deputy didn't convey the same level of confidence in him.

After he checked the handguns, he searched through the key ring for a little key that would unlock the rifle and shotgun. He unlocked them, took them down, and loaded and unloaded them one at a time, checking the loading actions. He took them out, aimed down the sights, and dry-fired them. Both were good weapons.

He liked the Winchester, but it would've been more practical if it was equipped with a long-range scope—it would be nice to pick off several of the enemies from a distance. But in the end, he didn't care. Stealth was better for Jemma's sake. And up close and personal was better for Widow's sake.

He laid out the weapons across the truck bench and stepped back, and pulled out the sheriff's cell phone. He dialed Cameron, gave his code to the voice on the other end, and waited.

Cameron said, "That was slow."

"What the hell are you talking about?"

"It took you long enough to get out of there."

"I had to escape custody and commit several felonies."

"So what? The Jack Widow I used to know would've been out of there ten minutes earlier."

Widow said, "I don't remember being that good."

"Are they alive?"

"Of course."

"So, you've gotten rusty and weak."

"You're suggesting I should've murdered two police officers?"

"Of course not. Still, it took you too long."

"I thought it went well."

Cameron said, "Anyway, I got some info for you."

"Go ahead."

"First, on the Leon thing. She hasn't called me back, but her captain said she's down there somewhere in the field."

"Okay."

"Soon as I speak to her, then you will."

Widow didn't respond.

"The next thing is that you might've stumbled onto something here."

"Go on."

"Auckland Enterprises is an international entity. It's big on a national scale, but small compared to the rest of the world's economies. It trades on the New York Stock Exchange only."

Widow shook his head, even though Cameron couldn't see him. He said, "Talk to me like I'm an idiot. I understand nothing about stocks."

"Are you still reading every day, or did you forget how?"

"As much as I can."

"It means that this is a rich company. It's rising."

Silence fell across the phone like she was waiting for Widow to react.

She said, "It means this is an ambitious company that was small a couple of years ago, but now they're aggressively competing to grow."

Widow asked, "What's illegal about that? Isn't that all of them?"

"Of course, it's all of them. Where do you think the expression 'corporate greed' comes from?"

"So, what's the connection? What's Glock's position?"

"Okay. It's circumstantial but interesting."

"Tell me."

"First, let me say that I don't know what evidence there is, but the FBI has been looking into them. It appears they've had no luck. They have something that piques their interest, but no evidence to warrant anything further than interest."

"I know what they got, what they *had*. It's the reason I'm here. They *had* a witness. A guy named James Hood."

"What do you mean they *had*? They lost him?"

Widow said, "They lost him, and now he's dead."

"Dead, how?"

"I killed him."

Cameron said nothing, but Widow could imagine her face.

"I didn't actually kill him, but I led Glock straight to him. They beat him to death and framed me with it."

"Okay. So now you want payback?"

"Yes. But that's not the reason for the urgency. He had a little girl. They took her."

"Oh, my god!"

"She's only six. They'll kill her or sell her. I have to get her back."

Cameron said, "Understood. You know I'll help in any way I can. I got a can of Red Bull here, and I'll stay by the computer to give you support."

"Thanks. I owe you."

"All right. So... there's no connection between Glock and the company. But Auckland Enterprises dabbles in many things, and there are two things that are across the board. And a third thing that's very interesting.

"First, they deal primarily in the construction business. Building things. Things that nobody really needs. They work in govern-ment contracts, which are more lucrative than drugs these days. Here's the second thing. They've been buying up all the construc-tion equipment and related businesses around the Texas border. They've also been purchasing a lot of the land along the border. Land that no one wants."

Widow asked, "What about heavy equipment?"

"Did you get hit in the head? Heavy equipment *is* construction equipment. That's what these businesses have."

"I don't know much about construction. What else?"

Cameron said, "About five years ago, they were acquired by a majority shareholder. A guy named Sheridan. Ever heard of him?"

"Sounds familiar," Widow said. He tried to recall the name in his head. It was right there on the tip of his brain.

He thought of the hotel chain, but before he could go any farther, Cameron said, "John Sheridan. AKA Texas Senator John Sheridan."

Widow said, "I've heard of him. He's pushing for a huge border wall."

"I'm glad to see you're paying attention to the world again."

Widow said nothing.

Cameron said, "This is where your friend Glock comes into play."

"How's that?"

"Sheridan has a squeaky clean political history. He's a real fringe in his party, but his constituents love that about him. Before he was in politics, he ran a unit of the DEA."

"DEA?"

"Yeah. You know, the Drug Enforcement Administration?"

Widow said, "I know who they are."

Cameron wasn't lying about being up all night. And probably not about the Red Bull either, because she was very snappy. And he had heard her like that before. Her job required her to stay up for long hours sometimes. He used to joke to himself that her moods were like the terrorist alert color warnings. Red was when her joking turned to insults. Right now, she was in the orange somewhere.

"In the DEA, he was head of some unit that operated with the Mexican government. A lot. Know what that means?"

"Yeah. It means they were in Mexico from time to time."

"Right. And that's where Glock comes into the picture."

"How so?"

"Your friend was a SEAL once upon a time. Not long, though. He was jailed for drug charges. But they couldn't make them stick, so he was discharged. Fast forward, and he went to Mexico. Dealing for some cartel. Enforcer work. He got arrested. And then his trail goes cold for a while. And then he pops back up here and there."

Widow said, "He's here now."

"Yeah. This guy, Sheridan, was in the DEA and now has a sterling political record. We have to assume he hired Glock. We have to assume they're partners."

"So Glock handles the criminal side of the business. And Sheridan is the public face. How much money is in this wall?"

Cameron paused a beat and gulped. Like the number was big, and it was. She said, "Widow, the wall has been estimated to cost twenty-five billion."

Widow stayed quiet. He thought, *Same as Leon said.*

Cameron said, "Sheridan is pushing for the border wall. He's out there convincing Americans. Glock is out there behind the scenes, probably buying up all of this construction equipment and supplies, which many failing business owners are probably selling. Happily."

"But the ones that won't, that's where he uses his talents of persuasion?"

"Probably. If I dig some more, I wouldn't be surprised to find some mysterious deaths involved."

Widow said, "Don't bother digging. Let the FBI worry about evidence. I've got enough for me."

"Auckland is out there buying up land or forcing out landowners and gathering all the local equipment. They're making it so that they're the only ones who can handle building the wall in South Texas. So when the time comes for bidding for contracts, the senator will be able to say, 'Hey, Auckland already has everything. Auckland is ready to build now.'"

Widow asked, "How much money is involved in just the South Texas part of the wall?"

"Texas has the longest border with Mexico. I'd say more than half of the money would go to them."

"Fifteen billion?"

"At least."

Widow said, "I need something else. I need your help to find the girl."

"I was just thinking that."

"Can you find out where they might've taken her?"

"I don't need to. I can tell you."

"Where?"

"Auckland owns a lot of the land along the border already."

Widow nodded to himself.

Cameron said, "About two hours from Romanth, to the northwest, they've got land with something on it."

"What?"

"Ever heard of the Jericho Militia?"

"No," he said, but then he thought and said, "Militia? Glock had a small force with him last night."

"They're typical militia gun nuts trying to police the border. But these guys differ from the usual. Most militias round up illegals that cross the border and then turn them over to the Border Patrol. Not these guys. They've never turned in a single one."

Widow said nothing, but he doubted they were capturing illegal aliens and just setting them free. He knew that the guys he saw the night before were probably killing them.

Cameron said, "The Jericho Militia's headquarters are on this land."

"Okay. I'm headed there now. That's where they have her."

"Want the coordinates?"

"No. I have no way of using them. This phone is outdated. No maps."

"It's a lot of land. How'll you find them?"

Widow thought for a moment. Then he said, "I need a favor."

"I'm already doing you favors."

"Yeah, but this is a big one."

"How big?"

"Are there some bases around here?"

Cameron said, "The Naval base is far."

"Not Naval. Air Force."

Cameron typed on the keyboard, and the clicks sounded over the phone. She said, "Near you, there's Laughlin and Lackland."

"Check them out. Bribe. Pull in favors. Whatever you have to do. But I'm going to need some air support."

"What the hell are you talking about? You know they'll never commit pilots or jets or helicopters to you!"

"Not that kind of support. But maybe one of them can spare a spy drone."

Cameron was silent for a moment, then said, "Lackland might have one. There'll be no payload."

"Don't need it. Just the recon. Tell them to call it a military exercise."

"It's possible."

"I know you must know someone high up the chain of command."

"Not in Texas, but maybe in the DOD's office."

Widow said, "Good. Make it happen. I need to know the layout."

"It'll take a while. What you gonna do for now?"

"You said it was about a two-hour drive from me?"

"Yep."

"Guess I'm driving. Call me as soon as you have the drone."

Cameron said nothing back.

He asked for Leon's cell number, and Cameron gave it to him. And then she hung up the phone and was gone.

Widow called Leon.

25

IT TURNED out Leon was only about ninety minutes away from a point between Widow and the Jericho location. He updated her, and she agreed to meet with him. She told him the whole thing sounded unbelievable, but her boss's boss had called him and explained to him that *his* boss had called him. And the chain of command had sent down the message that Leon was on loan to the Department of the Navy for the day, which was something she had never heard of before.

The reason she was so close to him already was that after she had gotten the message, she had been ordered to drive to Romanth, and so she had already been driving for an hour when he had finally reached her by phone.

Widow was still driving along a bumpy track of dirt road that didn't really qualify as a dirt road because grass had completely grown over it and died. Now it was a dead grass road more than anything else.

An hour had passed since he had spoken to Cameron, and a half hour had passed since he'd spoken with Leon. He was ahead of her, technically. But she was driving a much newer vehicle, and most of the road ahead of her was actual road. She'd be at the meeting place at about the same time as he arrived.

Widow was generalizing about the direction, but it wasn't hard because the dead grass road he was on didn't have many options other than straight.

Suddenly, his phone rang. He reached down and picked it up and clicked the green button.

"Yeah?"

"It's Cameron. Do you see it yet?"

"See what?"

And right then, as he answered, he heard it, a loud boom from overhead. He looked up through the windshield and gazed at the blue sky. A small, thin plane flew overhead. He took a second look at it and realized it was the drone, unmanned and hawkish, like a predator.

He said, "Great. I need to follow it to their headquarters. But first, I've got to meet Leon."

"Where is she?"

"I don't know, but we're meeting at a crossroads between a highway and this road."

Cameron said, "Okay, I'm sure we can locate that." And then she stopped speaking to Widow but left him on the line as she switched over to speak to someone else. She gave orders for someone to pilot the drone and lead Widow to the highway. Widow realized she was probably connected by phone with the Air Force pilot who was manning the drone. The guy was probably sitting in an old shipping container in Nellis Air Force Base in Las Vegas. Widow imagined that because most spy drones were operated from there. The Nellis base was a primary operating center for these drones. It was amazing. The drones were typically out on the sea, parked on Naval carriers. They'd launch from the ships and be piloted from way back in Nellis.

Things had changed a lot since Widow had first joined the Navy.

Cameron came back on the line, and Widow said, "What happened to pilots flying with their jets?"

"Everything's going digital now. Like a video game."

"I feel bad for him."

"He's the least of our problems."

"You should tell him he's helping to rescue a little girl."

Cameron said, "I could, but I don't know him. I'm not in his chain of command. He could blurt it out. He could get my guy who told him to do this in trouble."

"Guess we'd better keep him in the dark then."

"He's used to that. These guys fly missions all day long. They're always in the dark about them."

"All right, I see the drone. Will he fly it slowly?"

"He'll keep it in your eyesight."

Widow said, "Good. I can only go so fast on this road."

Cameron yawned a heavy yawn and said, "Widow, I've got to get some more Red Bull, or I'll be asleep before we even get her."

Widow said, "I'm okay for now. I can see the plane."

"Drone. Don't call it a plane. These guys hate that. It's like someone calling a battle carrier a boat."

"Drone," Widow corrected.

"I'm going to go offline for a while. I'll be back in forty-five."

"Got it."

Cameron hung up the phone.

* * *

WIDOW DIDN'T KNOW the model name for the drone. He knew little about them. It was just better than basic knowledge.

He knew there were different shapes and sizes. Widow knew there were different kinds built for different missions. He assumed this one was a spy drone because it had that bulky front end with windows around it like a little cockpit. But there were no pilots in it. It was equipped with powerful lenses for the onboard cameras. He imagined it had incredible zoom range and picture clarity. Widow had seen images captured by them in the past. He had been told that they never flew low. They usually flew so high in the sky that they couldn't be seen with the naked eye. And they were often painted to disappear into the sky. Night drones were black, and day drones were white.

Widow floored the truck and took it up to the highest speed he was comfortable with, which was about fifty miles per hour. He wanted to go faster, but the truck was already bouncing. The suspensions were working overtime.

He followed the drone, which kept flying low and then swooping away. When it got too far, the pilot circled it around, passing over the truck again and again.

He continued on past some more rock formations and grassy lands and dying trees to the north. He headed into this no-man's-land, always keeping the Rio Grande on the horizon to his left.

Occasionally, he passed far-off signs of life, like structures and windmills and power lines, but the cables on the lines weren't there. And the windmills were spinning, but the structures looked hollowed out. Everything was abandoned and lost and forgotten.

26

DONNA LEON STOOD outside her Tahoe and leaned on the front end. The windows were rolled all the way down, and Jake had his head stuck out the driver's side window. Even though she had left the air conditioner blasting inside, Jake was still panting. His head was huge, and his fur was thick. He was definitely hot.

She had her sunglasses on and her Kevlar vest and full uniform. She waited for Widow. Part of her was excited to see him again because she had thought about him a lot. The other part of her was curious as to what the hell was going on.

Her boss had told her to show up, meet him, and provide him with whatever support he needed. One unusual thing that had been relayed to her was that this was a no-questions-asked type of situation.

Leon continued to wait. She wished she had a cigarette. She had quit smoking three months earlier and was now regretting it. But she didn't have any cigarettes.

Just then, she heard a noise. It was loud, like a cracking or booming. She stared across the empty highway at the dirt road and saw nothing. Then she looked up in the air and saw a small jet barreling toward her. It was clearly a military jet. She surmised that because she had never seen a plane that moved like this. She stood up and took off her sunglasses. The thing was headed right toward her. She watched with her mouth open as it flew very low, and then was relieved when it jetted straight over her Tahoe. She followed it with her gaze and watched it yaw, and then the nose went up, and it flew straight up like it was making a loop.

A moment later, she heard a loud noise behind her. She turned and saw an old police truck bouncing on worn-out tires. Smoke rose behind it. The truck barreled up onto the highway. She saw Widow was driving it. No one had told her he was a sheriff.

* * *

WIDOW SWITCHED on the light bar, gunned across the blacktop and the median, and parked the truck in front of Leon's Tahoe. Smoke emerged from under the hood and shot out of the grille. The engine clicked. It was out of gas or out of radiator fluid, but either way, it was definitely out of time. It needed maintenance if it was going to continue on.

He stepped out and left the door open behind him. He walked over to her and gave her a hug, which was a little weird because she wasn't expecting it.

He pulled back and said, "Sorry about that. I've had a bad night. I'm glad to see you again."

She said, "Me too. You must have some friends in high places to get my boss all amped up."

"What did they tell you?"

"Nothing. They don't know a thing. All they know was that an order came down from someone higher than my boss's boss, and here I am." She looked back at his truck and asked, "Are you... like... a cop?"

Widow shook his head and said, "Forget about the truck. You don't wanna know that part of the story."

"What the hell is going on?"

"Remember, I was looking for someone?"

"Right. I thought you were a PI."

"Something like that. Turns out, this person I was looking for was into something deep and in way over his head."

"Where's this guy now?"

"He's dead."

"What?"

"Dead. Look, we're pressed for time. This is a clock-ticking scenario."

She gazed up at him and asked, "Are you okay?"

"More or less."

She asked, "More more, or more less?"

Widow paused a beat and said, "More less, I suppose, but listen. Long story short—there's a little girl out there, and there are some bad guys armed to the teeth, and they're gonna kill her."

"What? We gotta call this in!" she said. She reached into her pocket and pulled out her cell phone.

He clamped his hand on it gently enough not to scare her, but hard enough to make a point. He said, "We can't."

"Why the hell not?"

"Trust me. We can't. That's why I need your help."

She looked distrustful. She said, "I don't know, Widow."

"Look, these people are connected. We can't involve anyone. Not yet. After we get her, then you can call the cavalry."

"I don't like this. I don't feel right about it."

"Trust me," he said again.

The spy drone came swooping back around and buzzed over them. Leon watched it intently.

Widow said, "We're not alone, anyway. They're with us."

"Who? Who's with us?"

He pointed at the drone and said, "Them."

She looked at him sideways and asked, "Who the hell is *them*?"

"The United States Air Force."

"Are you serious? What are you, some kind of big deal?"

"No. I'm just a guy trying to do the right thing."

Her sideways look intensified, and he said, "I used to be something. Never a big deal. I had a long career in the Navy. I got friends left in the military."

"Where's this little girl?"

"That's why we got the drone. It'll lead us there."

"What am I walking into? How many bad guys?"

"That I don't know for sure. At least eight."

"Great."

"Ever heard of the Jericho Militia?"

She looked at him with disgust in her eyes. Widow watched them narrow, and she said, "You mean the Jericho Men?"

"I don't know."

"It's a militia that operates along the border. Their territory is about a hundred miles long."

"That could be them."

"It is. They're not a normal militia group. These guys are hardcore. They have firepower, and they're very, very racist. They think they're fighting for a cause, but their cause is white supremacy. We don't mess with them without at least four convoys with agents armed and strapped with Kevlar."

"Well, the good news is you'll probably get to kill some today."

"I'm not killing anyone."

Widow asked, "Have you ever fired your service weapon? In the line?"

"Of course."

"Ever shoot anyone?"

"No. Only warning shots."

Widow paused for a moment and then asked, "Can you shoot?"

"Of course!"

"I'd suggest that you let me do the wetwork."

"Wetwork?"

"Dirty work. I need you for backup."

She nodded and said, "They told me to do whatever you need. I guess I'm obligated now."

"Let's go. I'm going to ride with you."

"I'd guess so. That old truck looks like it should be taken behind the barn and shot."

"I agree," he said, and headed back to the truck.

Leon got into the Tahoe. She pushed Jake back and forced him to return to the rear bench. She waited, wondering what the hell she was getting into.

Widow reached into the cab of the truck. He shut off the engine and came out with several guns and slammed the door with his foot. He walked over to the Tahoe's passenger door, opened it, and asked Leon to pop the release on the cargo door in the back, which she did.

Widow walked around and stored the rifle, the shotgun, and the ammunition in the cargo area next to some of her gear. He also tossed in the M9 even though he didn't plan to use it. But he didn't want to leave it in an abandoned truck on the side of the highway.

~~He slammed the door and returned to the cabin. He dumped~~ himself down on the seat and said, "Follow the drone."

He adjusted the Glock, so it wasn't poking him in the lower back.

Leon whipped the Tahoe around and U-turned. She waited for the drone to circle again and then followed it down the dirt road.

27

THE SPY DRONE slowed its speed as much as it could and circled around several times to lead Widow and Leon to the Jericho Men's compound. Every time it flew too far, it circled back for them, which must have been hard for the pilot. Widow was sure he wasn't used to leading vehicles around. They drove for what felt like forever along a stretch of literally nothing but low grass, most of which was brown and yellow.

The sheriff's phone rang. Widow dipped his hand down into his pocket and pulled it out. It was a blocked number. He answered it.

"Widow. You're coming up on the compound now. It's about ten minutes ahead of you," Cameron said.

"I figured it was close. But Cameron, we got a problem."

"What is it?"

"From here, the land looks completely flat in all directions. Can you send the drone up ahead and check it out? We need to find some cover, or they'll see us coming."

Cameron said, "I can tell you just by Google Maps it's definitely flat. But I'll send the drone ahead. Just keep straight."

Widow hung up, looked at Leon.

She said, "What are we going to do, Widow?"

"I don't know."

"We gotta figure something out. If they got rifles and scopes, which I'm sure they do, they can just pick us off from a mile away."

Widow said, "How far can you crawl on your belly?"

She gazed at him with a half question on her face and shrugged.

"We might have to use the grass for cover and try to get to them."

"That's insane. This land is pretty flat."

"I know. But I don't see another way. Let's see what Cameron says. Pull up over there and park," Widow said, pointing to a patch of trees at the bottom of a slight hill.

Leon slowed and pulled the steering wheel. The truck glided to a stop, and they got out. She left the engine on and the AC blasting for Jake. Leon walked around to the back of the truck and popped open the cargo door, reaching in and grabbing something Widow couldn't see. She came back out with a box of dog treats.

Leon walked around to Jake, who had jammed his head out like he knew the time. She fed him a treat shaped like a bone. She said, "I don't know what your reason is for not letting me call in reinforcements, but I think it's a mistake. I've worked with the Border Patrol for years. These are good guys."

"I'm sure they are. I'm not questioning that. I've got a good reason."

"You gonna tell me? I mean, I'm here and about to risk my life."

Widow thought for a moment and then looked up at the sky for the drone. No sign of it. He looked at her, and he explained everything—Claire Hood, James, Jemma, Lucy, and the kill team. He told her about James's death and how he got the sheriff's truck.

She stared at him, mouth not wide open but closed. She said, "Whew! You just admitted to committing about a dozen felonies."

"After, you can arrest me."

She shook her head and said, "No need for that. I get it."

He said, "I guess there's no use in asking you for a date?"

She shot him another stare, tilted her sunglasses down so that he could see her eyes. They were nice eyes. She smiled and said, "I didn't say that."

He smiled back.

"But aren't you a homeless man?"

"Only technically. Don't they say that home is where the heart is?"

"Where's your heart?"

"Right here," he said, and pointed at his chest.

"I have no doubt. You're risking your life to save a little girl and trying to protect her citizenship as well."

Widow's phone crackled with a weak ring like it was running out of battery, or there was a terrible signal out here. He pulled it out and answered.

"I've got good news and bad news," Cameron said. Her voice sounded a little hoarse. She had probably been yelling at other people while they were off the phone. Cameron wasn't known for being a warm person. She had a reputation for being coldhearted. Widow had heard rumors about her before. He normally ignored them, but one nickname that stuck in his mind was Ice Queen. Some people used that to refer to her in code so they wouldn't get in trouble.

Cameron was a smart person, one of the smartest that Widow had ever known. She knew about her reputation. She even embraced it sometimes.

After having known each other for years, he had taken to calling her "Your Highness" occasionally and playfully. Because Widow had placed his life in her hands so many times, they were about as close to friends as anyone could be in a work relationship.

He didn't call her Your Highness this time, because she seemed too irritated to mess with. But he had been tempted.

Instead, he said, "Bad first."

"I've got photographs. The compound isn't complicated. It's a basic structure. Wood. A single-story house, but almost a shack. I saw a porch and a front door. There are no dogs visible. I told them to fly over so we could look at all angles. The windows aren't covered, and I saw pretty clearly into the house. We counted ten guys. That's the bad news. They're armed to the teeth. They've got a variety of rifles. I can't tell models. I don't see any snipers."

"Positions?"

"Four are out front, three walking the perimeter, and one on the porch. Two are inside somewhere."

"Did you see a little girl?"

"No. Sorry," Cameron said, and paused a long, long beat.

Widow stayed quiet, ground his teeth, then said, "She's gotta be there. What else?"

"Good news is that—remember I told you how they're buying up all of this heavy equipment?"

"Yeah?"

"Apparently, they've been storing a lot of it around their compound."

Widow said, "You mean we've got some cover?"

"Yes."

"That's good."

"Listen, I've got to send the drone back. I can't keep it there. If it records you shooting people, then this looks like an off-the-books op, and I can't cover that up—not through the Air Force. It's already involved three people. One officer, the pilot, and his copilot."

Widow asked, "They've got copilots?"

"Yeah. Of course."

"Tell them thanks. We got it from here."

"I'll dismiss them."

"Wait, I need one more thing."

Cameron asked what he needed, and Widow looked over at Leon. He told Cameron to hang on, and he walked away. Widow asked her for another favor out of earshot of Leon. He didn't want her to know.

Leon stayed leaning with Jake and let him lick her hand.

After another minute of talking, she saw Widow hang up the phone and return to her.

Leon asked, "What was that last part about?"

"Nothing."

"Secrets?"

Widow shrugged.

"Are we ready?"

"Let's go get her."

* * *

BLUE SKIES COVERED the earth as far as the eye could see. The heat was still there but dialed down from the day before. Widow figured it was partly a drop in temperature and partly the winds picking up and blowing across the rolling plains.

Yellowish, reedy grass blades swayed in a southern direction in huge, natural swooshes like rocking waves, which was not an advantage for Widow and Leon. The grass moving in one direction while they marched in another made it easy to spot them. If someone was looking, but nobody was.

They left the Border Patrol Tahoe out of the line of sight about a mile back, and walked in. They took with them the Winchester, the shotgun, the Glock, and Leon's service weapon. Widow tried to convince her to take the M9 instead. But she didn't like his reasoning. He had told her that her weapon was traceable back to her. He thought it better not to use an official weapon, one issued by the United States Border Patrol. In the end, he didn't press her too hard because the M9 was the personal weapon of a deputy, which meant it would've only required one or two more steps to trace it back to him and thus to her.

Leon didn't put out the vibe that she was on board with the whole idea of killing these guys, but Widow knew that when it came down to her life or theirs, she'd pull the trigger.

They stopped at a patch of young, leafless trees and surveyed their approach.

Widow smiled. He had been pretty happy with what he'd seen for about the last half mile. Cameron had told him they were storing heavy equipment here. She wasn't kidding. There were excavators, huge Caterpillars, and bulldozers. Monstrous machines—Widow didn't even know what they were all called—lined the property.

Jake was down low by Leon's side. He was a well-trained police dog. She had strapped him up with a tactical harness. He had extra ammunition for her weapon and the extra five rounds for Widow's Model 73.

The Winchester had a twenty-inch barrel and could hold ten rounds. It was fully loaded, giving Widow a grand total of fifteen rounds. Plus, the three Magnum shells for the shotgun. And a full magazine for the Glock and for Leon's H&K. He had plenty of bullets, as long as he made them all count.

"What's the plan?"

"I can't see the house, but it's gotta be in there somewhere. I'd guess it's in the middle. They got these machines stacked around it like a maze."

"Equipment. Not machines."

"What's the difference?"

"Sorry, my dad was in construction. I've seen a lot of this stuff before."

Widow said, "We can use the equipment to hide as long as possible. I don't suppose you got a silencer for that gun?"

She shook her head and said, "That's highly illegal."

"I figured. Just asking."

"I got a Ka-Bar."

"Let me have it."

She reached into a pocket on Jake's harness and came out with a tactical Ka-Bar, blade about five inches. She handed it to Widow.

"This'll work."

"What are you going to do?"

"I'm going to take out as many as I can."

"What do I do?"

Widow said, "You should stay back and come in behind me when the shooting starts."

"I'm not staying behind."

"You should wait. I've done this before."

"No way. I'm a girl, but I'm good with my weapon."

Widow said, "Okay. Your choice. Stay at seven o'clock."

She looked at him sideways.

"Stay behind me. To my left. Don't shoot until it's time. But don't wait for them to shoot at you. Got it?"

"I got it."

"What about Jake?"

"What about him?"

"Will he stay quiet?"

"He understands," she said.

"Let's go. We're gonna stay close to the equipment. Give me about ten feet of distance."

Widow gave her the shotgun. He said, "Use this first. It's loaded with Magnums. Three of them. It's gonna kick, but it'll blow away anything in your way."

"Got it."

Widow stayed low in a crouch and ran over to the edge of a big green excavator. He peered around the side and saw no one, only a trail of heavy equipment parked in no particular order or organization. He followed a zigzag path, taking a careful track, but walking fast.

They had plenty of cover, which was good, but as soon as the first shot was fired, everyone would know. The sound would echo on and on.

He looked up at the sky and wished he still had that drone. They could've used it as a distraction. They could've had the thing buzz over the compound for ten minutes. That would get everyone's attention. But he didn't have the drone. It was gone.

Widow hugged close to a huge black tire. It was enormous, bigger than any that he'd ever seen in his life. He had been close to tanks, but they didn't have tires. They had tracks. The only tires comparable to this were the ones on military cargo planes, which were big, but not like this. He didn't recognize the vehicle, but he guessed it was some kind of crane.

He leaned over and peered around the side.

Cameron had said there were four armed guys patrolling the perimeter. The good news was that Widow doubted there was any kind of pattern or professional training in these guys. They'd be scattered around. Maybe even out of earshot.

He saw one.

A lone guy, the obese one from the night before, was standing and facing the other direction. His AR-15 hung from a strap over his back. The guy was taking a leak about thirty yards away.

Widow had the Ka-Bar low in his right hand and the Model 73 in his left. He held the Model 73 with his hand down around the barrel and trigger housing. Widow glanced back at Leon and put out his hand as a signal to stop. He checked left. Checked right. Saw no one else.

He stayed low in a crouch and moved within five yards of the fat guy. He set the rifle down on the ground and launched himself to his feet. The Ka-Bar was tight in his right hand. He clamped his left hand around the guy's mouth and shoved the blade right into the base of his neck at the front, right above the collar bone—a nasty attack. Overkill, really. But Widow had no mercy for these guys. As far as he was concerned, they were all dead already.

He squeezed the hilt and jerked it to the right as he pulled the guy's head to the left. The guy didn't even struggle. He didn't struggle because he was dead in seconds. And it was a messy death. Blood shot out of him in a spray. It painted the side of a large cement truck. The huge mixing drum on the back was still and silent.

Widow waited for the guy to completely stop moving, and then dragged him back and laid him beneath the back tire. There was no use in trying to hide the body, not really, because the guy had sprayed so much blood.

One down, Widow thought.

He picked up the Winchester and returned to Jake and to Leon, who now had a different opinion of him. He could see that in her eyes.

He said, "What?"

"Nothing. Just nothing."

Widow stayed quiet.

Leon said, "That was really awful."

"That's the job. Remember, these guys aren't good people. Believe me, that guy deserved it."

"I'm not questioning it. It was just so violent."

Widow didn't respond to that. He said, "Let's go."

"We should take his gun."

"Nah. Leave it. Only take enemy property in the field if you need it. We don't."

"Enemy property?"

"Yeah."

"You really are a SEAL."

"I was."

Just then, they heard a noise to the south. Widow hushed her with his finger, and Jake perked up. He knew someone was close. But then the noise they heard sounded inhuman. It buzzed and sputtered and whirred. It sounded more like a far-off lawnmower or a remote-controlled toy car than an approaching human.

Widow whispered, "Stay here."

He scrambled back and moved behind, around an enormous excavator. He squatted down by the front end and peered around the corner, the Ka-Bar tight in his hand. It still dripped blood from the fat guy. Widow looked carefully, saw no one.

Then he heard a *whoosh* above. It sounded like the wings of a giant hummingbird. He heard a little motor. He twisted and searched the sky and saw it.

Flying about fifty feet off of the ground was a silver drone, but not like the one that they had borrowed from the US Air Force. This was a small one, like a remote-controlled helicopter, a kid's toy. It flew low and hovered over a row of dormant cement trucks.

The bottom of the drone had a big glass bubble that housed a camera. The drone's camera was shifting and clicking. It scanned the area around the cement trucks. It scanned the area where Widow had just killed the fat guy.

* * *

WIDOW RETURNED to Jake and Leon and said, "It's time to go loud."

"Why? What the hell happened?" Leon asked.

"They got a drone."

"Like we did?"

"No. It's the one you can buy at a sporting goods store."

"Damn."

"They're about to see the body. Let's move fast."

"Shouldn't we take it out first?"

"No. Leave it for now. Let them stumble around for a few minutes. If it gets close, shoot it."

Leon nodded. She said something to Jake in German, and he jumped to life like he'd been waiting all day to get to work.

Leon said, "What now? We blitz to the center?"

"We should split up. The moment we're made, Jemma's chances of being killed skyrocket."

"I agree."

"Take Jake and head south. Circle around on the outer perimeter. You see one of them, you shoot him. Use the shotgun. Same goes for the drone."

She nodded and said, "Good luck."

Widow said, "Wait. Put your phone on vibrate."

"It's on silent."

"Not silent. Vibrate. You kill one, text me."

She nodded.

"Remember, there were ten. Now nine."

"Okay."

"You find her, text me. You get into trouble, text me. Got it?"

"You do the same."

Widow nodded and headed up the center row of vehicles. He took out his phone and set it to vibrate. Sometimes it was necessary to split up in order to achieve an objective. Widow had no reservations about that, but the problem with splitting up was communication. They didn't have radios and headsets to stay in contact with, and he didn't want his phone ringing. Texting was the best way for them to relay information. He needed her to tell him if she killed one so he could keep up with the numbers.

Widow simultaneously kept his eyes on the sky for the drone and watched his twelve o'clock view. He stayed low, using the heavy equipment as cover. He heard the drone's buzzing blades echoing behind him. They faded and faded. He kept the Ka-Bar out for now.

He walked on for what seemed like a hundred yards, but was realistically more like sixty. Up ahead, he heard voices. He crouched down and stayed as close to a pair of bulldozers as he could.

He peered through a crack in the metal skirt around the midsection of one of the bulldozers. He saw two guys. They were standing by a white F-150 that must've been from the 1980s. The hood was up, and one guy had his head stuck in it checking out the engine, Widow figured. Just two guys talking over an engine, which was good. It meant the drone hadn't discovered the dead guy yet. The bad news was that there were about twenty yards of open clearing between his position and theirs. No way was he going to sneak up on them, but he could try. He put the Ka-Bar away, levered the action on the Winchester, and walked slowly toward them. The ground was worn and compacted from the traffic of the heavy equipment around them.

Widow pulled the rifle up, stock in his shoulder. He paced to about fifteen feet behind them and aimed down the stock. Then he paused. He noticed a half-empty bottle of tequila resting on the front tire. That made him smile because tequila was Mexican. For militia racists who hated Mexicans, that was rich.

The half-empty bottle also made him smile because he realized chances were they had been drinking it.

He didn't fire. Instead, he crept closer, keeping the rifle ready. No movement.

He moved in closer. Nothing. Now he was less than ten feet behind them.

Widow took two giant steps. Fast. He reversed the rifle and plunged the stock into the back of the first guy's neck. He toppled forward, nailing his face on the grille of the truck. Widow heard a loud *crack*. The chrome finish was smeared in red blood.

The guy's nose had broken.

The other guy pulled his head out from under the hood and jumped back.

Widow saw an AR-15 resting against the bumper. The stock was on the ground, and the muzzle was within inches of the guy's hand.

Widow reversed the Winchester and shoved it in the guy's face. He said, "Don't even think about it! I'll blow your head off!"

Widow didn't recognize the guy's face, but he knew instantly that the guy recognized his. He knew because he'd seen that look of terror in people before. Many times it was right before he killed them.

The guy said, "You?"

"Me, asshole."

"You're supposed to be locked up."

"I guess you were there then?"

The guy said nothing, but he trembled violently like most people would if they knew they were going to get shot in the face.

Widow looked down at the other guy. He tried to get up, cupping his nose, trying to stop the bleeding.

Widow said, "The girl."

The guy didn't even let him finish the question. He said, "She's alive. We didn't touch her. I swear."

"Where?" he asked.

The guy didn't answer. He just released his nose with one hand and pointed toward the house.

Widow wondered why Cameron hadn't seen her from the drone. Maybe it had been too high up.

"What about Glock?"

"Who?"

Widow shoved the rifle deeper into his face and said, "The guy with the voice."

"He's here too. He's out back. Near the girl."

The other guy stood up. His face was a mess. He held it with both hands, but that didn't seem to help. Blood was everywhere. The guy leaned back against the truck. His hair was so disheveled that Widow figured he must've had a comb-over because he now had one long section on the side.

Both men were over forty, maybe over fifty.

Widow said, "Get over. Next to your friend."

They both came in closer to each other.

The second guy asked, "What ya gonna do?"

Widow wanted to kill them, but he wasn't sure. He wasn't in the habit of killing unarmed guys. But they deserved it. He couldn't use the knife—it was hard to kill two guys who saw it coming with a single knife.

Suddenly, he heard Jake barking in the distance. Only a couple of barks, but it was certainly enough to announce that there was a situation on the property. At the very least, the militia guys would know there was a dog loose.

He didn't hear Leon discharge her weapon, and this worried him for about a half a second, but then his phone vibrated. He took it out and smiled at the screen. It read, "One down." But Widow thought, *Two down.*

He slipped the phone back into his pocket, one-handed. He looked at the two guys and said, "Bad news, guys."

"What?" they both asked. Only the voice of the one with the broken nose sounded jumbled and nasal.

"Looks like you don't get to live to fight another day after all," Widow said, and he shot them both through the chest. Quick. *Pop!* Lever the action. And *Pop!* It was fast.

The muzzle flashed, and a red mist sprayed against the front of the F-150. Neither guy screamed because both were dead before they hit the dirt. Widow had aimed at the heart. He watched them fall over and stared at the holes in both men. The proximity of the shots had burned through the front of their shirts. Blood pooled underneath them.

He moved away from the dead bodies, then jogged around the set of bulldozers and dipped down beside a large dump truck. He peered around the corner and saw mountains of heavy pipes of all different sizes. Some were big enough to be tunnels, and others were around two feet in diameter. They were stacked and piled in neat rows, but in no particular order.

He looked past them and saw the house. It was about fifty yards away. He stopped and pulled the phone out again. He texted Leon, "Two down," and "Go live." Then he wondered if she'd understand. She probably would, but civilian law enforcement was different from military. He texted, "Shoot to kill."

She responded, "Got it."

Then he heard the buzzing sound again. The little drone was coming behind him, flying over the dead bodies. Widow knew that now they would know someone was coming for them. It would be all hands on deck. And he heard them. Loud, angry voices. He looked back at the house and saw guys coming out of it armed with their AR-15s and whatever else.

He peered back at the drone, which was moving in his direction.

He texted Leon again and said, "I see the house. They're coming out. Wait until I shoot. Then fire two times. Into the air. Draw them away. Then head back to the Tahoe."

Widow turned and aimed at the drone and fired, levering the action after.

The drone didn't explode like in the movies. But the bullet ripped through the center, and tiny little flashes of electricity surged through it. It plummeted to the ground.

Widow turned back and aimed in the house's direction. Then he heard Leon's shots way off in the distance. She was a good two hundred yards away, at least. He dropped to a crouch and ran to the right, keeping his head low. Widow scrambled to cover behind a row of huge pipes. He ran around them, gripping the rifle with one hand. Widow pulled the Ka-Bar back out and lowered himself so he was out of sight as best he could be. He peeked around the pipes and saw the house. It was less than twenty yards now. He saw five confused faces standing in front of it.

Widow tallied five men, plus the four dead, which meant that there was one more in the house. But then he saw Glock and another man come out of the house. There were eleven, not ten.

The guy behind Glock was big, with a long gray beard, like the leader of a motorcycle gang. He must've been the head of the Jericho Men, the head guy. He had an open laptop in his hand. The head guy must've been controlling the drone, which made Widow suspect he was the one who had tracked him using the iPhone from the dead woman. Therefore, he was the reason Hood was dead.

The guy started barking orders at the men. Three of them ran off in Leon's direction, two others toward the fallen drone. All of them were armed with AR-15s, which made Widow wonder if they had a corporate sponsor, except that the AR-15 was manufactured by various gun makers, not just one. Then again, they did have a corporate sponsor—Auckland Enterprises.

Widow moved parallel, but in the opposite direction of the two guys headed for the fallen drone. He stayed close to the pipes and then crossed over to stand near a giant spool.

Between the spool and the house was nothing but beaten-up tracks of dirt. Heavy, thick tracks traced around the house to the back. He stayed there and texted Leon to be on the lookout for three guys headed in her direction. She responded with "Get the girl" and nothing else.

Widow raised the Winchester and aimed at Glock, who was about thirty-five to forty yards away. He was looking straight ahead and missing Widow to his left. Widow was tempted to take the shot, but he didn't want the rest of them coming down on him. Not yet. He lowered the rifle and ran to the back of the house. He made it to the edge and hugged the wall.

The walls of the house were wood siding—cheap and thin. He put his ear to the wall and listened, hoping to hear Jemma crying or even panting. He just wanted a sign that she was alive.

He heard nothing but music. It sounded like some remade Hank Williams, not as good as the original.

He kept the rifle ready for a shot from the hip and slid down the wall to the back corner. He leaned over and looked.

The backyard was a rectangle, wide and short. There were several personal vehicles. Over to the south was a long stretch of animal cages, like a dog kennel. They were dark, and the bottom half was blocked off by a long baseboard, which he guessed was simply plywood they had nailed on. He saw no dogs and heard no barking. But there was a stench unlike anything he'd ever smelled before. It was horrible. It smelled like there were dogs in there, only none of them were alive.

Troughs lined the back of the kennel, and there were holes where dogs could stick their heads out and eat. The smell was so bad that he wouldn't have been surprised if there was old, rancid dog food still in the trough.

Widow jumped around the corner and stood in the backyard. He scanned the area—no sign of life. He moved to the back door, which he expected to be unlocked. Why lock it way out in the middle of nowhere?

The bad thing was that the back door had a screen door on it, and screen doors were noisy. They squeaked when they were opened. The best way to deal with them was quick, like a Band-Aid. But Widow did one step better. He skipped it and checked out the windows. He figured he could find an open one. On a nice, windy day like this, why not?

He skipped the first two and found one near the other corner. It was open. The room was an empty bedroom. There was a double bed, pushed to the wall. On the big wall in the room, he saw computers—not one, but several. There were monitors and all kinds of computer equipment.

The monitors were all on, and he could see empty fields and portions of the Rio Grande. They were showing feeds from cameras that must've been placed miles away on the borders.

Looked like hard-to-reach areas, like those might've been areas the Border Patrol wasn't monitoring, because to cross them was a death wish. Widow imagined that if the stories of illegal immigration were true, these were the types of places where aliens crossed —the unexpected areas and, therefore, the least guarded by US Border Agents.

Leon had said that these guys turned no one over. Ever. Which made Widow think they did something else with them. Something worse. And he thought about the kennel. They had no dogs. He looked back at the kennel. And then he heard a noise. It came from off in the distance. It was gunfire. He heard AR-15s. Unmistakable. Jake barked. And he heard the undeniable sound of a Magnum blast from the shotgun—return fire from Leon. He smiled, but he couldn't leave her out there alone for long.

He pulled out the phone and called her. It rang and rang, and she answered.

"Not a good time!"

"Where are you?"

"I'm at the Tahoe."

"Get in and drive away. Keep going. I'll call you when I have her."

He expected Leon to argue back, to give him some crap that she couldn't leave him behind, but she didn't. She just said, "I'm starting it now! Call me back!"

He heard the engine start, and the line went dead.

He put the phone away and jerked out the Ka-Bar, cut through the screen in the window, and jumped in. Widow kept the rifle down at his hip. He searched the room, checked under the covers, under the bed, inside the closet, but there was no sign of Jemma.

He didn't want to call out to her because he wasn't sure if there were any other guys in the house or not. Cameron had only counted ten, but that didn't mean there were only ten. So far, he had seen eleven. Modern drones weren't perfect, and neither were drone operators.

Widow clasped his hand tight around the knob to the door and jerked it open. He panned down the hall. No one was there. There was one other door to his right and a living room at the end of the hall. He opened the other door and found a bathroom with a stand-up shower, a cracked white sink, and a steamed-up mirror. There was still steam in the air. Someone had just gotten out of the shower.

Widow looked at the carpet in the hallway. Wet footprints peppered the floor down the hall. Someone might've been just getting out when he heard the gunshots.

Widow stepped into the bathroom and flushed the toilet. It was loud. He stepped back into the bedroom, leaned the rifle down by the door, pulled out the Ka-Bar again, and waited.

Two seconds later, a barefoot man wrapped in a towel came running down the hall with an M9 in his hand and nothing else. There were twelve guys, not ten.

The guy faced the bathroom, gun out.

Widow reached out, grabbed a tuft of the guy's hair, and jerked his head back. He spun him around and swatted the gun out of his hand. It clattered off the doorjamb.

Widow shoved the guy into the wall and pressed the Ka-Bar against his neck, forcing him to look at the ceiling unless he wanted his throat cut.

"Where's the girl?"

"What? I... I don't know, man."

Widow looked at the guy's eyes, which were looking down at him because his face pointed to the ceiling. Widow recognized him. It was the guy who had shot him with the rubber bullet.

"Last chance. Where?"

"I told ya. I don't know."

"She here?"

"She was. She was with that guy. With the voice. I swear I don't know where she is now. I was asleep, and then I took a shower."

Widow pulled the knife back away from his throat, let the guy lower his head. He locked eyes with him. Widow said, "Look at the knife."

The guy looked confused for a long, long moment and then moved his eyes slowly down to the knife and the blade. It was still wet with blood. The guy squirmed.

Widow clamped his hand over the guy's mouth and said, "You lie."

He stabbed the blade into the side of the guy's neck, jerked it around. Blood sprayed out and across the wall. But the guy didn't die, not as fast as he should've. He tried to push away from Widow but couldn't. Widow stared into his eyes and watched his life slip away. He let go of the guy. His body went limp and inert, slid down the wall, and he was dead by the time he hit the carpet.

Widow stepped out into the hall and approached the living room. Then he stopped, realizing the shooting had stopped. He heard the leader yelling outside.

Widow slipped into the living room. A small kitchen was off to his left. He saw appliances, a cheap dining room table, and four chairs. On the table was another laptop, open. The screen showed a muted news report about one of the presidential candidates, the one pushing for the wall, Widow guessed. He really wasn't sure which was which, because he didn't even know who was running. The guy on the screen looked familiar. Could've been the other guy. He wasn't sure. And didn't care.

He turned and looked around the room. There was no sign of Jemma.

Two more AR-15s rested on a coffee table near a long leather sofa, which might've meant that Glock and the leader had run out

the door without them. Which might've meant that they were
unarmed or only had sidearms.

The front door was ajar, and Widow heard Glock's inhuman
voice. And then the door flung open.

Widow raised the rifle. Fast. He planted his feet, pressed the
stock into his right shoulder, took aim.

Glock and the leader of the Jericho Men walked in, and the looks
on their faces were the best part of Widow's day.

John Glock held a Sig Sauer in his hand, like the one the dead
woman had. The leader of the Jericho Men held a cell phone up
to his ear and the laptop that controlled the drone in his other
hand.

Widow said, "Hang up."

The leader of the Jericho Men didn't say another word into the
phone. He just hung it up and dropped his hand down by his
side.

Widow backed up and said, "Come in."

The two men stepped in through the door—first Glock, and then
the leader of the Jericho Men. They stopped three feet from the
doorway.

Glock spoke, but Widow said, "Shut up!" And he levered the
action, which spat out a live round, but he did it more for effect
than anything else. The only thing better than the sound of a
rifle's lever-action was the cocking of a shotgun. That *Crunch!
Crunch!* sound would've been something special, but he was satis-
fied with the Model 73.

He said, "Toss the gun. Slow!"

Both men tried to do as they were told, but Widow said, "Just
Glock."

The leader left his in his pocket.

Glock tossed the Sig on the sofa. Widow kept his eyes locked with Glock.

The leader of the Jericho Men asked, "Now me?"

Widow turned to him. "You the leader here?"

The guy said, "He's the boss."

"But you're the leader of this militia?"

The guy nodded.

"What's your purpose?"

"What?"

"What do you guys do here?"

The guy swallowed and said, "Border security."

"That's what the United States Border Patrol is for."

"Yeah, but they're no good at it. Them spics come across the border all the time."

Widow asked, "So you capture them and turn them over?"

The leader said nothing, but his eyes instinctively looked over Widow's shoulder, toward the rotten-smelling kennel. Widow imagined they caught illegals and caged them in the dog kennel. What they did after that, he could only imagine.

"What do you do with them?" he repeated.

"They breaking the law."

"Do you kill them?"

The guy repeated, "They breaking the law."

Widow shot him through the gut. The leader went flying backward, landing halfway through the doorway. He sprawled out across a doormat that read "Welcome." Which Widow thought was ironic.

He racked the lever again, twisting and pointing it at Glock in case he got any ideas.

Glock said nothing. He didn't move. He didn't even flinch.

Widow kept the leader in his view, but circled to the left, slowly. He said, "Where is she?"

"If I tell you that, you'll kill me."

"Where is she? I won't ask again."

"How do I know you won't kill me?"

"Is she alive?"

Glock said nothing for a long moment but stared in Widow's face. He said, "She is."

Widow lowered his gun. He asked, "Is she here?"

"Put the gun down, and I'll tell you."

Widow thought for a moment and asked, "What? You want me to put my weapon down, and we go at it like a couple of adversaries? Like in the movies?"

Glock said, "Yeah. You want to know where she is, then you can beat it out of me. Or try."

Widow cocked his head and looked over Glock's shoulder. The leader had his sidearm out, but he had lost too much blood to lift it. Widow saw him lift the gun and then drop it. His shirt was covered in blood. His jeans were covered in blood. He lay in a lake of black blood. Widow felt sorry for him because he knew a gut shot was a painful way to die, and really, Glock was the one who deserved it most.

"Want us to duke it out? The winner gets to live?"

"Yes," Glock said in his lizard voice.

Widow thought about it. There was something satisfying about the thought of tossing the rifle and pulling out the Ka-Bar knife and jamming it into Glock's neck, opposite side from his first stab wound. That thought lingered for a long moment.

Glock said, "Let's do it."

Widow said, "Tell me one thing first."

"What?"

"What about Lucy? The wife? She alive?"

"She's alive, but not for long. I got a guy there. Of course, killing her won't do much, anyway. It's really a mercy thing. I saw her. She's not gonna live much longer."

"When's your guy gonna act?"

"What? You want to save her too?"

Widow stayed quiet.

"Tell ya what. You win. Then you can go save her too."

Widow raised the gun, stock in his shoulder, eyes down the sight, and fired. The muzzle flashed, and the gunshot boomed through the house.

The bullet hit Widow's target and came out on the other side. The target was Glock's neck, which blew apart—completely. Red mist erupted, and heavy red blood shot out the back and painted the sofa and wall and the ceiling. It went in all directions. It splattered Widow's face. He had to blink his eyes to clear the blood out of his vision.

Glock's head didn't come off from the removal of his neck, not completely. It hung by a thread. He was dumped over on the floor.

Widow said, "I win."

There were still five guys left out there, and Jemma was out there somewhere as well.

Widow went to the window and looked out front. He saw two of the guys running back to the porch. They had heard the gunshots, but hadn't seen their boss's dead body yet.

Widow stepped back, muzzle two inches from the glass, and aimed. He shot the closest one first. Glass shattered and sprayed toward his face and chest. The bullet hit the guy right in the face, which Widow knew was dead-on because he saw that red mist again. Quickly, he racked the lever and aimed at the other guy, who he had thought he wouldn't have time for, but the guy stopped right in his tracks and stared at his dead friend.

Widow stepped right, took aim, held his breath, and squeezed the trigger. The bullet rocketed out and hit the guy square in the chest. Widow levered the action again and walked out. He stepped over the leader, who was deader than anything. Widow held the Model 73 down by his side. He had hit the second guy in the chest, but he was still alive. The guy was panting like he was trying to breathe, trying to scream.

Widow's eyes automatically went to the horizon toward the other three guys and Leon. He scanned the heavy equipment, looked in between the bulldozers, the Caterpillars, the dead cement trucks, and the heavy pipes. He heard no shots and saw no one coming.

He stopped walking just past the last guy, who wore a Kevlar vest and was desperately trying to take it off. Widow kicked away the guy's AR-15 and squatted down. He jerked an M9 out of the guy's hip holster and tossed it far away. Widow set the rifle stock down in the dirt and pointed the muzzle to the sky. He said, "Here, let me help."

He reached down and helped him pull off the vest.

He recognized the guy as the one who had shot him with the tranquilizer dart that put him to sleep.

The guy tried to breathe.

"Just breathe. You're okay," Widow said. He looked in the direction from which he expected the last three guys to come running, but no one came.

The guy tried to speak but still had not caught his breath.

Widow took out the Ka-Bar and stabbed him in the chest, in his right breast, puncturing the lung.

The guy got his breath back fast because he screamed.

"Relax. You're still alive."

The guy whimpered.

"You want to live, right?"

The guy nodded.

"What's your name?"

"Pat."

"Okay, Pat. You tranqed me last night, right?"

"No, sir. Not me."

Widow twisted the knife, but only slightly. Pat screamed again.

"Don't lie to me, Pat."

"Sorry. Sorry. Yeah, it was me."

"Good. Tell me you tranqed that little girl too. Tell me she's not dead." Widow squeezed his hand tight on the Ka-Bar's handle, letting Pat feel it. "Tell me she's not making any noise right now because she's heavily sedated."

"She's not! I swear! I shot her with a dart. She's alive."

"That's good, Pat. That's real good." Widow peered up and scanned the horizon again. Still, no one running toward him.

"Is she in the attic?"

"No. No, man. There's no attic."

"What about one of these machines? She inside one of those?"

"No, man."

"Pat, I'm thinking you don't understand this game."

"Huh?"

"Where is she?"

Pat shivered, and Widow was afraid he was going to go into shock, which wouldn't have been good. He calmed his voice and asked again, "Where is she?"

"She's out back. In the cages."

Widow said, "The dog kennel?"

"Yeah. The cages."

Widow thought about killing the guy, but he didn't. He jerked the knife out, and Pat screamed again.

"Put pressure on it," Widow said, grabbing his hand and putting it over the wound. Then he grabbed him by the collar and dragged him up to the porch and leaned him against the steps.

"Pat?"

Pat's eyes shot up at Widow.

"If I see you touch a gun, I'll kill you."

Pat nodded violently.

Widow dragged the leader out of the doorway and tossed the leader's gun into the living room. He locked the bottom lock and slammed the door shut, testing the knob. He walked over to the other dead guy, took both AR-15s and sidearms and ejected the magazines and the chambered bullets, stuffed them into his pockets, and left Pat there. He loaded the extra rounds into the 73 and headed to the kennels.

* * *

WIDOW WALKED along the other side of the house toward the kennels. He ran when he reached the backyard.

He reached the dog kennels and saw what he already feared. The kennels weren't for keeping dogs. They were for keeping humans.

He walked the length of them, searching for any sign of Jemma. Instead, he saw dried bloodstains on the fence wire. As he got near, he gagged when he saw fingernails stuck into the baseboard and human feces covered in flies. Someone had been there recently. He saw rusted handcuffs dangling from the fence wire. There were dozens of them. He saw piles of old, dirty clothes and used shoes.

The trough was full of slop. There were flies circling it—thousands of them.

He called out, "Jemma? Jemma?"

No answer. He followed the kennel to the end and saw nothing. He backtracked in case he had missed something. Then he saw movement. One of the piles of clothes shifted slightly. He ran over to it and saw it move again.

"Jemma?"

No answer.

He used the Ka-Bar to saw through the fence, but it was taking too long. He stood back and took the rifle, angled his hands, aimed upward, and fired into the underside of the kennel's roof in the next pen. The wood was old and dried out, and it exploded and splintered. He racked the action again and fired once more. More wood splintered. He racked and fired, and racked and fired, until he was out of bullets. A giant hole opened up in the roof, and he took the rifle, reversed it, and slammed the stock into the remaining pieces of the roof until it was a big enough hole. He dropped the rifle and grabbed the remains of the roof with both hands. He jerked and pulled at the opening, and after a long minute, the roof ripped off the nails. His hands were raw and full of splinters.

He reached in and picked up the heap of clothes and found a little body inside. It was Jemma. She was alive, like the guy had said, and was fast asleep.

Widow lifted her and carried her away from the kennels and the smell. He took her past a long area of dirt and a bulldozer that

~~looked like it had been recently used to dig up the ground. He~~
stopped and looked at the bulldozer and then back at the dirt.
And a horrifying thought occurred to him. A thought that didn't
come from his imagination, but from years of being on the job.
He'd bet anything that he was standing on top of a large mass
grave. He'd bet they used the bulldozer to dig it up, dump bodies
inside, and then cover them up.

Widow winced at the thought. His first instinct was to get Jemma
far away from there.

He kept walking and carried her over to a clearing far beyond the
heavy equipment and the vehicles and the dead bodies and the
house. He squatted down in the dirt and laid her across his lap,
propping her head up against his chest. She was breathing heavily
and, he hoped, was dreaming peacefully.

28

WIDOW CALLED LEON.

Her phone rang only once. She picked up and said, "Widow, where are you?"

"I'm at a clearing on the other side of the equipment. Are you okay? Where're the other guys?"

"They shot at me."

"Yeah, I heard."

"I ran back to the truck. I jumped in and hit the sirens. They ran as soon as they saw the truck. It must've been because they recognized the Border Patrol symbols."

"I'm sure. They probably heard the gunshots back here and figured you were a part of a bigger operation. They ran."

Leon said, "Yeah. Probably."

"Where'd they go?"

"They piled into a truck and took off. I started to chase after them, but I stopped because I figured you might need the help. This is a rescue after all, and not about arrests. But I got their plates. I can visit them later."

"~~You can call them in. Get highway~~ patrol out on them. I got the girl."

"That's great news! Is everything done there?" she asked, but in a way that suggested she wasn't sure how to ask if it was all clear.

Widow said, "We're fine here, but I'm not sure you should come in."

"Why not?"

"You've done nothing wrong. There's no evidence you were even here. No fingerprints. No tire tracks. I don't think you should come to the scene."

"You going to carry the little girl out of there? Want me to pick you up?"

"No. We got a ride. You've done great."

"I don't understand. You're ditching me?"

"Sorry, Leon. There's more to be done. And you can't know about it. You've already put yourself on the line for me."

She stayed quiet.

Widow said, "I need you to do me one favor."

"What?"

"Stay out there. Radio in those plates. Get those other guys picked up. Wait twenty minutes and call in the location to your boss. Get the agents out here. Bring them in and tell them to look at the dog kennel in the backyard."

"Why? What's there?"

"Just do it. Tell them to dig up the land around it. Tell them to look near a bulldozer parked back there."

She was silent for a moment. She asked, "Widow, what are we going to find?"

"My suspicion is that you'll find graves."

"Graves?"

"Yeah. These Jericho Men were up to no good."

"What about you? Don't you want to stay? We can take the heat off of you. Clear your name."

Widow said, "Also, one of them is wounded but still alive. He's in the front of the house. He's unarmed. He might still be alive when you get here."

She ignored him and repeated her question. "What about you?"

Widow said, "I'm not worried about my name. I'm sure that will get sorted out. I'm not much for sticking around. For paperwork and interviews and more paperwork. Not my style."

"What about the girl?"

"I'm going to bring her back to her mother."

"How? You gonna commandeer one of their vehicles?"

Widow paused, listened hard. He looked toward the skyline to the northeast. He waited a moment and then heard a distant sound.

"Widow?" Leon asked.

"Wait."

He waited another long moment, and then he saw it, a gray dot on the horizon, flying low, flying fast. It was a Bell 206 helicopter painted gray with US Navy symbols and a serial number on it. The chopper yawed, and the blades thrashed. It was a Navy chopper, but it had flown out of Laughlin Air Force Base. Apparently, it was on loan or had to make a special landing there for a reason Widow didn't know about. Perhaps it had needed mechanical work, which Widow didn't want to think about. Whatever. It flew now.

He had walked away from Leon earlier and asked Cameron to work her magic and send an airlift. He needed to get out of there fast. And Cameron had delivered.

Leon said, "Is that for you?"

"Yep. That's my ride. Sorry, I can't stay."

Leon said, "You didn't trust me to tell me earlier?"

"I didn't want to put you in a position that could compromise your career."

"You could've trusted me. I brought you here."

"You're right. I'm sorry. I'll make it up to you."

"How? When?"

"Someday."

There was silence between them, and the Bell 206 flew in closer. It stopped and hovered above the clearing near Widow. It came down for a landing. The rotor wash swooped up dirt and grime. Widow protected Jemma's face from it as best he could. The blades' *Whoop! Whoop!* sound came down louder and louder.

Widow said, "Look, I can't hear ya. I gotta go."

Leon said, "Good luck, Widow."

Widow smiled and hung up the phone. The chopper had a single pilot who wore a flight suit and had the sun visor from his helmet down over his eyes. He waved at Widow, who nodded back.

Widow walked around the chopper to the side door. He cradled Jemma with one arm and reached out and slid the door open. He stepped up onto the landing skids and stepped into the cabin. He set Jemma down on a rear bench and buckled her in. Her head fell to the side onto her shoulder. She was out cold.

Widow turned to the pilot, who handed him a headset. Widow put it on, and the pilot asked, "Where to, sir?"

"Take us to the hospital in El Paso."

The pilot nodded and said, "Strap yourself in."

Widow nodded and said, "We need to get there in a hurry."

"I'll do the best I can, sir."

All that sir stuff made Widow think Cameron had told the pilot he was a special officer in the US Navy, which wasn't completely untrue. He had once been an officer, technically.

Widow turned to the open door and looked over the landscape one last time. It looked like a graveyard for dinosaurs. The heavy equipment represented most of the well-known types. They looked like lifeless monsters.

Widow looked in Leon's direction and saw her sitting on the hood of the Tahoe. He slammed the door shut, and the chopper tilted and turned back north.

29

THE OLDER GUY from Kill Team A didn't know Glock was dead. He sat in the break room for hospital employees. It amazed him how easy it was to stay undetected with stolen hospital scrubs and a tray with half-eaten food on it.

He had stolen the scrubs out of the locker of an orderly he saw finish his shift. He had followed the guy down to his locker and waited for him to shower and leave. Once the guy left, breaking his combination lock with no one noticing was easy enough. A stolen screwdriver from maintenance used as a chisel and the butt of his Glock 17 as a hammer worked like a charm. The lock broke, and the scrubs were his for the taking, although he wished that the guy kept a clean set in his locker instead of tossing his old ones in there.

The older guy from Kill Team A had been in the hospital for twenty-four hours, but he wasn't tired, not at all. He had gotten plenty of sleep. Being a retired police officer had given him the ability to sleep anywhere. He had learned to sleep on stakeouts and on sentry duty when no one was looking. For him, sleeping wasn't a problem. He had seen a lot of cops who had a real problem sleeping on the job—not him. For him, it was never a problem. And actually, sleeping on the job wasn't the problem for other cops either. The problem was not waking up when they needed to. But he had a trick for that.

He had spent the night propped up in the waiting room, feet up on another chair, eyes shut. His trick was that he had his earbuds in, and the other end jacked into his phone. He listened to soft white noises to help him sleep, using an app he had downloaded. It played sounds of the ocean, which was okay with him, but not his favorite. He really liked rainforest showers. There was something about a rainstorm over a jungle that really soothed him.

He was Hispanic by birth and was well aware of the Principal's hatred of his people. He didn't care. There was no need to get one's feathers all ruffled over ideologies. Especially when one of them was a multimillionaire and the other one was not. He knew the Principal was John Sheridan. They all knew. Glock had told them.

Sheridan considered himself the brains of the operation, but he was really just the financier, the money. He was the originator. Sheridan wasn't a stupid man, and he was far from a saint. Back when the older man had first met Glock and worked with him, they were running drugs across the Mexico-Texas border a decade ago. And back then, the older man knew of Sheridan.

Sheridan worked for the DEA, but not in the tough, undercover sense that one normally thinks from hearing the acronym DEA. Sheridan was a pencil pusher. He was in charge of a small unit. How he had gotten that job didn't require police work to find out. He had gotten it from his daddy's connections. The Sheridan family tree had been full of well-connected scam artists.

Sheridan's unit did good work and got themselves noticed. Sheridan had taken all the credit, and then his career in politics had taken off.

Of course, some of the major busts his unit had gotten were from Glock tossing him a bone here and there.

Just then, the old man's trick worked because his headset rang with his phone. He answered it. "Yeah," he said.

"It's me," Sheridan said. Not Glock, which was very unusual.

"What's up?"

"Have you heard from Glock?"

The old man stopped and checked his phone in case he had slept through it ringing. No missed calls. He said, "No."

"He's not answering his phone."

"Maybe he's busy."

"No. No. He always answers. Especially now. We got too much riding to let the Hood situation go on."

"What do you want me to do?"

Sheridan was quiet for a long, long beat, and then he said, "I'm about to have dinner with my family. We've got company. Some people from our candidate's campaign are here. You know what that means."

"They want to talk with you about building the wall."

"Shut up! Don't say that over the phone. Just say yes."

"Relax. You're paranoid. No one is listening."

Sheridan didn't respond to that. He just said, "Give Glock thirty more minutes. Call him."

"What if he don't answer?"

Sheridan paused. The old guy could hear a little girl in the background calling him Dad and asking him to play with her.

Sheridan said, "If he doesn't answer, take care of it. Call me back after."

The phone went dead, and Sheridan was gone, to have dinner with his family, which turned the old man's stomach even though he was a killer. The image of this Texas senator acting squeaky clean in the eyes of the public and his family but really being one of the biggest mobsters in South Texas still affected the old guy. It made him second-guess who was the brains. Maybe it was Sheridan after all.

Either way, he shrugged. The guy was paying him to kill a dying woman. And that's what he'd do, but not yet. He still had thirty minutes. He looked up at a wall clock and then switched his ambient music back on. He set the phone's alarm, then put his head down on the table next to his tray and shut his eyes.

30

THE LATE AFTERNOON sun lit the sky with its earliest shades of red, which reminded Widow of the red mist he had seen from shooting Glock. He couldn't lie to himself that he hadn't enjoyed seeing it.

Widow looked down at Jemma. She was buckled in tight to his right. She had her head on his arm. Her hair rested out across his forearm. She was stirring. She had snored the entire chopper ride.

Her eyes moved, squinted, and her arms stretched out.

"Take your time," Widow said.

She opened her eyes and seemed disoriented at first. She looked up at him and asked, "Where are we?"

But he could barely hear her. He took the headset off and leaned in. He raised his voice and said, "We're in the sky. Over Texas. Want to see?"

Her eyes opened wide, and she looked around. She saw the rear cabin of the Bell 206. She was very surprised. Widow wondered how much she knew. Did she see them beat her father to death? He hoped not. He hoped she was shot with a tranquilizer dart right after him, which turned out to be the case because she looked very confused.

She asked, "Where's my dad?"

Widow's hope exploded into disappointment, fast. He didn't want to be the one to answer that question for her. He looked out the window and then looked back. He said, "Have you ever been in a military helicopter before?"

She shook her head.

"This is a Navy chopper."

She was quiet.

He said, "Hey, you wanna ride in the cockpit?"

"Cockpit?"

"Yeah. It's up front. By the pilot. He might let you fly it."

She perked up and seemed to forget about her dad, at least for the moment. "Okay," she said.

"Okay. Let me check with the pilot. I got good news for you."

"What?"

"Guess where we're headed?"

"Where?"

"We're going to see your mom," he said. Then a thought struck him and made him regret saying it. What if it was too late? What if she was dead? He couldn't bring himself to tell her that her father was dead, plus her grandmother, and now he might have to tell her she lost her mother too.

He felt about as bad as he ever had felt for someone. Jemma would have to be a tough little girl to endure the news that she had lost three family members all in one night. He shook those thoughts off. No need worrying about the unknown. Right now, he saw a huge smile on her face, and that was good enough.

He put his headset back on and asked the pilot.

"That's not permitted, sir," the pilot said.

"None of this is permitted," Widow said.

"That's true. But I don't know."

"Just do it. You can blame me."

The pilot said nothing back.

Widow took off his headset and unbuckled his harness and Jemma's. He led her to the cockpit. She shook and stumbled the whole way, partially from the conditions of the flight and partially from side effects of the sedative they had drugged her with.

Widow helped her to the front, past the pilot, and into the copilot seat.

The pilot said, "Hey there, miss."

Widow put a headset on her so she could hear.

The pilot said, "So you're going to help me. Be my copilot. My name is Mr. Michelle."

Jemma laughed and said, "You got a girl's name?"

"No, no. It's my last name. I'm a Navy pilot. We call each other by our surnames."

She looked confused and asked, "Surnames?"

Widow said, "It's your last name. But why not give you a code name?"

The pilot said, "Yeah. A code name. We use those too."

She asked the pilot, "What's your code name?"

"Mine's Maverick, like *Top Gun*."

She looked at him funny.

"You know. The movie."

She shrugged.

Widow said, "She's only six. She doesn't know that crap."

The pilot nodded, reached out, and flipped a couple of switches in a row. He asked, "What do we call you?"

She said, "Call me, Pip. That's my code name."

Widow stayed quiet and looked out through the windshield. They were over El Paso.

Jemma asked, "What's your code name?"

Widow said, "Call me Black Widow."

"What's that?"

"It's a poisonous spider."

"But aren't those bad?"

"Only if you mess with them. If you leave them alone, then they'll leave you alone."

Jemma was all strapped in to her harness in the front next to the pilot. She looked out at the city below and looked like she was calculating or processing this new information. She was a very inquisitive girl; Widow knew that once she'd gotten through all of this tragedy, eventually she'd grow up to be something special.

She said, "Black Widow, thanks for taking me to my mommy."

Widow stayed quiet, just politely smiled. He felt the way he imagined Babe Ruth must've felt when he was asked by a dying little boy to hit a grand slam for him.

The pilot said, "Better sit back. We're almost there."

Widow nodded and returned to his seat, strapped back in, and waited.

31

HOSPITAL SECURITY WAS ALREADY on the roof when the Bell 206 descended. Two security guards, one in uniform and one in a uniform that included a brown windbreaker with no logo on the front, but a simple word printed on the back in yellow block letters—SECURITY.

The chopper's rotor wash blew and kicked up wind and Texas dust from the roof as it went in for a landing.

Widow hadn't thought about it, but he was rather grateful they didn't already have a chopper parked on the roof, which was often the case whenever it wasn't in use.

The landing skids touched down and bounced slightly and returned to touch the concrete.

Widow faced away from the pilot and from Jemma and pulled the Glock 17 out of his jeans, racked the slide, and chambered a round. He didn't have to click the safety to fire because the Glock 17 had no external safety. Its safety action was internal. Therefore, it was ready to use right out of his pocket. He slid it into the front of his jeans, which wasn't the most inconspicuous place for it, but it made it harder for someone to disarm him. He didn't know what the last guy posted here to kill Lucy looked like.

Widow figured the last guy didn't know what he looked like, either.

Widow had already lost two innocent members of Lucy's family. He wouldn't lose any more.

The pilot pulled up his visor, exposed his face, and slowed the propeller blades. After a long moment, the noise from the engine settled, and he said, "I was told you might need a ride back. So I can wait here."

Widow said, "Yes. Stay here and keep watch over her. I'll be back."

The pilot looked a little reluctant, but in the end, he shrugged it off. Widow figured the guy would much rather be doing this than flying some admiral to his golf game or whatever these guys did during peacetime.

The pilot said, "Sure thing. She'll be fine here."

Jemma said, "I want my mommy!"

Widow said, "And you will see her soon. I need you to stay here for a moment. She doesn't know you are coming."

"It's a surprise?"

"Yeah. Like a surprise," Widow said, hoping that he wasn't lying. He turned and jerked open the side door and jumped out.

Security was standing twenty feet from the chopper.

The front guy without the windbreaker said, "You can't land here. What's going on?"

"I'm with NCIS. We've got a situation at your hospital."

"NCIS?" the guard asked. Many people didn't know what NCIS was. In fact, if it wasn't for a long-running TV show, almost no civilian would know what NCIS was.

Widow said, "Navy police. We're like Homeland Security."

That last part made the guy light up. He looked at the word "Navy" written on the side of the chopper and needed no more proof than that. He asked, "Are you like a cop?"

"Special agent."

"What's going on?"

"Sorry we didn't radio you. We're here to apprehend a suspect. I can't tell you more than that."

The security guard asked, "Do you have jurisdiction here?"

"NCIS isn't a military agency. We have jurisdiction. And I've got no more time to explain."

"What do you need?"

"I need to know the floor and room number for a patient."

The guy said, "What's the name?"

"Lucy Hood. She's a cancer patient. She'll be somewhere critical. She's on her last leg."

"Okay. Let's go. All the cancer patients are on seven."

Widow followed the guards to a metal door that led to a staircase. They wound down a couple of flights of stairs to an elevator. The guard pressed the call button, and they waited.

He got on his radio and asked another guard to radio back with the room number for Lucy.

The elevator door opened, and they got on and pressed seven. The ride was short because the building was only twelve stories high. They rode the elevator down. The bell dinged, and the guard on the other end of the radio came back and gave Lucy's room number.

They entered a large lobby area with a nurse's station out front, like a toll booth to enter the cancer ward. The walls were a yellow-white. There was a thick carpet, and red cushioned chairs welded together, and a sofa. A wide-screen television was implanted into the wall frame—custom made.

Generic potted plants and flowers were scattered along the walls and corners and next to a square pillar. The floor was well lit from bright bulbs under a tiled ceiling. Widow looked at the wall clock. It was nearing sundown, and it was two minutes before the end of the hour. And less than two minutes before the hour meant Lucy might be out of time. He'd killed John Glock. There was no one left to give orders except for the senator. In Widow's experience, whenever someone gave a tactical kill order, it was on the hour or the half-hour mark. No one ever ordered a kill at ten minutes till or five minutes after. People everywhere started work at the hour mark. Same went for hit men. They killed at the hour mark. But less than two minutes to go wasn't encouraging because many people acted early. When someone's a target, what was the difference between two minutes before and two after? It was all around the same time.

Widow looked at the faces in the waiting room. He saw an older couple sobbing. A doctor stood over them. He'd probably just given them some bad news. He saw a pair of small children, a boy and a girl—a brother and sister. They were arguing over their mom's purse. Not loud, just the way kids do. She was ignoring them and reading a magazine.

There was a man seated in the corner. Widow stared at him. It wasn't him. No way. There was a sadness on the guy's face that couldn't be faked. He was about to lose someone close to him as well. No doubt.

The security guard without the windbreaker asked, "What now?"

"How many exits are there from this floor?"

"There're the stairs and this elevator."

The guard with the windbreaker spoke for the first time. He said, "There's the service elevator too."

Service elevator.

Widow said, "I need one of you to stand by the stairs and one to stay with this elevator. Get another guard to stay at the exits downstairs. No one leaves. Not yet."

"Should we call the police?"

"They've been notified," Widow lied.

The guard in the windbreaker took off to the stairs, and the other stayed behind. He told Widow the room number again. Widow nodded, even though he had remembered it.

He started off down the hall, following the signs to that room number. The nurse at the station didn't stop him. The security guard waved at her.

Widow ran through a pair of double doors, and onto a tiled floor that had been recently mopped. It was dry, but not all the way. He slid running down it and stopped at another corner. He passed busy staff members as he ran. Doctors talked to nurses, and nurses made their rounds.

He saw orderlies pushing carts and moving patients and making beds.

He came to another turn that was near a public restroom with a water fountain out front. Widow turned and stopped in front of Lucy's room.

He pushed the heavy green door open and busted in. The door's hydraulics stopped it from slamming, and it closed sluggishly behind him, making a slow swoosh sound.

The lights in the room were dim, but they were on. The bathroom door was wide open. Widow gazed around the room, his hand on the hilt of the Glock. The entire room was empty.

32

WIDOW LISTENED hard to the silence in Lucy's room. There was the low hum and the beeps from a machine near the bed. He saw that there was a heart rate monitor, but it was off.

The bed was disheveled. The comforter was on the floor. The hospital bed's arm rail was down. And Lucy's IV was detached and leaking fluid on the floor. But she was gone.

Next to the bed on a nightstand was a framed photo of Jemma. So Widow knew he had the right room.

He turned and walked out of the room. He breathed in and breathed out. Fury and fear filled him at the same time. He feared he was too late. The fury was in case he wasn't.

He turned left, looked back the way he came. He turned right, stared down a long corridor. There was a corner at the end and a right-hand turn that disappeared.

Where did she go?

A door opened in front of him, and a nurse in blue scrubs backed out.

Widow said, "Excuse me."

She turned and asked, "Can I help you?"

"Where's Lucy Hood?"

The nurse was a short twenty-something with thick red hair piled up in a bun. She said, "She should be in her bed there."

The nurse pointed to the room that Widow had just come from.

"She's not."

"That can't be!" the nurse said. She pushed past him and looked for herself. She came back out and said, "She's gone."

"I know," Widow said.

He didn't know what the killer looked like, but he knew what Lucy looked like. He had seen that photo of her. He took away her healthy, happy demeanor and tried to picture a sicklier version of the same woman. Hispanic. Hair had possibly fallen out. And she'd be very thin.

She hadn't passed him in the halls, not so far. He was certain of it.

He asked, "What's that way?" He pointed straight ahead at the turn.

"That way's a dead end."

"Where does it lead?"

"I told you it's a dead end."

"Listen, I'm a cop, and this is a matter of life or death. Now, where?"

"It leads to a closed-off section of this floor. We've been under renovations there."

Widow looked back at the corner and asked, "Is anyone down there?"

"Not after that corner. It's closed. I told you."

Widow said nothing and ran to the corner. He heard the nurse call behind him. She said, "What should I do?"

He didn't care.

* * *

AROUND THE CORNER, Widow stared down a long, dark hallway. There was a makeshift plastic covering that was hung as a deterrent. It flapped open and closed, and Widow felt a draft. The lights stopped about ten feet in front of the flap. There were no warning signs or "Keep Out" signs and no tape blocking the entrance—just the plastic flap.

Widow pulled out the Glock 17, shoved his finger into the trigger housing, pressed firmly on the trigger because the Glock had the internal safety system, which meant that the trigger had to be squeezed all the way down in order to fire. He didn't want even the tiniest fraction of a second stopping him from putting a bullet in the last guy.

He kept the muzzle straight forward, none of that pointing at the floor crap. He wasn't worried about safety. He wanted to save Lucy. He was in a shoot-first mood.

He moved to the left side of the wall because that was where the windows were. There were no doors on that side for him to worry about. It was the edge of the building.

Widow moved slowly through the flap. He had no light but the city lights from outside. A neon sign flashed somewhere nearby because a red light blinked from the farthest corner of the hall. It was every two seconds. Flash. Dark. Flash. Dark.

Several window frames were missing glass, and the wind blew in hard. Long sheets of plastic were draped down the walls and across the floor. Some rooms were missing doors. The others were wide open, and none of them had knobs.

The same square pillars were on the left side of the hall. Here, only three sides were exposed. The other side was inside the wall. There was a ladder left behind by the construction crew. It stood in the far center of the hallway. Loose wires hung from the ceiling. He saw a red-painted sprinkler system. Steel spigots protruded downward like stalactites.

Widow looked down at the floor. The plastic was mostly smooth but bumpy in certain places. The thing he noticed most, the part that jumped out at his cop brain, was the trail of grooves that ran from the tile onto the plastic. It looked like tire tracks or wheels.

He stayed back against the wall and let his eyes follow the tracks. They led down the hall, turned into the last room on the right. No door.

The trail was promising and probably legitimate, but he wasn't a complete idiot. If he had noticed them, it was likely that they had been placed there for him to notice, to follow. Maybe, or maybe not. It depended on how good this last guy was. His friends hadn't proven to be very good. At least not the man and woman back in Uvalde.

Widow walked toward the first room, keeping one eye on the last doorway. He stopped and jumped in, ready to fire. No one was there, which was what he had expected. He wasn't sure what room the last guy was in, but he was sure it wasn't the first. He would've checked the first and then headed to the last, briefly checking the others. The last guy was in the room between the last and the first.

Widow examined it. Plastic covered furniture and an empty bathroom with a toilet and no sink.

Widow stood in front of the toilet. It had a lid, which was good for what he planned to do.

Widow was a tall guy, six feet four inches, but the ceilings in a hospital are high. This one was ten feet, at least. He couldn't reach it from the floor, but he could by standing on the toilet.

He lifted his foot and quietly stomped on the toilet seat, testing it to see if it would take his full weight, and it did. He stood up on it and looked at a single fire sprinkler spigot that came out of the ceiling. He reached up and grabbed the end of the spigot.

Most people think sprinklers are programmed to only go off in case of fire. Not true. In the movies, actors always light a cigarette lighter and press the flame up to the spigot. And the spigot goes off. This would work, but Widow didn't have a lighter. And he didn't need one.

Fire sprinklers go off if pressure is applied to them as well. He grabbed the end of the spigot and jerked it down as hard as he could. Water rumbled through the pipes and burst out of the spigots all across the seventh floor.

Widow had to listen carefully. He knew that he only had seconds after to hear what he needed to hear. And he did. He heard the last guy grunt and shuffle from out of the way of the spraying water. He was in the next room over—the second room, which had been his guess. And it was a good thing Widow heard him because five seconds later, the fire alarm sounded—loud and blaring.

Widow jumped down from the toilet, ignored the water spraying violently against his face. He was a trained Navy SEAL. For him, water was no big deal, but he doubted the last guy had the same advantage.

He leaped through the next doorway, Glock muzzle pointed out. Normally, he would've checked his corners fast, but there was no need. The last guy stood in the middle of the room. He was dressed in green scrubs, like an orderly. He rubbed his eyes, trying to see. The water was everywhere. It came down like a torrential downpour. It leaked across Widow's face in rivers, but he kept his eyes open and his gun steady.

"Drop the gun!" he shouted.

The last guy didn't even fight back. He dropped a gun, which splashed in a puddle of water so fast that Widow couldn't tell what kind of gun it was.

"Hands up! Don't move them!"

The last guy opened his hands and shoved them toward the ceiling. He was grunting and squinting. Water was clogging his eyes, and his nose too. He was spitting and trying to breathe.

Widow said, "You going to shoot her? Is that it? Sounds sloppy."

"No," the guy said. He said nothing else. No protests. No plead-ing. He was caught, and he knew it. That part, he got right. The next thing he said, he got dead wrong. He asked, "You FBI? Going to get a big promotion over this?"

Widow ignored the accusation and said, "How were you going to kill her?"

"I'm not speaking until I get my lawyer."

Widow entered the room. The water sprayed against him and bounced off.

The last guy opened one eye. The other was paralyzed from the water. Some people are no good at opening their eyes underwater. He watched Widow enter the room. The red neon light flashed and lit him up every two seconds. Widow looked more like some-thing out of a Stephen King novel than an FBI agent. As Widow got closer, the guy realized he might not be FBI.

And he asked, "FBI, right? Where's your backup?"

Widow shot him in the kneecap. The bone shield at the front of his knee shattered and splintered. The red mist that Widow had seen many, many times before exploded out more like a thick smoke because of the water.

The guy screamed in a watery agony as he half gurgled water. He stumbled over and grabbed at his missing kneecap.

Widow bunched up the guy's collar and lifted him back up, almost completely off the ground.

"I'm not a cop."

The last guy opened both eyes and stared into Widow's, only seeing them every two seconds and in red. He said nothing for a long moment, and then a flicker of recognition came across his face. He had never seen Widow before, but he knew who he was.

He said, "You? You're that guy. The one Glock went after."

Widow stared at him but didn't respond.

"You killed him." It wasn't a question as much as a realization.

The guy moved quickly, lifted his left hand, and came out of his pocket with a syringe. He stabbed it at Widow. Even though the guy was fast, he was badly injured and had already lost blood. Plus, he was having a tough time with the water beating down on his face.

Widow caught his hand by the wrist. He jerked it out, hard to the left, extended his arm all the way, then dropped and broke the arm over his knee.

The guy screamed again in pain that Widow hoped hurt worse than anything he'd ever felt before.

Widow reached down with his free hand and picked up the syringe before it got lost in the water. He held the needle in his hand with the Glock, pinched it between the grip and his thumb. He lifted the guy up and held him one-handed.

Widow asked, "Lucy is in the last room?"

The guy nodded, said, "She's in a wheelchair."

Something Widow already knew. He said, "I assume she's alive. The plunger on this syringe is still out."

The guy nodded.

Widow said, "Tell me about Sheridan."

"He's a senator. Texas."

"Go on."

The guy's working hand grabbed onto Widow's wrist. A natural reaction. His other hand dangled at the end of a broken arm.

"It's about building the wall. The border wall."

"I got that. Tell me more."

"Government contracts are worth more today than the drug business. Sheridan and Glock are trying to get the bulk of the contracts for the Texas border. The money is in the billions."

Silence fell between them, and the water from the sprinklers hammered down. The fire alarm blared and echoed through the halls.

"Where is he now?"

"He's at his home."

"Where is that exactly?"

"He's got a house in Lake Hills. It's the biggest one. It's on the lake. But you'll never get to him."

Widow said, "Everyone can be gotten to."

"Not Sheridan."

"Why do you say that?"

"He's a US senator. It's an election year. He's got Secret Service around him."

Widow stayed quiet.

The guy said, "I didn't want to kill her. It was going to be quick. She's not going to make it, anyway. I was doing her a favor."

Widow stayed quiet.

"Putting her out of her misery."

Widow didn't respond.

"It would've been quick."

Widow lowered the gun, stuffed it into his pocket, but kept the syringe in his hand. The guy sighed in relief at first, but then Widow plunged the needle into his neck and released whatever the hell was in it into the guy's bloodstream.

He said, "Let's see."

The guy let go of Widow's wrist and grabbed at the syringe. But it was too late. The entire contents were in his neck and veins now. He struggled and slapped at Widow's face. It did no good. He was dead before he could take another breath. Whatever was in the needle had been fast-acting.

Widow released the guy and let him fall. His head landed in the water. If he had still been alive, he would've eventually drowned if the water level had been high enough, which it wasn't, not yet. Widow knew little about sprinkler systems or how long they sprayed water. The one thing he'd learned from this experience was that the water in the systems was not clean water. It probably needed to be flushed in order to stay clean. He figured this one had not been flushed out in a long time because it smelled horrible.

Widow reached down and searched the guy's pockets. He found his burner phone and pocketed it.

He looked one last time at the guy. Then he turned his face down to keep the water out of his mouth and eyes. He dropped the syringe into the water and ran to the last room, where he found Lucy Hood.

33

WIDOW COULDN'T IMAGINE what he must've looked like to the hospital staff when he came out of the gloom and pouring water, carrying Lucy like a monster carrying a woman he'd abducted from a nearby village.

Members of the staff ran over to him, one of them the security guard without the windbreaker. He asked, "Did you do that?"

Widow said, "No. I found this woman back there." He handed her over to an orderly and said, "Take her."

"Did you find the guy you were looking for?"

"No."

"Maybe he pulled the fire alarm, trying to escape."

Widow said, "You might be right. I gotta go after him. Come with me back to the chopper. I need to ask something else of you."

The security guard without the windbreaker nodded and headed toward the staircase.

Widow said, "Let's take the elevator. There's no fire."

"We can't. It locks down during a fire alarm. We gotta take the stairs."

Widow didn't argue. He followed the security guard into the stairwell. He was glad not to have the water beating down on him anymore, but now his clothes were soaked. They climbed the stairs fast.

They burst out onto the roof.

Widow looked at the pilot and twirled his arm, hand toward the sky, index finger pointed up—the signal to prepare for takeoff. The pilot had been sitting next to Jemma, explaining the parts of the chopper to her. He nodded at Widow and returned to the cockpit, strapping in and gearing the Bell 206 for takeoff. The rotors started spinning and whipping up gusts of wind.

"I need you to take this girl. Her mother is the woman I found."

The security guard asked, "How's that? I thought you found her by accident?"

"I know. Sorry. I can't explain. Take the girl. Bring her to her mother."

The guard protested, but in the end, he decided there was no point. As far as he knew, Widow was some kind of agent with the Navy. How was he supposed to argue?

Widow went to Jemma and said, "Come out of the chopper, Pip."

She got out of her seat, scrambled over to Widow, and hugged him. "What's this for?"

"You're a good guy."

"How do you know that?"

"You've brought me to my mommy."

She said nothing about her dad, which made Widow wonder if she knew anything about what had happened to him. He hoped she didn't, but something told him she knew.

She pulled away from him and said, "You're all wet. And you stink."

He smiled and said, "I stink a lot."

"Am I gonna see my mommy now?"

"Go with this nice man. He'll take you to your mommy."

"What about you?"

"Pip, I'll see you later. I gotta take care of something."

She let go and hopped out of the chopper. Widow jumped in and waved at her. He said to the pilot, "Lift off."

"Where we headed?"

"Just lift off. I'll tell you in the air."

The pilot didn't question him. He hit buttons and flipped switches and grabbed the flight stick. The rotors spun and whirred. In seconds, they were in the air over the hospital. Widow didn't strap in. He stayed at the open door and watched Jemma for a long time. She stayed on the roof, waving at him.

He watched until she was a tiny speck.

He turned to the pilot and told him where to go.

34

OVER THE HEADSET, the pilot said, "I'm not authorized to land anywhere else for you. If you need me to land, I'll have to radio it in."

"Don't worry about it. You don't have to land," Widow said into his headset.

The pilot said nothing to that. He looked out over the sky. The sun had gone down, and now it was full dark.

Widow got out of his seat in the back and leaned into the cockpit. They were five thousand feet up, which was good. It kept the houses below from hearing the chopper. He craned his head and looked out the windshield, down at the landscape at Lake Hills. They had circled it twice until they found the right house.

Widow asked, "Where's the escape package?"

The pilot turned his head and looked up at Widow.

"You can't use that."

"Why not?"

"It's meant for emergencies."

"Where is it?"

The pilot didn't respond for a moment and then looked at the copilot seat. "There's an extra one under the seat. Look under the back."

Widow returned to the rear cabin and looked down under the seat. He moved a loose metal flap and pulled out a parachute. It was white, which wasn't good, but the night sky was fairly cloudy, maybe enough to not worry about it.

He pulled off the flight helmet and the headset. He took out the package and strapped it on. Then he went back to the pilot and yelled over the noise in the helicopter, "You got a tactical bag onboard? A waterproof one?"

The pilot said, "I don't know. I didn't prep the chopper. Check under the back bench."

Widow turned, stopped, and yelled back to the pilot, "Lower us to three thousand feet."

The pilot knew that was a low drop altitude, normally designated for emergency jumps, but he didn't protest.

Widow went to the rear bench and pulled up the cushion and looked in a small cargo space. There was a small bunched-up bright orange bag. The color wasn't appealing to him, not for night work, but it was made to be waterproof, and he needed to protect the dead guy's cell phone. So he took the bag, opened it, and pulled out some stuffing that must've been left inside from when it was first opened. He put both phones in and inspected the rest of the cargo space. He found a small tactical flashlight, which worked, and a pair of small field glasses. Both would come in handy. He put the field glasses and the tactical light in the bag, as well as the Glock 17.

Widow took the bag and walked over to the side door. He kicked off his shoes and socks and stuffed them into the bag, zipped it closed, and pulled the strap tight around him—shoulder to under-arm. The bag was tight to his chest.

The chopper yawed and tilted, and in seconds, the pilot said, "We're here."

Widow jerked open the door, and the metal scraped along the track. The door came open, and immediately he was slapped in the face with a cool wind. He looked out over the terrain. There were some thin clouds beneath him.

Luckily, Lake Hills wasn't a major town. The lake was called Lake Medina. From a bird's-eye view, it looked like a squid with only two tentacles. They waved in different directions, the legs to the west and the south and the head to the north.

At the head, he could see Sheridan's family house. He jumped.

The freefall was only three seconds, or it should've been, but he held off pulling the chute for an extra two seconds, which was dangerous. He pulled the ripcord, and the chute blew out and jerked him back.

The wind wasn't too cold, but he was still damp from the fire sprinklers. He shivered. He fell slowly, like a kite that hung in the air. He aimed for the center of the lake between the squid's head and its legs. As he fell, he kept his eyes on Sheridan's house. He didn't want the Secret Service to see someone parachute in.

On his way down, he checked the bag, made sure it was still zipped shut and secured to his chest. He needed everything in it and couldn't afford to lose it.

He waited until he was about fifty feet from the water and then snapped himself out of the chute and hell dove the rest of the way —feet extended, legs straight, to break the water's surface.

He curled in his toes and took a deep breath. The air filled his lungs, and he held it. The water engulfed him. Bubbles erupted and fizzed around him like a stomach tablet thrown into a glass of water. He let himself sink about ten feet, and then he checked his chest for the bag, which was still there.

The lake water wasn't cold, but it wasn't warm either. The temperature was somewhere below being called chilly. A month later and it would've been cold, but it was still October.

He kicked with his legs and swam north. He made it about twenty yards before he stopped. Widow had been a SEAL, and even though he was undercover, he'd still had to learn how to swim deep and hold his breath for long periods of time. But he was no longer a SEAL, and long breath-holding is a perishable skill. He needed air. He looked up at the surface, then back at the ground he had covered so far. He didn't want to come up under the parachute. He thought he had passed it, but wanted to be certain. He saw the edge of the chute floating in the water. One good thing about jumping with a white chute was that it was easy to find.

He swam up and broke the surface, took a deep breath, and breathed in and breathed out. He stayed on the surface for several long seconds. He twisted and turned, scanning, and got a three-hundred-sixty-degree awareness of his surroundings.

No sirens. No flashlights. No loud shouting or even newly lit windows on the houses around the lake. No one had seen him come in.

He stayed in the water for another twenty seconds, flipping the pages of his old SEAL playbook in his head, searching for a tactical move. He had to deal with an unknown number of Secret Service agents, with whom he didn't want to engage in combat. Secret Service weren't the bad guys here. Plus, they were not a group of law enforcement guys he wanted to tangle with. He doubted he'd get away from a group of them like he did the two small-town cops back in Romanth.

After ten more seconds, the right play came to mind.

Widow looked back at Sheridan's house, which was pretty big, the biggest on the block. It was three stories—red brick and white pillars with white shutters. There was a large wooden deck built around the back. Widow imagined it had a barbecue pit and a porch swing, maybe even an outside, fully-stocked bar.

There was a T-shaped pier over the lake, about a hundred feet from the water's edge. Two boats were roped to the pier. One was a huge boat, like a yacht. This only made sense to Widow if there was a river or canal that led out to the Gulf, but Lake Hills was pretty far from the Gulf. That made Widow think the yacht was just for extravagance. Then again, Lake Medina seemed pretty big. Not Great Lake size, but big enough.

The second boat was a twenty-footer—good boat.

Widow made a one-hundred-eighty-degree turn and swam to the opposite shore from the squid's head.

35

THE SOUTHERN BEACH WAS BEAUTIFUL. Widow had never heard of this lake before, but he had discovered that Texas had a lot more diverse terrain than he had thought. It had greenery, mountains, lakes, beaches, cities, and deserts. It reminded him of California in that way.

He came up on shore, lay back on the sand, and stared at the sky. He had swum too hard, plus he was soaking wet again. Being a Navy SEAL once didn't mean he was still a champion-level swimmer. He felt out of shape. Swimming muscles differed from others, and he hadn't used his in a long time.

He caught his breath, sat up, and looked back over at the north end of the lake. Sheridan's house had lit windows, but no backyard activity that he could see.

Widow stood up and looked around. The nearest house was several football fields away. He figured the beach was natural and not man-made because there were large disc-shaped rocks jutting out of the sand. He left his shoes in the bag because he was going to be back in the lake in a moment. He opened the bag and took out the dead guy's cell phone, checked to make sure that it hadn't gotten wet. It worked fine.

He placed the phone back in the bag and took out the flashlight, flicked it on. The beam fell down across the dirt. He looked around. There was a hill, a small parking lot with three rows of three spaces, and a small cluster of trees. He walked up the hill, watching the ground, avoiding stepping on sharp rocks and debris. There wasn't much debris. The locals kept the beach clean.

At the top of the hill, he scanned the area. No one was around. He turned back and looked at Sheridan's house. It was the same, but he eyeballed it for a long second. He moved over to the west side of the hill and eyeballed the house from there as well. Then he went to the east, near the forest, and checked out the house and the rest of the lake. He found the angle he was looking for and turned toward the trees. He didn't have to look far to find the right one.

He walked over to a younger tree, studied it, and looked back over his shoulder at the Sheridan house and then back at the tree. He pointed the flashlight beam at the ground and flicked the switch again, changing the beam. The first setting was a straight, low beam. The second was a bright beam. And the third was strobe flashes. He left it on the strobe and jammed it into a hole in the tree's side. He tugged it around to make sure it would stay, and it did.

Widow stared back at Sheridan's house. He took the dead guy's cell phone out of the waterproof bag, looked through the missed calls. He saw a contact labeled *"Principal."*

36

JOHN SHERIDAN TRIED to call the last member of the team he had spoken with, and there was no answer. There was no answer from Danny's. No answer from Glock's phone. No answer from Kill Team B. He called several times, each phone number. He even tried to call from the house phone, which was dangerous. The burner phone masked his identity even though both kill teams knew who he was. But no one else in their organization did. That's why he always insisted that he be referred to as the Principal. Now, no one was answering him. Therefore, no one was calling him anything.

He sat in his study on the second floor of the house and held papers in his hand like he was reading them thoroughly, in case one of his extended family members walked in. Downstairs, he was having a party, a family gathering. It wasn't anything too big, just about twenty people, including his wife, her family, his kids, and his brother. None of them had any idea who he really was. Well, they knew him, but only part of him.

Like most great men in history, Sheridan had great flaws. That's how he thought of himself, as a great man. Only he hadn't been given a chance to show how great he was. Not yet. So far, he had to play the politics game the way it had always been played, like he was concerned about every citizen in his constituency. He had to behave and act like no one else mattered more to him than them. He had to pretend he didn't have foreign influences in his life. To be fair to what was left of his conscience, he had started out caring about all Americans. He used to believe all men were created equal.

But the Mexicans? They shouldn't be here. He knew that. He'd always known that. Why couldn't they stay in their own country? Make Mexico great. That should be their focus, not coming over here and stealing American jobs, stealing American women, stealing the American dream.

He didn't hate them, not necessarily. He liked to keep himself in the dark about what Glock's crew did. Those boys were worse than he was. He knew that. Sometimes he had problems sleeping, but the money helped. Knowing that Auckland Enterprises would secure border wall contracts would help his bank account. Then he could provide a good future for his children, right?

These were the thoughts he focused on. He tried not to wonder where the hell Glock was.

* * *

WIDOW CALLED THE CONTACT LABELED "PRINCIPAL" in the dead guy's phone. The phone rang, not even a half second, and a voice answered. Not a lizard voice like Glock's, but a normal Texas voice with a deep accent, almost like it was fake.

It said, "Where the hell have you been?"

Widow didn't answer. Instead, he panted, in and out. He wanted to put some fear into Sheridan, and he had seen this trick work in one of the *Rambo* movies.

It seemed to work here because Sheridan said, "Who the hell is this?"

Widow hung the phone up and slipped it back into the water-proof bag.

He looked through the field glasses out across the lake at Sheridan's big backyard. He clocked a figure in the dark on the second-floor balcony. It was a Secret Service agent standing near a set of French doors that led in to the second floor of the house. The agent was good. He looked left, looked right, and stopped at the center of the backyard each time. He was like a robot. He wasn't leaning against the wall, but had his back close to it. Widow couldn't see his eyes or the details of his face because he stayed out of the lights over the backyard. Well-trained.

There were lit houses and boathouses and piers all around the lake, not enough to light up the lake but enough to distract the agent from the flashing tactical light. Also, the distance was too far for him to notice it with the naked eye, which was good because Widow didn't want the attention of the Secret Service, just Sheridan.

Widow slipped the field glasses into the bag and zipped it up, checked it again to make sure it was strapped tight around him, and then returned to the water. He took a deep breath and dove in. He targeted the north shore, Sheridan's house, and swam.

The lake was calm, which meant Widow had to either swim slowly or stay underwater for most of the trip across. He chose the latter. He stayed as deep as he could and swam at a nice, steady pace. He made few waves. He came up four times for air, which wasn't bad for as long as the lake was.

Widow swam to the surface and lifted his head out of the water slowly, like a crocodile—eyes first and then nose and mouth. He stared ahead and saw the bottom of the yacht and then the other boat. He looked up at the house. He saw the Secret Service agent.

The agent was still swiveling his head from side to side, with no notice of Widow. Widow took a breath and dove back underwater and swam toward the yacht.

He swam for less than another minute and was at the bottom of the yacht. He kept his head behind it and out of the agent's cone of vision. He moved around and saw a pair of WaveRunners he hadn't noticed before. He took another look at the agent from around the double motors of the yacht. He waited until the agent looked to the east, then dipped down and swam across the surface, past the WaveRunners, to the twenty-foot boat. He reached up with his right hand, hauled himself up, and rolled into the boat. He stayed on his back and waited. He knew that if the Secret Service had noticed him, all hell would break loose.

He waited, but nothing happened. No floodlights. No alarms. No shouting. And no shooting, which was the most important thing.

He lay on his back and unzipped the waterproof bag. He felt around for the phone and pulled out the sheriff's phone by mistake. He tossed it back in and felt around for the other one. He found it and hauled it out. He had several missed calls—all Sheridan.

He called back.

Sheridan said, "Who is this?"

"Listen carefully."

"Okay."

"Are you alone?"

Sheridan said, "Yes."

"Got a pair of field glasses?"

"A pair of what?"

"Binoculars?"

"Yeah."

"Get them and walk outside. Backyard."

Sheridan said, "Okay. One minute."

But one minute was really about five seconds. Widow leaned up against the side of the boat and peeked his eyes over the side. He watched the house.

The French doors next to the Secret Service agent opened up, and a man stepped out. It was Sheridan, must've been. He wasn't a young guy, but he was far from ancient. Maybe in his fifties. A bit of a belly—nothing that a month of walking and eating better wouldn't cure. Widow couldn't tell if he was bald or not because he wore a baseball cap—Rangers, maybe. He looked clean-shaven, wore a button-down Oxford, sleeves rolled up to the elbows. A black or brown sweater vest over the shirt and a pair of chinos, maybe navy blue. He looked like a typical politician trying to look casual.

Sheridan had a cell phone in one hand and a pair of heavy black binoculars in the other. The binoculars were twice the size of the ones Widow had.

Sheridan said, "What am I looking for?"

Widow said, "Look straight across, south side."

Sheridan looked through the binoculars and didn't need to look long. He said, "I see it. The flashing light."

"Yes."

Widow watched the Secret Service agent, who was just out of earshot. He moved closer to the senator.

Widow said, "Get rid of the Secret Service."

Sheridan turned to the agent and said, "I'm all right, Steve. Can you give me some privacy?"

Widow watched carefully. He didn't want Sheridan giving the agent any signals or signs that he needed help.

Steve said, "No problem, Senator. I'll head to the front. Do a sweep of the perimeter."

"I told you to call me John," Sheridan said, and he smiled at the agent.

"Sure thing, John. Holler if you need me."

And the agent walked in through the doors and was gone from sight.

Widow said, "Good."

"Who are you? Where's Glock?"

"Glock's dead."

Silence fell across the phone.

"That got your attention?"

Sheridan gulped and said, "Yes."

"Good. 'Cause they're all dead."

"All?"

"Yeah."

"How?"

"I killed them."

Sheridan said, "You? Alone? Who are you?"

"I'm nobody. Just a guy interested in one thing."

"What's that?"

"Got any money in the house?" Widow asked.

Sheridan said, "What?"

"Money. Got any money?"

"Yeah. In a safe. Not much though."

"How much?"

Sheridan was quiet for a moment, and then he said, "About fifty thousand."

"You lie. You got more than that."

Sheridan said, "I've got over a hundred thousand in cash. There's more in jewelry."

"Forget the jewelry. I only care about the cash. That's all I want, John. Cold, hard cash," Widow lied. "Bring all of it."

"Bring it where?"

"Across the lake, John," Widow said.

Sheridan was silent.

Widow said, "Put the cash in a bag. Get in your boat and come straight across to the flashing light. Otherwise, I'm sure the cops will be interested to know what I know."

Sheridan asked, "What do you know?"

"Oh, I know everything, John. I know about Hood. I know about Glock."

Sheridan was silent.

"I know about the wall, John."

More silence.

"I know about the Jericho Men, John. I have proof. Lots of proof, actually. I have so much proof that I'm sure it will do much, much more than put you in prison for the rest of your life. I'm sure that your kids' kids won't be able to outlive the shame. In fact, I bet their lives might be in danger as well."

"What? What do you mean?"

"John, didn't you think this through? Building a border wall will do a lot more than prevent illegal immigration. It will prevent drug running. Do you know how much money that will cost the cartels? Not to mention your friends in the DEA, the crooked agents. Didn't you ever think about their pockets?" Widow said, purposely playing into Sheridan's motives. Lying to reaffirm a suspect's position was a good undercover cop tactic. It was the quintessential ploy of the *good cop* part of good cop, bad cop.

Sheridan said nothing.

Widow said, "I doubt you'll live long after the truth is exposed. I doubt your kids will even live to see their kids."

"Okay! Okay! I'll bring the money."

"Good, John. That's real good," Widow said, putting a special emphasis on the word *good*, which he had heard somewhere before, a movie maybe, one of those old 1980s action movies. Stallone or Schwarzenegger.

"Okay. I'm getting it. I'll call you after."

"No, John. You think I'm an idiot? Get the money, bag it up. Leave the line open. I want to hear you the whole way."

Sheridan said, "Okay."

He set the binoculars on the railing and walked back inside. He shut the doors.

Widow heard walking and the sounds of a desk drawer running across the tracks. Then he heard the sounds of a safe's lock, the clicks and mechanics. The safe door opened, and he heard papers shuffling around—the cash. There were some other ambient sounds, and after a long moment, Sheridan came back on the line.

He said, "Okay. I got it."

Widow said, "I've got binoculars too. I better see a big bag."

"Okay. Now what?"

"Get in your boat. Tell no one. Come across. Bring the cash. We'll talk."

Sheridan said, "Okay. What do I tell my family? I've got a bunch of guests here."

"Tell them nothing. Just come. You'll be back before they notice."

"I should hang up the phone. They'll wonder why I'm on the phone."

Widow said, "Fine. Don't make me wait."

He hung up the phone.

37

SHERIDAN GATHERED ALL the cash out of his safe and piled it into a backpack. He left the safe open and hung up the phone from the guy who was trying to blackmail him. He cursed Glock's uselessness under his breath.

Behind the cash in the safe was a snub-nosed thirty-eight special —two-inch barrel. Brown handle. Spurless, model 206. It was a gift given to him by a past president.

He kept it loaded, but he opened the cylinder and spun it anyway. It was fully loaded.

He put it under the front of his sweater, tucked into his chinos. He slung the backpack, one strap, over his shoulder, and left the study. He walked out with no intention of paying this guy. He'd let the guy count the money, and shoot him the first chance he got.

Sheridan was a politician and a damn good one, by his own admission. Therefore, he knew how to fake smile and fake talk to people. He was an expert in social encounters. He saw his family and extended family's faces, all familiar. And two or three new faces he didn't recognize. Normally, he would approach the new faces, talk with them, listen to them. That was his secret. When he met new people, he focused on them, homed in on them like a bullet to a target.

This time, he had other things on his mind. He waved at his wife and pointed to the back door like he was saying, *I'm gonna step out for a second, hon. Be right back.* And he thought he would. He'd pull his gun on the stranger and shoot him. A gunshot would echo across the lake. That was true, but this was Central Texas. And over there, the lake was surrounded by woods. Gunshots weren't uncommon. One of the Secret Service might get their tail feathers all riled up, but once they saw he was okay, they would forget all about it. He could throw the guy's body into his boat, cover it with a tarp, and then weight it down with rocks early in the morning and dump it in the lake. Tomorrow was Sunday anyway, and he was always sneaking out to go fishing.

Everything would be fine.

He walked out of the house, dismissed another agent who offered to follow him, and closed the back door behind him. He looked off in the distance, across the water, but couldn't see the light flashing.

He carried the backpack down a long gravel walk to the water's edge and stepped onto the pier. Once he left the lights from his house behind him, he could see the light strobing across the lake. He walked past a tarp his kids used to cover up their fishing gear to protect it from rain. He took it and balled it up. He would need it for the body. He tossed it on the twenty-foot boat and stepped on board. He tossed the backpack into the passenger seat and started up the engine. The back motor roared to life, and water sputtered and bubbled behind the boat. Sheridan untied the ropes to the pier and kicked off. He kept the lights of the boat off.

He pulled the thirty-eight out and placed it on his lap as he hit the accelerator. The boat jumped to life and blew across the water. Not fast, not slow.

When he got farther from shore, he hit the accelerator. The engine roared, and the propeller rolled.

At full speed, it took about five minutes to get close to the southern shore. Once he neared the shore, he slowed the engine to a hum and moved in slowly. He was going to have to jump into the water and walk to shore. Explaining his wet shoes and socks and pants to his wife was the least of his concerns.

He scanned the shore with his eyes, saw no one. He took off his ball cap, revealing a full head of brown hair with graying temples. He tossed the cap on the passenger seat and killed the motor.

The anchor was manual, which meant he had to throw it over the bow and let it catch at the bottom. He waited, and the boat gently rocked to a stop.

Sheridan walked to the rear of the boat, ready to jump into the shallows and wade over to the beach, but he stopped. He looked down. Under the tarp he had tossed into the boat was a pair of shoes he didn't recognize. They couldn't belong to his kids. They were huge. He bent down and picked up a left shoe, held it up, and stared at it. It must've been a size thirteen, but he only wore a ten.

Then he heard a noise behind him. He spun around and saw a giant hand reach up onto the bow from the water. A second later, a large man was standing on the boat.

Sheridan went for his thirty-eight but stopped cold when he saw a Glock 17 staring at him.

The large man said, "Don't!"

38

WIDOW SAID, "Don't! Don't move!"

Widow had hung onto the front of Sheridan's boat, waves slapping him across the face, for the whole five minutes until they reached the beach.

Sheridan said, "What? What is this?"

"You've done some very bad things, Senator."

"I brought the cash," Sheridan said and tossed the backpack between them, hoping the large man would follow the bag with his eyes. Sheridan figured he just needed the large man to look down for a split second, but he didn't.

Widow said, "A little girl lost her father because of you."

Sheridan said, "Wait a minute. Take the money. Aren't you going to look?"

"No. This isn't about money."

"It's all there. Take it!"

"This isn't about cash. This is about people."

Sheridan said nothing. He just shivered with his hands up. His wedding ring faced out.

"You a married man?"

"Of course."

"Got kids?"

"Of course."

"Know who Jemma is?"

"I don't know."

Widow said nothing, just stared at Sheridan.

"She's Hood's spic daughter," said Sheridan.

"What's that?"

"Nothing."

"What's that word you said?"

"Spic. You know, beaner."

"Ah. I see. So this wall is more than just money. It's about Mexicans?"

"We gotta keep 'em out!"

"You know, Jemma lost her father because of you. And now I'm thinking we can blame losing her grandmother on you too."

Sheridan said, "I don't care about those people. Why should I? Bunch of wetbacks. Illegals. They aren't even supposed to be here." He lowered his hands closer to his waistline. He asked, "What's it to you?"

Widow stayed quiet.

"Don't kill me. Take the money. I brought it for you."

Widow said, "You think you can get to that gun? I'm aiming right at you. Center mass. And I'm a good shot. You think you can beat a bullet?"

Sheridan stayed still.

"You want me to lower mine? We can draw. Like the Old West. This is Texas."

Sheridan said, "Yes. That's only fair, right? You're supposed to be some kind of good guy here. Like the cowboy who just blew into town? Like John Wayne?"

Widow nodded and said, "Okay. Like the Old West."

He lowered his gun.

Sheridan smiled because he might not have been the get-his-hands-dirty type, but one thing that he could do was shoot straight. He watched like a dog with hungry eyes as Widow lowered the Glock.

"Ready?" Widow said.

Sheridan asked, "Really?"

"Just kidding," Widow said, and he shot him right in the sternum, center chest. The red mist exploded, and blood gushed and burbled out of the nine-millimeter hole in his chest.

Widow watched as Sheridan stumbled forward and toppled back, landing against the rear wall of the boat, near the motor. His body crumpled over like a sinkhole imploding in on itself.

Widow looked to the shore and saw lights flick on all over the place. The gunshot had been noticed by the residents of Lake Hills. He had little time. He guessed maybe he had fifteen minutes.

He stuffed the Glock into his waistband and walked over to Sheridan's body. He lifted it up and over to the side of the boat, tossed it overboard.

He pulled up the anchor in a rush, which reminded him of SEAL training when they had to pull huge truck tires with ropes. After he got the anchor in the boat, he dumped himself down in the driver's seat and sped off, down the west leg of the squid, and to the farthest shore.

The boat continued to run. Widow stood up, half crouched so that he wouldn't fall out of the boat. He let it continue to go, and he grabbed the backpack, dumped the cash into the waterproof bag. He took his shoes and put them back on. He left the backpack in the boat, and he dove into the lake. The boat continued on without him, driverless.

Widow swam as hard as he could in the opposite direction, away from the boat, away from Sheridan's house, and down the opposite leg of the squid. He swam east and then followed the winding tentacle south.

39

THE SOUTH TIP of the lake led Widow to a quiet suburban street with single-story family houses with lush amateur gardens and uniform mailboxes and porches with porch swings. It looked like the kind of neighborhood where everyone knew everyone else, and no one locked their doors. He came up on the street and shook his pants, which clung to him. He slipped off the waterproof bag and pulled his shirt off. He wrung it out and cracked it like a whip several times, trying to dry it off. He slipped it back on.

He pivoted and looked back at the lake. He had swum a long, long distance. His legs hurt. His arms hurt. Even his chest was sore from holding his breath for so long. He had actually lost count of how many times he came up for air.

Behind him, far in the distance, across the lake, just over the trees, he could see red-and-blue lights. He imagined neighbors had heard the gunshot, came out to investigate and dismissed it. But the senator's Secret Service detail wouldn't have dismissed it. They'd probably investigated and noticed the senator was missing, and his boat was missing. They wouldn't have freaked out over it, but an unexplained gunshot at night, plus the missing senator, would make them worry.

Widow had swum for over ten minutes. The boat had probably crashed on the opposite shore. Maybe it had crashed into someone's yard or even their boat. Whatever happened, someone had called the police. Those lights were police lights.

None of that mattered. He was ahead of them so far, and no one even suspected he was involved.

Right now, the police had probably discovered an empty boat. Probably saw the blood. The Secret Service would show up, recognize the boat. They'd start searching. First, they'd focus on the water, dispatching boats, and maybe a car or two to circle the lake. But Lake Medina was a big lake and not a circle. It had many snaking twists and turns and canals. Therefore, there was a lot of lake to cover, a lot of shoreline, and a lot of homes.

Widow would be long gone by the time they thought to drag the lake. By the time they found the senator's body, no one involved would name Widow.

40

WIDOW HATED humping it over seven miles of woods and grassland, but he had no choice. He wanted to be far from Lake Hills, and hitching a ride wasn't an option because he was not only a man who looked like a creature that belonged in a lagoon, but he was totally drenched from head to toe. And looking the way he did, combined with his wet clothes, made it smarter for him to take his chances going east through the woods.

Eventually, he found his way to a road and walked alongside it a while. His clothes dried to the point of damp, but not dry. He followed the road for a long, long time but gave up on finding a town. It was a lot of nothing, and he saw signs that pointed to another lake called Diversion Lake.

He was about to give up all hope when a Ford Bronco, an old one, pulled alongside him.

The window rolled down, and a decent-looking blonde woman said, "Howdy there. You sure look like a fish outta water."

Widow leaned down and smiled at her. He didn't get too close to her window—no reason to take a chance and blow a ride. He said, "You have no idea."

"You from around here?"

"No. My girlfriend abandoned me back near the lake." Everyone who hitchhikes likes to embellish the truth sometimes. Why not?

"Girlfriend, huh?"

"Yeah."

"What, y'all fighting?"

"No. We're done."

"Really?" she asked and smacked gum in her mouth, which annoyed Widow, but she had a great smile, and he wasn't one to turn down a ride, no matter who was driving.

He nodded.

"You need a ride?"

"I do."

"Pitch in for gas, and I'll give ya a ride."

"Not a problem," he said. He scrambled around the rear of the truck and took out a small wad of hundreds from the bag and zipped it back up before she could see it.

He hopped in the passenger side and handed her a hundred-dollar bill. He said, "How far will this get me?"

She took it and examined it and said, "Hell, that'll get you to San Antonio."

"Seriously?"

"Well, I'm actually headed in that direction. I was gonna go to a local dive. Have a beer. Look for a friendly man like yourself. A man with some extra cash. If you catch my meaning."

She was a hooker, a hooker with a Ford Bronco. This made Widow smile, and he gave a slight chuckle. After everything he'd been through, with the cops and probably the Secret Service two steps behind hunting for him, a hooker had come to the rescue.

He said, "Tell ya what. I don't know how much you charge. But I'll pay you two hundred to drive me to San Antonio."

She looked in the rearview mirror and then back at him and said, "Two hundred?"

He nodded.

"You got it."

And they were off.

Six minutes later, his phone rang. It wasn't the dead guy's phone —it was Sheriff Harks's. He almost didn't answer it because he figured that by now, the sheriff might've gotten out. But it was Cameron.

"Hey," he said.

Cameron said, "Everything okay?"

"Yeah. It's good."

"The pilot said you didn't return with him. Said you exited on your own. Wouldn't talk anymore about it."

"Yeah. About that," Widow said.

"Yeah?"

"There might be some cleanup."

Cameron said, "I already told them I didn't know who you were or what they were talking about. And I encouraged them to forget as well."

"Thank you," he said.

She asked, "Where will you go now?"

"East, I think."

"Why east?"

"Why not?"

She didn't respond to that.

He said, "Get some sleep. I'll see you around, Cameron."

"See you," she said, and he hung up.

He sat back and stared out the window.

"Everything all right, hon?"

"Yeah."

"Who's that? Girlfriend?"

He said, "Yeah."

"You want to talk about it? We got a long drive still."

"Nah. Actually, I want to take a nap. Would that be okay?"

She said, "Sure. I won't bother you until we get there."

"Thanks. Thanks for everything. What do I call you?"

"Michelle."

"Jack Widow," he said, and he racked the seat all the way back and closed his eyes.

THE NEXT MORNING, a forgiving sun rose over El Paso, Texas. Sunbeams fired through the windows of the hospital. Patients were sleeping all over the hospital, because the night before, they had to be moved around and were up most of the night because of a false fire alarm. Parked in the lot were a firetruck and an El Paso police car, both on reserve.

A local detective had been on the phone with the US Navy all morning trying to track down a helicopter that had landed on their roof, but the Department of the Navy was denying any such event. It was proposed that perhaps one had been stolen, but they vehemently denied this.

The police still felt it was good to leave an officer at the hospital. All of this wasn't due solely to the false fire alarm. It was mostly because after a mysterious man had arrived in a Navy chopper; the staff discovered an unidentified dead orderly on the seventh floor.

The waiting room on the seventh floor was completely empty, as were the staff area and the rooms. This wasn't because of the dead body or the crime scene tape. It was because of the fire sprinklers spraying out water for an hour. Machines were ruined, carpets were stained, beds were drenched, and the doctors were concerned about germs. So the patients were moved to the third floor and dispersed into shared rooms with other patients.

Jemma Hood was fast asleep on a hospital bed next to her mother. Machines and a heart monitor beeped and whirred and provided white noise for her to sleep deeply. She had slept and dreamed better than she had in weeks, maybe months.

A familiar voice broke her sleep. She heard a voice say, "Pip. Little Pip. Wake up."

Jemma squinted and turned and opened her eyes.

She saw her mother looking back at her with a big smile on her face.

Lucy Hood said, "Hey, Pip. Are you going to sleep all day?"

The first thought Jemma had was that she was still dreaming, until her mother kissed her on the forehead.

Jemma said, "Mommy?"

"Yeah, dear. It's me. Who else would I be?"

Jemma jumped up and hugged her mother tight.

"What's wrong, dear? You act like I've been in a coma," Lucy joked.

* * *

A WEEK LATER, Lucy Hood was still in bed, but she had been moved to a standard shared room. She had a nice younger girl in her room, a preteen. Jemma liked her. Lucy kept Jemma out of school, and the two were inseparable and might remain so for a long time.

Lucy's cancer had become manageable. Doctors said it was a good sign that she came out of her coma. Although she still had cancer, the growth had subsided, and for the first time in months, they felt optimistic about her chances to live longer.

In the last few days, she had visitors from the FBI, the US Marshals, and the local police. She had been asked the same questions over and over. They were about her husband. But she had been in a coma for months. No way did she have the answers they wanted.

Of course, she had cooperated out of fear of someone asking about her citizenship. When she couldn't help the FBI, she had expected to hear from Immigration and Customs Enforcement. She just knew they would be the last ones to visit her. She knew they would come and take her and Jemma away. But they weren't the last to visit her.

She had gotten a strange visit from the Naval Criminal Investigative Service, and only one agent came. The agent had explained he was a new agent just doing a routine follow-up interview. It was no big deal.

The questions weren't major or anything. Most of them were to Jemma. The agent asked if she remembered the man who had helped her. That sort of thing. Unfortunately, she had little information.

The agent left a bag with Jemma and Lucy. He had said it was from his boss, and he didn't know what was in it.

Lucy was astonished to find that the bag was full of cash, and that wasn't all. It also had birth certificates and social security cards for both her and Jemma. And both were from the United States Government, proving they were US-born citizens.

* * *

AUSTIN, Texas was more than just the capital of the Lone Star State. It was Donna Leon's home. But she wasn't at home. She sat in a Starbucks, doing more than avoiding the pouring rain. She turned in her seat and stared out the window at a long line of people hiding and hunching together under their umbrellas and rain slickers. The line was so long that she couldn't even see the end.

Widow stood at the counter, ordering two coffees. Unlike when he was in Las Vegas, this time he knew that the second one would make it to the intended woman.

His coffee came, her coffee came, and he took them and returned to Leon's table. He had thought she was something special in uniform, but he was wrong. Because in her casual clothes, she was far more spectacular—jaw-dropping.

"Here's your coffee," he said, and sat across from her.

"Thanks."

"They get the money?" he asked.

"They got it."

"Did you get the IDs?"

She nodded and said, "I've got better news than that even."

"What's that?"

"Lucy Hood woke up. They say she'll be fine."

Widow smiled a long smile, all teeth. He hadn't smiled that way since Las Vegas, which was over a week ago.

He said, "That's great."

Leon was quiet for a moment, and then she asked, "What's next for you? Where will you go?"

Widow stayed quiet.

She asked, "Or will you stay?"

Widow said nothing.

Leon said, "Maybe you'll stay awhile?"

"Maybe."

"What would make you stay?"

He looked deep into her eyes and said, "Give me a reason to stay."

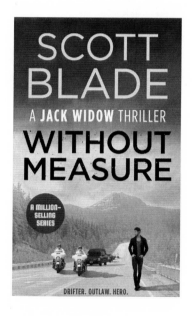

Out Now!

WITHOUT MEASURE: A BLURB

Shots fired on a remote Marine base.

The shooter killed himself.

The Military Police's #1 suspect?

An outsider named Jack Widow.

Hitchhiking all night. No sleep. Widow stops in a diner in a California mountain town with only two industries left: a small arms manufacturer and a forgotten Marine base.

Wanting to drink coffee in peace, Widow can't ignore his cop senses warning him about a man seated at another booth. The man is Arabic, Islamic, and a decorated Marine. But, there's something else. Something off. Something troubling.

Later, that same Marine walks onto the base, shoots five innocent people, and then himself.

The Military Police want to know why? They want someone to blame. All that's left is Jack Widow.

Read the explosive, bestselling whodunit today!

★★★★★ *Full of brutal justice!*

★★★★★ *Scott Blade is his best book yet.*

CHAPTER 1

HIS NAMETAPE READ: "TURIK."

He looked like a lone gunman. The kind who walks into a school or airport or, in this case, a military base, shoots five people, turns the gun on himself, and pulls the trigger.

Lone gunmen stick out like sore thumbs. The very definition of a lone gunman is a lone man with a gun. Easy enough to spot.

Turik was as close as any other lone gunman that I had seen before. And I had seen them before. Plenty. These guys have two dead giveaways. They're quiet—thus, the lone part. And they've got guns. Simple enough.

I was staring at a guy who fit the bill, but there was also another element to consider—targets. What were the intended tactical targets for a lone gunman? I was near one of the traditional targets for a lone gunman. I was near a military base, not a stone's throw away, but close. Arrow's Peak Marine Base was only ten miles away, by my guess, in a north and uphill direction. I had never seen it before, but I knew it was an old Marine installation, canvased behind thick, snowy woodland areas and built in the valley of long, rolling hills—white in the winter and green in the summer.

Arrow's Peak took its name from one of the region's most notable natural sculptures. The tallest mountain in the county had a crude, rugged arrowhead-shaped peak. It was especially easy to spot in the cold of winter when the peak was painted white with snow. I'd seen it walking in above the tree lines.

The mountain didn't stand alone, but it stood out. It didn't appear to be reachable by road. The terrain surrounding it comprised thick, high trees, also heavily sprinkled in snow.

The Marine base wasn't in the mountains, but north of town.

I saw many road signs for it on my way along the highway.

The guy I was staring at had a gun strapped to his side. It was a military-issued M45 MEU(SOC), which is a .45 ACP, originally based on the M1911 handgun designed by the famous gunmaker Browning, from way back in the day in Utah. The MEU (SOC) was a heavily modified version of that firearm.

His was well cared for. It looked well worn too, like a firearm that had been fired many times in its career. This wasn't a feature that most men noticed, but I did. I had been trained to notice things like that until it became second nature. The M45 is a tactical gun issued to Marine Special Forces. This gun is used by MARSOC, which stands for United States Marine Corps Forces Special Operations Command. The Corps loved long titles that made for bad acronyms. Unlike the Army or the Navy, which was better at it. Like SEAL, which means Sea, Air, and Land teams and is a much better acronym.

The Critical Skills Operators are also called Marine Raiders. The Raiders have gained credibility in the last several years. In many circles, they are as deadly as the SEALs, not a claim that I agreed with. Then again, I was a little biased because I'd spent most of my career with the SEALs.

I sat in a worn vinyl booth next to the window at a dive called the Wagon Hash Diner, a well-kept but old diner built on a wagon trail off a small two-lane highway, the 96. Green, lush landscape towered around it; only I couldn't see much of it because it was half-covered in snow. I was in a small mountain town called Hamber, which the locals believed to be the first gold rush settlement in the forty-niners' era. The locals believed this, but no one else did. At least, I had never heard of it, but then again, my history on California gold mining wasn't just dusty; it was practically nonexistent. The only thing that I could recall about the forty-niners was that I lost a hundred bucks on the football team's game about twelve years ago to an old CO, when we were at sea for six weeks.

I never cared for them again.

All the information that I knew about Hamber was what I had read on the back of the Wagon Hash menu.

When I was done reading, I leaned across the booth and picked up a newspaper left behind by another patron. I liked newspapers, liked to hold a physical copy of something that, long ago, was the coveted way to get the news. Once upon a time, the newspaper was the only form of media besides word of mouth, but still equally reliable.

The newspaper used to be the first and last line of defense. But one day, capitalism came along and did what capitalism always does. It squeezed the life out of newspapers and smothered the pages with ad revenue, exploiting newspapers until they were bled dry. Then capitalism moved on to the internet, which is where most people get their news these days. Smartphones have allowed instant news coverage and unlimited ad buy revenue.

The *New York Times* is still considered today's paper of record, but most of their income comes from online ads. Ironic, I guess.

I didn't have a smartphone or a tablet or a PC. I owned little anything. All my possessions were provisional. I was a minimalist in the truest sense. For me to keep up with current events, I had to read newspapers.

I opened the paper. It was a day-old copy of the *LA Times*, far from home, but the pride of the entire state. Therefore, it was read here.

There was a lot going on in the news today. A new president had come into office. A new Congress was holding cabinet confirmations, and the DOD was upsetting people because they had blown their budget last year and were up for a hearing on a bigger one. Washington business as usual.

I didn't vote for this president, and I didn't vote for the other guy either. The Washington shuffle bore little weight on my life. I didn't care either way. One political party argued this, and the other argued that. One party won and one didn't. Life went on.

In my mind, it was a bad choice versus a bad choice, like choosing between getting shot in the head by a total stranger or being shot in the head by a loved one. In the end, what difference does it make?

I flipped to the sports page, checked the games, checked the scores. Nothing of interest except a university basketball game. It was the LSU Tigers, which wasn't particularly interesting to anyone else, but I was born in Mississippi. It raised my eyebrow; that was all. They had lost.

I flipped back to the front page, ignoring the local politics until I found a story of interest. Another terrorist attack in Berlin. It was a story about a hijacked truck that rammed through a busy square and killed dozens of people. Witnesses said that the driver drove the truck in an erratic and dangerous way. The cops were still searching for the driver. He'd escaped. A massive manhunt was underway. The Germans had good cops. I'd been stationed there more times than I could remember. The German police back then didn't mess around. I had faith that they'd catch the guy.

ISIS claimed the attack.

I presumed Interpol would find a dead body if they hadn't already. The body would belong to the truck's owner, not the hijacker. The hijacker drove erratically because he probably didn't know how to drive the complicated sticks and gears of a commercial truck.

Lately, ISIS terrorists have used trucks in Europe to kill innocent civilians. In America and Turkey, they have used gunmen to shoot up public places, which was part of the reason I was more than concerned about Turik.

A waitress came over and ignored the lone gunman, who was seated two booths in front of me.

He stared straight on, not looking at me, not making eye contact. The waitress hadn't noticed his gun. I figured because she had her back turned to the door when he walked in and sat down. The M45, holstered at his right side, was now out of sight under the tabletop.

No one else seemed to have noticed it either.

The waitress asked, "Sir, would you like a refill of coffee?"

I looked at her name tag. A quick glance. Her name was Karen.

I didn't want to cause alarm, so I said nothing about the lone gunman. I answered, "Yeah. And let me get a fresh mug as well."

The one I was drinking out of just didn't quite look so clean once I had drained it to the bottom.

She paused and stared at me. She stared at my lower sleeve tattoos, two American flag gauntlets, one covering each forearm, masked with multiple other designs that meant nothing to anyone but people in my line of work and me. Tattoos are usually either an occupational hazard or a spiritual totem—or both—depends on who is making the assessment.

Because I had been an undercover cop, of sorts, to me, they were both. I had once been an NCIS agent—a Navy cop—assigned to Unit Ten, which was a highly secret black ops unit. We investigated the things that no one else would investigate or even knew or cared about. Often, we were used as a surgical instrument for the military to uncover things that no one wanted uncovered. We investigated crimes involving the SEALs and Black Ops teams involving the Navy and Marine Corps.

As far as I knew, there were only a handful of us. I'd only known a few agents from Unit Ten, which I had zero contact with.

Because most NCIS people were civilians, they needed military agents who could penetrate military units undercover and hold credibility all at the same time with other military personnel. I was the only agent ever to penetrate the SEALs. Which meant that I had to live, eat, and breathe like a SEAL. There was no margin for error. For years, I lived a double life, sixteen years. But a double life was never the right description of who I had been, because a double life implied that I had two lives.

In fact, I had no life. I had only double identities, one real and one fabricated. I didn't have a real life, not until I stopped living how they told me to live, how I had been expected to live. Now, I lived nowhere, a man without a home. I was a drifter—homeless but not in poverty, although I looked it from time to time.

I considered myself to be wealthy enough. I always had food, clothes, shelter, and I found enough money to get by, continuing my chosen lifestyle. If I ever was hard-pressed for money, there were ways of making it. I had a passport. I could get transient work if I had to. Pay-by-cash sort of work was always available.

Karen was still inspecting the coffee mug like I had said that there was something wrong with it. I saw her expression as she searched for a defect on it.

I coughed involuntarily, a kind of under-my-breath cough because I had caught it right at the beginning, and I attempted to staunch it out right before the end, like catching yourself saying something inappropriate halfway through the words. I failed.

The cough that would've counted for nothing suddenly turned into a big ordeal. Everyone in the diner looked my way, like I was choking. But then, after a long few seconds, the cough subsided.

Karen stopped looking over the coffee mug and asked, "You okay, sir?"

"Ye-Yeah," I said, covering my mouth. I got too caught up in the cough just to flat-out answer her straight.

She stayed quiet and stayed where she was, like she'd been at attention in front of a commanding officer. She had good posture.

"I got a little cold," I said. And I wasn't lying. I was fighting a cold, nothing bad, not yet. It was still the beginning stages. I felt a soft, irritating tickle in the back of my throat and a headache that felt three days old, but I knew it would only get worse and last at least three more days.

"Okay. I'll get you a new mug. Do you want some soup? Today, we got chicken noodle."

I shook my head. I hadn't eaten since the day before. Not much appetite. It wasn't like I was sad or depressed or something; I just had no desire to eat, maybe because I wanted to sleep more.

I had been up most of the night before.

Even though I had come in here originally intending to order breakfast, I changed my mind as soon as I sat down. I just wasn't hungry.

I watched Karen walk across the square tile floor and over a long, black rug, back behind a long countertop with one of those old-fashioned cash registers perched on it. They had no computer system in sight. All business was done with handwriting and paper.

Over the food window, between the kitchen and the front of the house, I saw one of those old tin spinning wheels, where the wait staff stuck in a paper order, called out that they had a new order, and then spun the contraption toward the kitchen. Once the meal was completed, the ticket spinner was spun to the front again. No tickets were on it. I doubted that they even used it. They probably bought it at a flea market.

I turned and looked again at the guy who fit the gunman profile, trying not to stare. I pretended to look over everything in the diner casually.

The rest of the diner was relatively empty. Two other tables had patrons. One was a pair of truckers who had been here since before I walked in the door. They sat far off, near a unisex bathroom entrance. They laughed and kidded each other in hearty tones, like they were old friends who stopped on this route every six months and reunited in the Wagon Hash diner.

The other table was a young married couple; the wife was somewhere between the ballpark of seven months pregnant and delivering a child. I wasn't sure. I wasn't an expert on the subject. Never had I ever been a parent or had a child or a wife. I had girlfriends but never got as far as a wedding conversation—not even close—hard in my line of work.

I looked back at the guy who fit the lone gunman profile. Two other things jumped out at me about him. First, he looked Arabic, which meant nothing, not necessarily. But being that this wasn't the Middle East or even near a major city, and this was basically the backwoods mountains of California, it was safe to assume that the overwhelming majority of townspeople were white, mid- to lower-class Americans. Not that they weren't welcoming of strangers, just that it was unusual for a Muslim to stop for gas here, much less live here. I'd spent a lot of time overseas, and some of that was in tours in Iraq, Afghanistan, Qatar, and even a couple of unrecorded missions in Iran. Over there, I was the one who stuck out.

I'd seen so many Middle Easterners that I was good at spotting their localizations. This guy, minus a beard and Islamic attire, looked like he had gotten straight off a plane from Tehran, or possibly Istanbul. He was clean-shaven and somewhere in the neighborhood of his late thirties, not much older than me, if I had to guess. He had thick, dark hair in a style that must've originated as a jarhead cut, but now was grown out from that.

On the table in front of him was a bunched-up Marine cap with woodland camo patterns. It looked like it had been folded and pinched and thrown around for years. It was a part of the second thing about him, the most obvious thing.

This guy was in the United States Marine Corps. No doubt about it. He wore a woodland-pattern combat uniform.

A WORD FROM SCOTT

Thank you for reading A REASON TO KILL. You got this far—I'm guessing that you enjoyed Widow.

The story continues in a fast-paced series that takes Widow (and you) all around the world, solving crimes, righting wrongs.

The next book (one of my personal favorites) is WITHOUT MEASURE. Hitchhiking all night. No sleep. Widow stops in a diner in a California mountain town. A chance meeting with a Marine officer. A short conversation. And an hour later, the Marine walked onto a military base, shot and killed five random people, and committed suicide. Now, the MPs want to know why. All suspicion is on the outsider, Widow.

In this exciting mystery, Jack Widow digs deep under the surface to uncover the truth. As he turns over rocks, he finds dark secrets crawling underneath.

After that in ONCE QUIET, Widow gets stranded because his bank account is empty, a banking error (or is it). He finds temporary work/housing on an isolated cattle ranch where a seductive wife maybe be hiding secrets more deadly than anything Widow's faced before.

On vacation in NAME NOT GIVEN, wanting to surf the waves on Cocoa Beach, Widow finds a pair of Army dog tags discarded and abandoned. If that's not strange enough, someone has filed the name completely off. Before he knows it, a serial killer is on the loose, killing women who have gone AWOL from their posts and suspect number 1 is Jack Widow.

If you love Tom Clancy, then THE MIDNIGHT CALLER must be your next read. This one has Jack Widow in a NYC hotel, when the phone rings from an internal line at midnight. A woman with a Russian accent pleads for his help. Saving her will propel Widow into an international conspiracy with Russian spies, American conspirators, and a missing nuclear submarine.

What are you waiting for? The fun is just starting—once you start Widow, you won't be able to stop...

THE SCOTT BLADE BOOK CLUB

Building a relationship with my readers is the very best thing about writing. I occasionally send newsletters with details on new releases, special offers and other bits of news relating to the Jack Widow Series.

If you are new to the series, you can join the Scott Blade Book Club and get the starter kit.

Sign up for exclusive free stories, special offers, access to bonus content, and info on the latest releases, and coming soon Jack Widow novels. Sign up at www.scottblade.com.

THE NOMADVELIST
NOMAD + NOVELIST = NOMADVELIST

Scott Blade is a Nomadvelist, a drifter and author of the breakout Jack Widow series. Scott travels the world, hitchhiking, drinking coffee, and writing.

Jack Widow has sold over a million copies.

Visit @: ScottBlade.com

Contact @: scott@scottblade.com

Follow @:

Facebook.com/ScottBladeAuthor

Bookbub.com/profile/scott-blade

Amazon.com/Scott-Blade/e/B00AU7ZRS8

Made in United States
North Haven, CT
22 April 2023

35769268R00200